Yuri Andrukhc... requires an exceptionally talented translator in order to be appreciated in English. Happily, Andrukhovych has found just such a wordsmith in Vitaly Chernetsky, who has managed to accomplish the well-nigh impossible: staying true to the original text while producing powerful and persuasive English-language prose. Read this novel, both to experience one of the most important recent Ukrainian literary texts and to bear witness to Chernetsky's emergence as a great translator. Kudos to both!

ALEXANDER MOTYL

Twelve Circles is a flamboyant meditation on the history of everything. Don't expect the trains to run on time but (in their own time) they arrive and depart and in due time the story of Karl-Joseph Zumbrunnen unfolds before our eyes. Andrukhovych is the ultimate omniscient narrator and his mile-long sentences chart their own unbroken course, fearlessly, with no end in sight. It's all in the details, the unspoken truths, the sidelong glances, and the marvelous translation by Vitaly Chernetsky brings it to life on the wide screen.

LEWIS WARSH

Для
Галини,
щиро —
[illegible]

03-21-16

Twelve Circles

Yuri Andrukhovych

Translated from the Ukrainian by
Vitaly Chernetsky

Spuyten Duyvil
New York City

ISBN 978-1-941550-44-1

Library of Congress Cataloging-in-Publication Data

Andrukhovych, IUrii, 1960-
[Dvanadtsiat' obruchiv. English]
Twelve circles / Yuri Andrukhovych ; translated from
the Ukrainian by Vitaly Chernetsky.
pages cm
ISBN 978-1-941550-44-1
I. Chernetsky, Vitaly, translator. II. Title.
PG3949.1.N296D8913 2015
891.7'934--dc23

2015006957

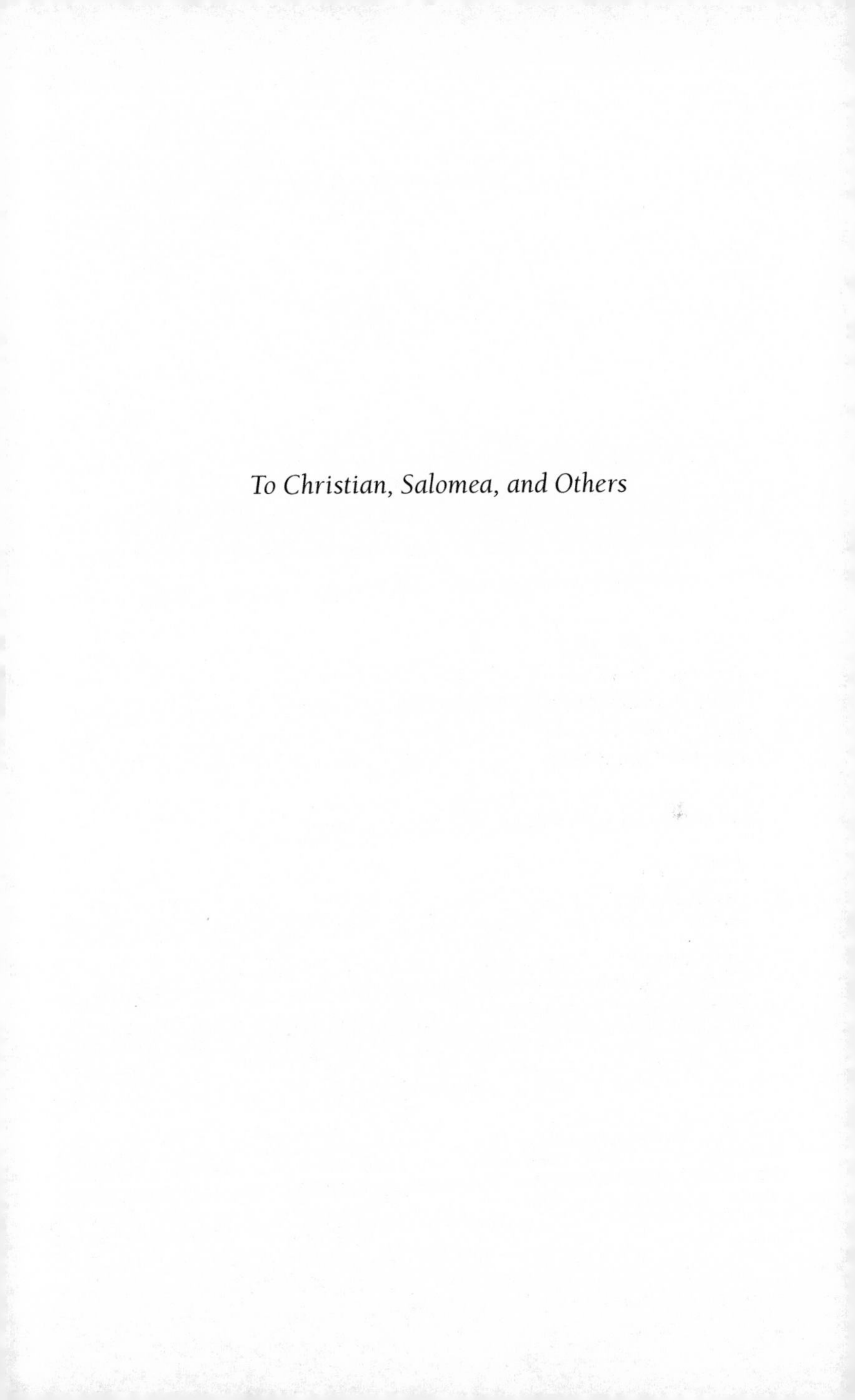

To Christian, Salomea, and Others

Lonely friend,
Enveloped in the world's mysteries
Like a belt of the night—
On this springtime evening, come with me,
Have a few drinks in a tavern on the Moon.

Bohdan-Ihor Antonych

I.

Fortuitous Guests

1

In his letters from Ukraine Karl-Joseph Zumbrunnen wrote, "Everything that we want for ourselves, what we think about and what we hope for, happens to us without fail. However, it always happens too late and always in a way that is somehow wrong. So, when *it* arises before us, we do not even recognize *its* face. Thus we are mostly afraid of the future, afraid of traveling, of children, of changes. I do not know how to resist this, but I pretend with all my strength to resist. Recently they again started cutting off electricity here for long stretches at a time."

None of his closest friends ever succeeded in getting from him a clear answer to the question of why he kept traveling there. The young woman whom he dated for eight years (her name was Eva-Maria, and no one knew whether there was more of Eve or of Mary in her personality) one morning told him she had had enough. Seeing her off at the gate, he also saw most of his youth off—the time when one meets other people's gazes with astonishing openness. But Karl-Joseph Zumbrunnen did not stop traveling to Ukraine even after this breakup. He—as only his closest friends noticed—just started stooping a bit, plus the eye doctor had to increase his prescription glasses by one diopter.

Also, he did not stop going there when the Ukrainian government considerably complicated the visa procedures and noticeably increased the visa fees. Karl-Joseph still kept crossing the threshold of their embassy, sitting for hours in the waiting rooms next to coarse-voiced bordello escapees and various other illegals, registering with the corner of his eye the sometimes curious but usually disdainful glances of overweight Russophone secretaries each new time covered with an even thicker layer of makeup, and when finally allowed an audience for the umpteenth time reminded the forgetful government official his name, *nature of activities*, and goal of the trip. At a certain stage in the conversation, the bureaucrat would finally remember him and, with a watery stare somewhere downward, promise to help.

Karl-Joseph undertook his first journey at the very beginning of the nineties. At the time, this brand new state formation attracted many eastbound travelers. "If they survive this winter," wrote Zumbrunnen in his letters, "they are fated to have a good future. Now everything creates tremendous difficulties for them, there is a shortage of the most basic goods, including vodka and matches, the provisional pseudo-money keeps devaluating every minute, but we mustn't forget that this is the East, hence the material side of life will never acquire the decisive role here. I've had conversations with some young intellectuals and a few students; they are incredibly interesting people and they are ready to radically change their country." The addressees of his letters only shrugged their shoulders: all these ecstatic *notes of a traveler* seemed at best banal and naïve, if not lifted wholesale from the complete works of some Romain Rolland or some Rilke. Returning to Vienna in early summer, Karl-Joseph brought with him a lacquered wood-carved eagle, two traditional kilims from Kosiv (one of them for his girlfriend), and a pack of Vatra cigarettes. Karl-Joseph did not smoke, but from time to time he treated some of his guests fond of extreme adventures to these cigarettes; in this way, in a few years the pack lost about half its contents.

He published his photographs of the Carpathians and the city of Lviv in several obscure magazines, although the solo exhibition with the planned title "Europe: the Decentered Center" never materialized. Even Karl's readiness to change the title to a compromised one, "After Roth, after Schulz," was of no help. At the last moment some higher authorities from the Museum of Archeology and Ethnography interfered and everything fell apart. But Karl-Joseph Zumbrunnen kept on traveling.

In this sense he was entirely whimsical, which could not help deriving from his twisted genealogy that was, all the same, unexceptional among his Austrian compatriots. During the last four or five centuries his ancestors had mixed so much—in terms of estates, ethnicities, religions, political affiliations, to a completely explosive degree of incompatibility—that Karl-Joseph could with equal justification consider himself a descendant of Bavarian Anabaptist brewers, Sudetan mule herders, Tyrolean cheesemakers, bankrupt Salzburg moneylenders, Sopron salt merchants, a few suicide bankers, as well as a few suicided bishops, and also several other remarkable persons, including a certain fire and sword eater from Laibach, a cross-eyed owner of a puppet theater from Tarnow near Krakow, burnt at the stake as a witch, a famous compiler of farmer's almanacs from Mattersburg, and a no less famous feminist journalist, also cross-eyed. One of the distant branches of the Zumbrunnen clan included the composer Buxtehude and another, the artist Altdorfer. But it is entirely probable that Karl-Joseph undertook his first trip to Ukraine under the influence of the family myth about his great-grandfather, a fanatically active forest ranger from Vorokhta, later transferred to Chortopil.[1] Strangely enough, the great-grandfather was also called Karl-Joseph. Indeed, each nine out of ten male Zumbrunnens bore the name Karl-Joseph. The name of Karl-Joseph Zumbrunnen the great-grandfather was inscribed in gold in the history of Austrian (or maybe even the world's) forestry as the person who, in the middle of the nineteenth century, planted conifers and beech

---

1 i.e., "Devilville," the fictional town where Andrukhovych's first novel, *Recreations* (pub. 1992, English trans. 1998), is set (all notes are translator's, except where marked "author's note").

over enormous spaces of bare Carpathian mountain-tops. "Here no one remembers about him anymore," wrote Karl-Joseph, his great-grandson, in his letters, "and all my attempts to learn more about him end in failure. Here it appears the twentieth century did bring a horrific catastrophe, something like a tectonic break, as a consequence of which everything that had happened and existed earlier—say, before 1939—fell into oblivion. I spoke to some young historians here and they assured me they would seek to have one of the departments of the local forestry academy named after my great-grandfather. But that's not what I'm asking for!"

In ninety-two he went twice, in ninety-three only once, but for an extended stay. It appears he spent the entire three months allowed by his visa in Lviv. In ninety-four, having learned about the consequences of Ukrainian elections, he decided he would never again be able to go there. His letters from that time are marked by particular harshness and bitterness: "This country had excellent opportunities to change and to leap, lightning-like, from a state of permanent monstrosity and oligophrenic helplessness to a state of almost *normalcy*. It turned out the numbers of those people who did not want this, who did not even want this country to exist as such, greatly exceeds all acceptable limits. It seems two years ago I was severely mistaken. In the end, this is not my business but theirs; they make their personal choices every day. I only feel sorry for the tiny handful of the *different* whom I had a chance to meet and with whom I had good working relationships. Nowadays all of them have frozen, filled with somber foreboding of liquidations and cleansings. Someone among them has uttered the word 'emigration'; someone else, 'separation, border along the Zbruch.' I do not think it was the amount of alcohol consumed that mattered. These utterances were made in a fully sober state. Of course, such entities like the Danube Club (a historical and cultural society) will not be folded right away—at least not tomorrow. Therefore, while one still can, one should try to do as much as possible." Thus in the second half of July of the same year 1994, Karl-Joseph Zumbrunnen disappears into the Carpathians for a long while, photographing mostly old cemeteries for a future exhibition entitled "Memento." He spends almost a month between earth and sky, orienting himself with old military maps he had prudently brought from Vienna, moving sometimes along riverbeds, sometimes along dirt roads, sometimes along mountain ranges, pronouncing from time to time the strange word *Gorgany* which sounds like an incantation. He enters villages only to buy a little food. A dozen Ukrainian words plus gesticulation fully suffice to get him understood. Other words assure that he already has with him an interpreter, but this does not compute with the content and mood of his letters from that time, all of them concerned with loneliness underneath a starry sky. That summer was unusually hot, grass had already yellowed before August, and Karl-Joseph Zumbrunnen got a serious tan. He came to like most plunging into countless mountain streams and lying there, concentrating on the intense blue and completely cloudless abyss above him. It had not rained for a long while, thus the streams had far less water than usual. However, the water was also much cleaner, greenish and transparent, and warmer than usual. Karl-Joseph Zumbrunnen, like all my characters, loved water very much.

He originally came from the town of Sitzgrass, somewhere either in the east or the south of Austria (here you go, explaining it for the second time already, but what to do: the Gothic-style church; the clock on the belfry; a street with a post office and a wine tavern; the morning cooing of pigeons; the hikers—half of them on foot, the other on bikes. The old estate of a baron on the hill—a *Schlösschen*, now a museum of engraving and lake fishing. A chestnut alley. The Eastern Alps on the horizon. A water mill and some swimming in the greenish waters). Yes, exactly this water, the swimming until late in the evening near the old mill, somehow not destroyed by bombing in the final days of World War II, and the diving into the greenest warm innards of water with the cheerful secret idea of never coming back, lost forever in the deep, is what periodically overwhelmed Karl-Joseph Zumbrunnen in his happy dreams, while in his unhappy dreams he only heard some howling music and could not understand a word of what was being said to him.

Returning from the Carpathians that summer he noted with surprise that nothing terrible had happened as yet. All of his Lviv acquaintances remained free. The anticipated wave of arrests and the folding of patriotic structures had unexpectedly been postponed. A few acquaintances even suggested that things had turned out for the better and that one could and should find common understanding with the new authorities. At the very least, they were pragmatic, which wasn't a bad thing plus one could see the noticeable lowering of the average age of those in power: precisely what the society had needed for a long time. "It is people of our generation that are now coming to power," said one German Studies specialist, a temporary interpreter of Zumbrunnen, although in the greater scheme of things he interpreted Heidegger. "A few of them I know, or rather used to know, personally. Life is becoming interesting." Karl-Joseph Zumbrunnen did not hasten. He silently sipped the overly sugared Moldovan wine, but his heartache did not go away. His "Memento" exhibition was shown in several Galician cities, accompanied by throngs of visitors and insanely generous opening receptions. Each time, official ladies and gentlemen opened these events with speeches about the new modern European Ukraine. Moderately sexy young women, as if following a director's signal, began swirling like odalisques around the *popular Viennese photographer*, seemingly accidentally bumping into him with their tensed buttocks. Once again Karl-Joseph was enjoying himself in this warm country.

In the fall of that very year, as it has already been mentioned, his Viennese girlfriend dumped him, having learned that for Christmastime he was yet again headed for Lviv.

They say that at five thirty-four in the morning Eva-Maria barely touched her lips to the still tanned crevice underneath his Adam's apple, and that was it. At the time, he wasn't yet wearing a small silver rectangle engraved with his name and address on a choker around his neck. Thus it was the last summer when her favorite crevice could have gotten tanned. The last summer, the last fall.

However, the following summer he wrote from Lviv, without trying to conceal the euphoria he was forcing upon himself: "Decent beer has appeared! New coffeehouses and even decent restaurants! Some things are indeed changing, for instance a few building façades. I have even begun thinking about a temporary switch from black-and-white to color—not for the sake of *beauty*, of course, but for the sake of history. This stuff could make a rather cheerful new book: *Lviv: The New Skins*. These attempts to cover local surfaces with questionable paint brought over from nearby Polish markets would indeed look comical, were it not for the idealist yearnings of local new business-persons. These are indeed young people who, above all else, want to change their country and—knock on wood—they seem to be succeeding!" And a bit further down: "I was seriously mistaken when in the early nineties I wrote that they would extremely quickly master the favorable tendencies for development and instantaneously change the country's situation for the better. The years that followed showed this country was too big, too sluggish, too complicated for instantaneous change. Fortunately, I was mistaken when, a year ago, I decided it was time to draw a large cross over this whole picture. The farewell to youth is not so tragic when it is followed by maturity."

The final phrase did not quite fit the earlier context of amateur analysis, and Karl-Joseph's friends yet again shrugged their shoulders when they reread it. However, I believe I have figured out what happened. But we'll talk about that later.

His letters during the second half of the nineties were a strange mixture from a private journal, contradictory diary entries, and entirely unmotivated emotional breakthroughs into spheres bordering on the metaphysical. "It is terribly frustrating to talk to some local authorities," we read at one point. "A few days ago, one of them, a former prisoner of conscience and author of samizdat poetry, who through the irony of higher powers and local palace intrigues landed in an enviable office, tried convincing me his nation was nearly ten thousand years old, that the Ukrainians had direct connection to the cosmic forces of Good, that the shape of their skulls and brow ridges was rather close to *the Aryan standard*, due to which there existed a certain global conspiracy against them whose direct actors were the closest geographical neighbors and certain *internal corrupting ethnic elements*—'You know what I mean, Mr. Zumbrunnen.' Later, he exerted considerable effort to demonstrate to me the complete and utter worthlessness of Russian culture. It seemed to him that he reduced Mussorgsky, Dostoevsky, Semiradsky, and Brodsky to ashes. ('And the surnames, the surnames alone are worth their weight in gold,' he screamed, in his ecstasy spraying me with his bluish-yellowish foam. 'Rubinstein! Eisenstein! Mandelstam! Mindelblat! Rostropovich! Rabinovich!') The most comical thing was that he had to formulate all this in Russian since this *true Ur-European* never bothered to learn any other language. I was forced to interrupt his chaotic lecture with a few uncomfortable questions, to which he only senselessly blinked his eyes. 'All right, if your culture is truly so ancient and powerful, how come your public toilets are so filthy? Why do your cities look rather like rotting garbage heaps? Why do historic city centers die in rapid succession, one neighborhood after another? Why do balconies collapse, why is there no light in the doorways, and so much broken glass underfoot? Who is to blame for this? The Russians? The Poles?

Other *internal corrupting elements*? All right, you don't bother with the cities, but what about the natural environment? Why do your villagers—according to you, carriers of a ten-thousand-year-old civilization—so doggedly throw all their shit right into rivers, and while hiking through your mountains one finds five times as much scrap iron as medicinal herbs?' I barely resisted the temptation to ask something more personal: why did he, recently awarded the Order of St. Vladimir, have so much dandruff on his shoulders. But what I had asked aloud was entirely sufficient for him to noticeably cool down and, scrutinizing with suspicion the shape of my skull, let me know in a confused and wordy way that he saw no possibility of financial support for our expedition this year. All this leads to especially depressing conclusions, when an *étatist* figure of this sort, seemingly mockingly lifted lock, stock, and barrel from the archival underbelly of a terribly vulgarized nineteenth century, is contrasted with the local present-day state of affairs. I write this letter from the very heart of a forgotten Europe, from the legendary premises of Hotel Georges, reeking of abandonment, cold, mold, and endless fake repairs. Here local types with the unmistakable stooping gait of secret police informers pass me notes from my acquaintances. Here deformed corpulent bartenders, sleepy and unwashed, serve me vile overly sugared coffee. While this is going on I am forced to listen to loud and empty music, to see insolent faces, necks, and butts (I do not look in their direction, but it is impossible not to see them, that's the problem!), breathe in their sweat, their perfume, the smoke of their cigarettes. I am forced to fall ever deeper into this tragicomic entourage, into this cynical despair—and I must somehow believe they are descendants of ancient Egyptians or Etruscans, which is proven by their national colors and calendar rituals, reflecting *all the beauty and harmony of relations between Man, Nature, and the Creator* (everything capitalized, of course, as notes one local author with irony)."

However, in another letter, not too distant chronologically from the one just quoted, we find expressly different accents: "Who gave me the right to sermonize to them, to point out to them all these potholes and gold teeth? They live the way they want to, for they are at home. I am unreasonable in this already because I am a traveler. And the main thing one cannot take away from them is their kind, vodka-infused warmth. In some ulterior sense they are immeasurably more humane than we. By humaneness I understand the capacity to open up unexpectedly, to see even in a stranger someone who is your closest kin. Yes, it takes the trains here some thirteen hours to cover the distance of 400 to 500 kilometers, which our Intercity express trains can do in less than four. But at the same time, in their uncomfortable, intentionally cramped train compartments people take out food and drink, get to know each other, share each piece of bread, and tell each other highly important, often entirely intimate things. Life is too short all the same, so why hurry? The most moving moments, when one unexpectedly stumbles upon this suddenly uncovered vodka-warmed truth, are much more important than official business rapidity and closed-off fake politeness, behind which hides only emptiness and mutual indifference. I like it that all of them at times resemble one giant family that spreads over many branches. Offering their food and vodka, they become unbearably insistent if you start refusing it. And I think this is not because food and vodka are much cheaper here than back home, but because people here are truly more honest and generous in their souls. Therefore, when you refuse their offer of food and drink, it is like you refuse them the right to be mutually understood. How unlike the atmosphere of our Eurocity trains, well ventilated, sterile and healthy, impeccably heated, yet simultaneously devoid of true human warmth—only the superficial gliding of smiles and an artificial silence, broken only by the clicking of lighters and the rustling of aluminum foil!"

Yes, beginning in the second half of the nineties Karl-Joseph Zumbrunnen did start remarking that he was getting used to things and growing to like it in this country. Once, suddenly and definitively—at the time he was walking through the impossibly rickety train on its way from Ivano-Frankivsk to Kyiv, from his car number eighteen to the restaurant car (number nine)—so, right there, right at that moment, suddenly and definitively he realized he liked walking in large steps, imitating self-assuredness and awareness of the situation. He enjoyed passing by others in the too-tight train aisles and passageways. He liked the drunken gazes and gold teeth of the train conductors. He liked knowing the name of the upcoming station (Zdolbuniv). He liked that at that station people would bring onto the train cheaper beer. He liked being able to handle everything so well. That the compartment doors were almost fully open, and that when he would finally arrive to car number nine, he would enjoy the unhealthy train food, the poorly baked bread, the half a glass of vodka expertly divided into two gulps, the faces of others at the restaurant, already rather deformed by drinking, the tights on the hips of loudmouthed women, their vulgar jokes, of which he understood not a word, but still exploded into most sincere laughter together with other accidental companions and—who knows?—perhaps even their loud and vulgar music, in which he deciphered only occasional Russian-language phrases like "my gal," "but I don't have," and "you hugged her" . . .

This is probably why in one of his letters soon afterwards he wrote, "The path of a foreigner is full of trials and dangers, but there is nothing sweeter than the feeling of putting down roots in the Foreign. One fine moment you suddenly realize, without exaggeration, you actually *could live here.* And it is not out of the question that tomorrow you might already want to live *only here*."

It became increasingly clearer to the addressees of his letters that the Eternal Feminine had something to do with all this. Ukrainian women of that era—utilized not only as sexual slaves, but also in traditional matrimonial relationships in several North European countries—had already acquired a certain renown in the West. "These chicks are cool," joked one of Karl-Joseph's café acquaintances, a dentist whose name is of no importance here. "They are as sexy as prostitutes and entirely unspoiled by feminism." It is worth remarking that after a while, Karl-Joseph no longer adequately responded to jokes of this kind. This amused and intrigued his pals who gathered each Friday, following an old bourgeois custom, at the "Alt Wien" pub, long run by the Croatians. There he involuntarily transgressed the unwritten rules of this male-only circle, especially those of obligatory verbal ease and a pretend attitude of lighthearted and elegant cynicism. Old Charlie-Joe lost his sense of humor, they made a mental note. The situation is entirely clear even without an analyst's couch. Good-bye, Charlie, you got stuck like a fly. You got sucked in, head and all, into some cunt. How do you feel there, Charlie?

In reality things were the way they were: the decline of eyesight, the unfamiliar autumnal loneliness, the general deadening, the passive waiting for a trip to

Lviv for the Julian Calendar Christmas, the four-hour search through his belongings at the Chop border crossing—*goal of the trip*, one of them kept asking in a Russian-style fur hat with flaps down (although the somewhat stunned citizen of the Republic of Austria answered the well-memorized "*shournalist, photo*," at that moment he still did not quite fathom his *true* goal). Then a thaw, warm rains, limb-breaking sliding down Lviv's hilly streets, shoes and trouser legs splattered with dirt, frequent falls. A Christmas party in some mansion on Lysenko Street, old acquaintances, new acquaintances, new temporary interpreter, a university teacher ("No, Karl, not a *bleacher*!"). Too much drinking, too much food; shepherds with a lamb. Ms. Clumsy—to begin with, in the very first moments, spilled a glass of red wine on herself, having knocked it over with the sleeve of her folkloric-style dress. Secondly, she elbowed Zumbrunnen painfully when sitting down, returning from a *barbershop* ("No, Karl, a smoke shop!"). Thirdly—and as everyone knows, third time's a charm—she twisted her foot, almost falling down the spiral staircase at a pub where everyone had been invited to look at the artwork by the party's host. Karl-Joseph managed to catch her—and probably not only because he was standing one step above her. In this way, for five minutes, he became the hero of an old-fashioned movie, the One Who Rescues the Lady from Mortal Danger. "You are velcome, you are very velcome," he answered to her words of thanks instead of making a dashing gesture and doing something genuinely or parodically chivalrous (for this his command of Ukrainian was insufficient). He kept repeating his "velcome," and everyone else next to them fussed uselessly and pushed around in search of first aid for the injured foot. Some rather drunk mustachioed director (inspector? detector? erector?) finally succeeded on the third try bandaging it ("We are old Carpathian scouts!"). What do sprouts have to do with this, wondered Karl-Joseph. Finally a taxi was called, and Ms. Clumsy—in reality, Roma Voronych—disappeared, limping into the slippery humid night, accompanied by her husband, who was drunker than all the others. It turned out she *did* have one.

Then a few more festive days and nights passed, equally splattered by rain and leftover snow: some threadbare mummers that rather resembled scattered remnants of an army that had just lost a battle. Intrusive children with shaved heads hurriedly caroled in false mutant voices—in their pockets one could discern the outlines of knives and firecrackers. Then the heating at the hotel stopped working. Then it got fixed, just in time: masses of icy air returned from the Arctic. On the Julian Calendared New Year it snowed, and Karl-Joseph dialed her number, suddenly realizing she was fluent in his language, and this meant he could feel more relaxed and even ask about her foot and its recovery.

They immediately felt at ease with each other. She

assisted him wonderfully by bringing several new projects to fruition, not only as interpreter, but also as experienced advisor well versed in peculiarly Lvivian labyrinths of interpersonal relation. However, from the time of that first phone call *concerning the twisted foot* there had to pass two years of mostly *professional collaboration*, or better put, bittersweet uncertainty. Karl-Joseph had to return to Vienna twice and come back to Ukraine twice until one day *the inevitable happened* (some uninvited author of romance novels has popped out snake-like here—shoo!). So, it was a room at the Hotel Georges where they jumped each other with such astonishing haste that Ms. Clumsy pulled down the window curtains together with the wood-worm-eaten cornice, and Karl-Joseph had it confirmed yet again that he did not know how to deal with bras. Behind the wall some maladroit Giants continued making repairs to the neighboring room, mercilessly hammering into the wall their hypertrophied Bolts and Dowels and quarrelling with each other about something in their Professional Language. *What followed* happened more or less—in fact rather more than less—that is, quite nicely. But when she soon afterwards fell in the bathtub, probably having slipped, and with her arm knocked down the bathroom shelf with all the aftershaves, shampoos, deodorants, and other sundry objects, Karl-Joseph Zumbrunnen, suddenly feeling very lonely on the rumpled sheets covering two twin beds pushed together, turned to the hotel room's high ceiling with a rhetorical question: how was it possible to *screw* a woman who already had an almost grown up daughter? Instead of the high ceiling, he answered himself, "Apparently it is indeed possible."

They did everything they could, but the external circumstances kept getting worse. At the end of the nineties Ukraine landed simultaneously on several blacklists, introduced by the excessively unbiased observers from various international institutions. "When crossing the Ukrainian border we recommend having ready a ten- or twenty-dollar bill," advised their readers the compilers of the guidebook *The Southern and Eastern Carpathians* (London, Paris, and Berlin, 1998). "This is the everyday norm of *stimulating* Ukrainian customs officers, thanks to which you might be able to avoid customs inspection's lengthy and often degrading procedures. If you actually succeed in getting onto the territory of this country, a former Soviet republic, remember to be especially alert: all kinds of crime, including theft, carjacking, and even kidnapping have reached unheard-of proportions. It is of no use appealing to the local police with its horrific professional and technical levels of efficiency. Its officers do not speak any European languages, so you simply won't be understood, but in the meantime they will make numerous attempts at swindling you." In and of itself all this, just like the power outages during long autumnal and winter evenings, did not make a tragedy for Karl-Joseph—the increasing insolence of the state powers-that-be, and with it the rekindling of that internal hell one calls fear, constituted a much worse symptom. "It seems to me," he wrote in one of his letters, "that the happiest decade in this country's history is hopelessly slipping away. Some of my friends feel their phones are being tapped again. However, a complete return of the past would be impossible: if the former state power destroyed *those who were different* with the help of the courts, the camps, and so-called psychiatry, the present-day totalitarianism could be described as a creeping one; it indeed creeps up on you in the darkness, using entirely criminal methods. It's one thing to be sentenced, even at a closed, unjust but, forgive me, still somehow legitimate procedure, where with a dissident head held high you beautifully and loudly challenged the system, bearing in mind that sooner or later the West will find out about it. It is a very different thing to be cynically kidnapped by some unknown masked thugs, strangled during torture, then have your headless body thrown into a dump. Politicians, journalists, moneybags disappear. Even if any of them are eventually found, they are invariably dead. Behind all these *unclear circumstances* one clearly discerns textbook *suicides* or *car accidents*. Others are gunned down in elevators or on the steps of their own homes. Besides, with such a conducive background the ordinary, *non-political* crime also surged: no one can guarantee the safety of an ordinary citizen, and the black market in guns will soon see its golden age here. For now, it is darkness: darkness everywhere, power outages that last for hours, and dismembered bodies in trash-filled dumpsters."

And a bit further: "I involuntarily came up with something like an aphorism: a police state is where the police are as omnipotent towards honest citizens as they are powerless towards the criminals."

But even after these confessions Karl-Joseph Zumbrunnen did not stop going to Ukraine. He did not stop, even though the governments of the European Union member states *no longer recommended* their citizens visit it. But what could those governments know about stony mountain ridges open to all the winds, about the color of clay on boots worn out by a weeklong hiking trip, what did they know about the scents—of wooden churches, old cemeteries, mountain streams? And they certainly could not know anything about Ms. Roma Voronych, how she smoked in bed, how she looked for the bathroom in the darkness, how she simply breathed next to you, or how she turned off all light when undressing, for like most women her age she started becoming self-conscious about her body.

Therefore Karl-Joseph Zumbrunnen didn't have the slightest intention to follow the *recommendations* of Western governments. The reward for the constancy of his likes found him with an unequivocal decisiveness of a miracle: the previous year he was contacted by one of the senior editors of a large prestigious publishing house that specialized in contemporary art photography, multimedia projects, and documentary reportage, and asked to do a photography book of Carpathian landscapes with the working title *The Motherland of Masochism*. The recently popular current of Masoch research in cultural studies was finding its development in the *dead*, or rather, *violated nature* of destroyed landscapes. The editor was first and foremost interested in depictions of natural environments damaged by the *industrial*, and since in the East the industrial was perishing at just as catastrophic a scale as nature, this meant ruination squared. "You see," said the editor, "we are interested in all these cisterns and pipes overgrown with thorns, the banks of poisoned rivers, the dead slagheaps, etc. Poland? Slovakia? Romania?" "If the context of Masoch is important for you, then Ukraine," answered Karl-Joseph with as indifferent an intonation as possible. Like all knowing old birds, he remembered not to sell out too cheaply. "Oh, so Masoch's not from Poland?" the editor arched his pierced eyebrow. "Sorry, here in Düsseldorf we sometimes are not fully versed in your Austrian affairs," he added, scratching his fiery purple Mohawk. The amount of the advance allowed Karl-Joseph to perform, an hour later, the czardas of a victorious bear in his apartment in Praterstern, a dwelling far too tiny for such victorious dances.

Thus in the next letter from that year, Karl-Joseph Zumbrunnen had reason to write, "All the mystery of this world comes from our unwillingness to accept things the way they are. However, only one order of things actually exists in reality. Thus we are afraid of the future, afraid of traveling, of children, of changes. I do not know how to resist this, but I pretend with all my strength to resist."

2

Now the time has come to reveal them all. In one of the books I know this is called "The Arrival of the Heroes." However, I am not sure whether they are really heroes. Or whether this is truly an *arrival.*

But to start with, it is necessary to visualize a bird's-eye view of a small railway station in the mountains—one of those façades that, despite countless and senseless changes, still reminds you of Viennese Secession architecture. Someone told me once that Bohumil Hrabal supposedly said he would be happy to live anywhere one could find Habsburg-era train station buildings. So, Bohumil Hrabal could live here as well.

Thus we are going for a sharp descent.

So, we have an old tile roof with a few tiles missing, a low turret with a forever stopped clock, in whose rusted mechanisms lives a whole family of cuckoos, or perhaps crows, who rhyme with a train the clock emits, and a narrow platform paved with chipped yellowish bricks, and a few nonworking streetlights, formerly gas. There also must be a cracked stained glass window with intensely blue decadent petals and the first spring flies on the protruding iris leaves, a waiting room with two or three wooden benches with graffiti carved in with knives or pieces of broken glass

(*DMB-84, PTU-18, Alyona = cunt, Murmansk-95, Said = stupid fucktard, Angela + Tomato = LOVE*), a black cast iron furnace, in case winter snows lay siege to the place, and a laconic timetable of the trains—or rather the train: there is only one that comes through here—hanging above the usually closed window of the ticket office. The window opens twice a day, at 7:15 in the evening and at 4:03 in the morning, when, clinking with keys dating from the Habsburg-Hrabal era, a small dried-up woman, wrapped in a kerchief and, this time, wearing rubber boots, comes down from a house on the hill above the station. She comes to sell her ancient tickets, these little brown rectangles of hard cardboard, these passes to some train-station-proximate childhood. Although almost no one buys tickets from her.

Anything else? Yes, a hammer and sickle relief above the doors from the platform to the waiting room and a half torn-off ad "Obey your thirst" on one of the walls.

There is only one train here, and in the evening, at approximately 7:33, it is supposed to arrive *from below*, as they say here, that is, from the lowlands. Its stop, according to the timetable, is supposed to last two minutes, but usually lasts longer because five to seven crates of bread are to be unloaded from it. At the end of April—and we found ourselves here precisely at this time of the year—it is still light outside, but the train is going to arrive only when darkness will have long fallen. The thing is, the little woman in the little window got a call that the train is running almost two hours late, because somewhere on the span between the stations of Upper Butt and Middle Butt there was a cow lying *on the tracks*—the dark ebony phone, as well as the far from perfect diction of the dispatcher still leave one with doubt as to whether it was really *a cow* (*a sow? a bow? a plow?*). However, this is of little import, it is the actual fact of the two-hour train delay that matters. From this follows the little woman who can now once again close the ticket window and return to her house chores on the neighboring hill, not yet covered with berries, and the carter in a rabbit fur hat and a Turkish sweater can let out his bay, Rocinante, into fresh grass by the station and stretch out on the graffiti'd bench, waiting for the five bread crates to arrive (no fish today).

A quarter hour of complete silence passes, and from the side of the highway comes the roar of a car that jumps madly on the stones and potholes of the final stretch before the station that is not yet asphalted, and finally brakes in a very cinematic fashion on the tiny square by the main entrance. It is an SUV, or perhaps a minivan; something Japanese, American, or perhaps from Singapore; something in the style of Safari, Western, Action, or Fiction—in other words, a *foreign make*, but judging by the roar, possibly a KRAZ military truck engine. The driver runs out (big ears, thick neck, black leather jacket), swiftly crosses the waiting room, opens the door to the platform with his foot, gives a kick to a lamppost, looks around at all the great emptiness, spits in annoyance, grabs his cell phone from his belt, but before dialing the number notices the unharnessed cart, and then the freely grazing Rocinante, and thus makes a reasonable decision to dash back to the waiting room. There apparently he has a chat with the unceremoniously awakened carter, and afterwards, noticeably calmer, slowly walks out on the platform, squats down, and lights a smoke. Or he returns to the SUV, and in fact dials the number. Or turns on the music in the car (a question for our audience: what friggin' kind of music might he be listening to?) and reclines his seatback, or closes his eyes.

This way two more hours pass, during which time we can attend to our own business.

And now it is really here—the *arrival of the heroes*. It happens right before ten o'clock: the locomotive's headlight pierces the train station darkness, the clanking of train wheels slows down, then comes on screeching and gnashing, and the heavy shudder of the train cars. No need for us to watch the unloading of bread and how the carter, his face swollen from sleep, with the words "Later, Masha!" for the last time slaps the shapeless butt of the train conductor lady, a pencil and a bill of goods in her hand.

For us it is much more important to turn our attention to the *exit of the heroes* from the train. While we are at it, let us remember there are eight of them; four come from one car, three from another, and one more from yet another car. The gender balance in the first group is two to two, in the second one to two, in the third one to zero. Thus we have four representatives of the fair sex and just as many of the sterner sex. All of them, stumbling on the rails and sleepers, finally make it to the narrow platform, after which the train does give, say, a whistle and heads onward, and they are left all alone in the midst of mountains and darkness at a small station somewhere between Galicia and Transylvania (certainly not Pennsylvania!). They are a bit confused. Not all of them know each other, but, it seems, they begin to suspect it might be a good idea to engage in a conversation, for all of them have been brought into this night by some common great goal, once and forever, since only this night something will happen to each of them—oh no, sorry, this is *Recreations* suddenly spilling out of me. So, let's write it one more time, from the beginning: for all of them have been brought to *one and the same place.*

The hesitation about establishing relations is put to rest by the arrival of the black leather jacketed driver. The entire group follows him in a file, in the same order, across the waiting room to the train station square, where in an excited and disorderly fashion, stepping on each other's toes, they start packing themselves into the SUV that now looks armor-clad.

While we were away it came to be decorated with a billboard bearing the slogan "Charitable Program *Heroes of Business for the Heroes of Culture*". They do not see it in the dark, but it is important for us, since we find proof that they are indeed *heroes* and this is indeed an *arrival*.

At last they take their places and the hypothetical Ford Aerostar, roaring mercilessly with its KRAZ or quasi-KRAZ engine, dashes forward, or rather, away from the station, without skipping a single pothole or stone on the road. Nobody knows why—either because of the unusual circumstances, or because of darkness inside the car, or because of the large ears of the driver, or because of his friggin' music, everyone falls into a prolonged uncomfortable silence, which gives me an opportunity to pause and invent for them all a more interesting means of transportation.

It is undoubtedly true, in fact I agree one hundred percent with the pertinent reproach that in at least two thirds of my novels produced up to now, the heroes are *transported* somewhere. In the past I had successfully summoned for them trains, Ikarus buses, a momentously symbolic Chrysler Imperial, and also—the pinnacle of phantasms—an infernal semi-airborne "Manticora" capsule, designed possibly in Beelzebub's subterranean design bureaus and tested at fire-drenched ranges under a storm of stones, sulfur, and excrement.

However, I keep in reserve the possibility of a ship.

Let it sail somewhere across the ocean, but not here and not now.

For now the driver of the SUV so poorly described by yours truly, having covered less than ten kilometers along the nighttime highway, where on his left the rocky outcrops hang menacingly, and on the right down below is the River, without any warning also turns right and downward (the heroes bounce like corpses in a sack) and, crossing without second thought the above-mentioned River, jumps out onto a weathered forest road, and drives down it in an ever more aggressive manner (what else can he do?). The billboard on the roof breaks off small forest branches, and the headlights comb the uncertain path a few hundred yards ahead of him. However, this whole *ride into the unknown* cannot last forever—for I have found a new means: let it be a helicopter!

And thus the car brakes at some anemone-filled clearing bathed by the moon (that is, illuminated by moonlight that anemically breaks through the clouds here and there), and there is indeed a helicopter vibrating impatiently in a state of frenetic charge—a weighty giant, a war veteran, directly historically involved in troop landings, storming operations launched from the air, punitive aviation raids, national security and defense state coups, extermination of one's own POWs, and environmental protection. The pilot, of a military officer type, headphones over his ears, helps with the luggage, while the driver transfers over to him all eight in accordance with the list, and without even saying good-bye dashes back in his KRAZ Aerostar, its wheels splattering dirt in all directions.

Only then do they rise into the air, their behinds vibrating, and glue themselves to the rigid soldier seats, thinking about such things as parachutes, propellers, pelerines, packs of paper bags for barfing, and plenty of other things starting with a "p" . . .

Being inside a helicopter is not terribly conducive to conversation, and the situation is getting even more idiotic since they inconsiderately sat down facing each other (four against the other four). Now all they can do is look to the side, down below, or turn their heads, feigning interest in the helicopter's unsophisticated interior.

Artur Pepa, a man of letters from Lviv, has found the wisest solution, reaching for some strange-looking newspapers he bought back on the train. Of these, one (*Excess*) is of an inordinately regionalist variety; another, *Path of the Aryans*, is far too militant; and the third, *All the Colors of the Rainbow*, is in Russian. The latter turns out to be a gay and lesbian publication. After examining the photos, Pepa sighs and puts it aside, focusing his attention on the first two, which he had thoughtlessly already perused on the train. Thus now he is forced not so much to read but to pretend to read. For the hundredth time now his eye glides over the traditionally tawdry headlines in *Excess* (AS ALWAYS, FIREMEN WERE TOO LATE! GAS WILL GET EVEN MORE EXPENSIVE, BUT HRYVNYA'S VALUE WILL FALL! DECORATED WAR AND LABOR VETERAN MURDERED WITH A SYRINGE STRIKE BY HIS 17-YEAR-OLD GRANDDAUGHTER! NO LESSONS LEARNED FROM MOONSHINE TRAGEDY! THE BARANIUKS WEREN'T THE ONLY ONES KIDNAPPED BY EXTRATERRESTRIALS!). He makes a mental note that all this could comprise an entirely decent poem, turns over the culture page with an endless interview of some Shevchenko Prize winner, I ALWAYS SPOKE NOTHING BUT THE TRUTH TO THE PEOPLE, and finally turns to a half-page ad, which he finds actually witty:

YO! Hey YO: "Gurt!"
The Gurt Company—
Best YOGURT
from the Carpathian mountain meadows!

Then he picks up *Path of the Aryans*, studies for a while the not entirely clear motto "The Nation's Strength Is in Its Future!" and, skipping with indifference over the most typical headlines (NATIONAL LIBERATION REVOLUTION AGAINST CRIMINAL REGIME INEVITABLE! and CHORTOPIL AREA VETERANS OF UKRAINIAN INSURGENT ARMY SUPPORT CURRENT PRESIDENT), immerses himself in finishing the slow reading of an article on the penultimate page, WHAT EVERY UKRAINIAN WOMAN MUST KNOW TO AVOID UNWANTED PREGNANCY, starting with "Copulation during the menstrual cycle by no means constitutes a 100% guarantee of . . ." and continuing with the rest.

To his right sits Kolya, a young woman now aged eighteen, in a skirt so short that one feels like asking which feminine hygiene products she uses. Her full name (which she hates) is Kolomea. People consider her Artur Pepa's daughter, but actually she is his stepdaughter. She has already managed to dart a few seductive gazes at some long-haired redheaded goblin (that's how she described him mentally) sitting across from her, as well as to lick her lips in an erotic movement with the tip of her tongue, just like in the movies, and to re-cross her legs several times. The goblin turned out to be not only long-haired and redheaded, but also surprisingly shy, because each time he either lowered his gaze or turned it to the side, until he finally focused on some picture book he had with him. As a result, Kolya has grown indifferent and now just sighs.

To her right sits Ms. Roma Voronych, her mother, an interesting woman of the age that is considered *the better side of forty*. Ms. Roma, Artur Pepa's wife, is feeling slightly unwell—she never liked flying, even in the days when Aeroflot was at its pinnacle, and the flight attendants who looked like Nadia Kurchenko[2]

2 Nadia Kurchenko, an Aeroflot flight attendant, was made

ceaselessly served the sedated passengers sparkling water and mints. Back then she was even younger than Kolya is today (and Kolya is indeed already a grown-up girl!), and she flew with her parents to Kyiv, Simferopol, and Leningrad. She has no idea why she is thinking about that now. Perhaps this is a reemergence of a suppressed psychological trauma dating back to when she scraped her knee on the ramp to one of those planes. Ms. Roma sometimes works as an interpreter at various post-Freudian conferences at the Danubian Club; thus she knows a thing or two about stuff like that. But now she feels only nausea.

A citizen of the Republic of Austria, Karl-Joseph Zumbrunnen, who looks somewhat younger than Artur Pepa (although according to their passports, it is the other way round), completes this row. Karl-Joseph is probably the only one here who is generally cheered by the situation when it is almost impossible to talk. His understanding of spoken Ukrainian is very poor. Things are a little better with Russian, but as far as speaking is concerned, he is all but incapable of it in any language. Which is why in a company fully or halfway composed of strangers he prefers to stay silent. He does have another language, or rather, another speech organ: his camera, of which he never lets go,

---

into a heroine of the Soviet propaganda machine during the Brezhnev era; she was killed when trying to stop two hijackers who turned a passenger plane towards Turkey. Her story looks at least somewhat doubtful from the vantage point of today (author's note).

including now, lovingly holding it in his lap. Besides, his eyeglasses fog up easily, and he is almost unable to see the people who sit across from him.

And across from him sits two *gal pals* who look entirely identical. Yes, I did say *identical*, although one is a dyed brunette and the other, a dyed blonde. No, their sameness is not like that of twins; they are actually quite different, but also the same. This sameness is of the sort that makes all pop stars, tarts, fashion models, high school seniors, vocational school students, in other words, all our *female contemporaries* almost indistinguishable from one another, since this sameness has been created by television, magazine covers, and *our Soviet way of life.* They are called Lilya and Marlena (I do not think they meant the old pagan goddesses Lada and Marena), although their real names are Svetka and Marina. At this moment (but is it only at this moment?) both of them are not thinking about anything—with the only difference that while inside Lilya there is complete silence, broken only by the roar of the engine, inside Marlena's cortex spins the phrase "from the sea the wind was blowing, from the sea the wind was blowing, from the sea the wind was blowing."

To their left sits an individual we have already mentioned, the redheaded, long-haired guy definitely of an artistic appearance (a rough sweater that previously belonged to a famous woman actor from a German youth theater, a shirt previously worn by a Kurdish freedom fighter who was also a Lviv University student, absurd-looking trousers that came from someplace like Malta, a ring in one ear—the rest you can figure out on your own), so this increasingly popular (but where and among whom?) music video maker and TV designer, whose first name is either Yarema or Yaromyr (difficult to know for sure since he always introduces himself as Yarchyk) and his last name, Volshebnik, i.e., "Magician"—which gives the entire local beau monde a reason to call him Magikstein, and those who do not belong to the beau monde a reason to suspect that his name is actually Magikov and examine with suspicion the shape of his nose and his somewhat bulging eyes. He has decisively—as it seems to him—contemptuously, turned his eyes away from the frankly stupid seduction attempts of the little rail-thin slut sitting across from him, and following the example of a writer he has recognized from newspaper photos (*what the heck is his name? Biba? Buba?*), concentrated on the colorful little brochure from the Jehovah's Witnesses, *Make Yourself Worthy of Salvation*, acquired on the train from the same weird guy who was selling the newspapers. He is on his way to film a music video. This video will feature Lilya and Marlena.

And finally one more type, a somewhat short and fairly stout gentleman, yes, a *gentleman*—one of those who seems to be tailor-made for this definition. His noticeably professorial body shape and the delicate curvature of his posture point to his belonging to the species of a teaching professor, but not of the version profaned by the Soviet and post-Soviet style of *higher* education (a narrow-minded career-focused Cerberus, a student herder who is—let's be frank—hopelessly corrupted) but of an old (Viennese-Warsovian style) third-generation educator, an expert in dead languages and interwar-era anecdotes, affiliated most likely with some Catholic educational establishment or a secret scholarly society. This is Professor Doktor (yes, in Galicia one can find last names like this) who studies the alchemy of the word; an Antonych specialist, although he himself prefers to call himself an Antonychian. With an amiably benevolent smile on his thin old man lips he peers from time to time into the eyes of some of those present, as if seeking among them the most outwardly appropriate listener for the brilliant introductory lecture ready to fly off those lips, complete with lyrical digressions and swinging intonations: "The personality of Bohdan-Ihor Antonych (1909–1937)—a poet, critic, essayist, translator, and a promising prose writer—is undoubtedly among the most important ones in Ukrainian literature of the modern era. The emergence of Antonych at the beginning of the thirties at the very heart of Ukrainian literary life was just as desirable as it was unexpected. Due to the mysterious and never foreseen twists of his personal fate and the aberrations of social reception linked to these, Antonych may be considered a poet that for a long time was erased from our memory. At the same time the circumstances during his lifetime were rather favorable. In 1928, a young man endowed with many talents, coming from an obscure corner of the Lemko region where he was born and brought up in the family of a Greek Catholic parish priest, moves to Lviv, the uncontested social and spiritual heart of Galicia, and enters the local university. Almost immediately he attracts the attention of his teachers and classmates, demonstrating his considerable talents and impressive industriousness. Already during his student years he makes his debut in literary periodicals; by the age of twenty-two he publishes his first poetry collection, *Salutations to Life* (1931). Upon graduating from the university in 1933 (the Faculty of Philosophy, Department of Slavic Philology), thanks to his educational accomplishments he receives simultaneously several offers, notably a state scholarship to continue research in the capital of Bulgaria. Nevertheless, Antonych chooses the path of a free man of letters. Free in all the aspects of this complex notion. For as soon as we begin to recall Bohdan-Ihor Antonych, we inevitably feel the powerful captivating intrusion of a secret, a mystery, an enigma. Before reaching the age of twenty-eight, the poet departed for *the better world*, leaving us with numerous questions, or—to put it more correctly—with the sensation of a space saturated to the limit with almost subtropical vapors of conjecture and supposition. Ukrainian literary scholarship has paid relatively little attention to the problem of Antonych and otherness or, rather, of Antonych as an *other*, concentrating its efforts at the opposite end. Now I would like to reveal this *otherness* at least partially, limiting it to the notion of the exotic, and prove the presence of Antonych himself in this exoticism."

But the professor does not succeed in revealing Antonych's otherness any further, because the unforeseen flight ends—how long did it last, a quarter of an hour?—so, the helicopter lands at the elevation of six thousand one hundred fifty-five feet. The subalpine zone transitions into the alpine one, the alpine into the Tibetan, and the Tibetan into the Himalayan. Therefore juniper and dwarf mountain pines, and boulders eaten away by the wind, because there is always wind here, coming from all directions, and the moon again hides behind a torn swiftly flying cloud, and then jumps out only to hide immediately behind the next one, and you must see this: making their way through the gray and hardened snow, they walk in a line up the hilly alpine meadow, swallowing bits of wind and choppy moonlight reflections, led by the army officer type pilot towards electric flashes and dogs choking on their barking.

Have you ever heard Bull Terriers bark? I have heard the bark of the Rottweilers and the Pitbulls. But I am not sure if Bull Terriers bark at all. Growling—

yes, this they can do—but barking? And in general—why would I need Bull Terriers there, why hints, why these stereotypes? There were no dogs of any kind there, including Carpathian Shepherds. Therefore, no one choked on the barking.

But there were electric flashes, light signals—yes, definitely. There was an alpine resort, where at long last all eight of the so-called heroes dragged themselves, and where now they wait indecisively on a porch drenched in warm light. And what if not on the porch? Perhaps in a lobby, or how about a lounge with a lit fireplace, with deer horns and boar heads on the walls? And how could I forget about the bearskin of an unseen-before size, filling almost the entire floor?

And how should I introduce the ninth, Vartsabych? Perhaps in the form of a giant business card, a billboard-sized business card on which from a hundred yards away one can read:

Pan V*artsabych*, *Ylko, Jr., Owner,*
and on the reverse,
Варцабич Илько Илькович, власник?
and may on this card come to life
all the things that the heart knows so well:
oil, of course, and hard currency also,
blood—and in a near-rhyme with it, love.

And then everything will reveal itself as it is, an entire empire with all its causes and constituent parts: a chain of gas stations; a chain of resorts and *forest cabins*; a chain of Marzhyna currency exchange offices; the Gurt Company and its yoga-organic yogurts; the Chemerghes[3] distillery with its balsams of eternal youth, extracts of eternal joy, and mouthwashes; two or three animal farms with their temporarily alive furs; two dozen markets, both grocery and housewares—all of them covered, that is, *under protection*; one more farm, but with ostriches; then a few small miscellaneous holdings—some roadside diners, pool halls, public restrooms, kiosks selling expired Transylvanian beer and Snickers; sponsorship of beauty contests; nightclubs; vendors on commuter trains; highway robbery; a network of beggars in three district towns; two former factories that used to make furniture and candles respectively, and now are just used for packing supplies; three miles of a dead-end railway line; a bit of a gas pipeline; underground gas cisterns; missile silos; mushroom and berry patches in the forests; river pebbles; car junkyards . . .

(But all of it just for show, for human eyes. In reality one should remember the *free economic zone* and the play without rules, thus endless caravans of long-haul trucks without any registration, nighttime timber and cement transportation, endless click-clack of sealed cargo trains, metaphysical locomotive signals at small cargo platforms by the border, the red and green eyes of train signals, eternal disquiet and transit in one direction—to the southwest, towards Transylvania. Although we are located almost in the *center of Europe*,

3 A variety of moonshine.

everything here always bumps into Transylvania. It shines to us from everywhere—well, at times there's also *rotten Warsaw*, but mostly it's Transylvania, and that's the end. But he—Ylko Vartsabych, the Owner—has long managed to overcome the consequences of this geographic hopelessness and reach financially different, fairytale territories: Kexholm, and Heligoland, and the terrible Solomon Islands. Although personally I do not believe in those illegal Bangladeshis, a few dozen of whom supposedly suffocated under the freshly laid fake floor of a refrigerator truck—this is just idle talk.)

And that's it, not another word on this.

(Although one could also mention in passing an altogether different, mysteriously exotic line of business: ferns in bloom, a gathering of meteorite fragments, ghost hunting, and rinsing blood off antique jewels. For there exist two versions of equal weight of the story of Ylko's lightning-like ascendance to the peaks of finance and property ownership. According to one of them, he, then nothing but *dirt under the fingernails*, made a timely play on inflation and, having invested his first fifty bits of silver into a creaky Pakistani stereo system, opened the first disco in Chortopil that had a cover charge. According to the other, the only direct descendant of a prominent line of Carpathian Robin Hoods, he was initiated into the secret of the largest treasure in Eastern Carpathians, from which he freely partook by the fistful, not refusing himself or his country anything.)

So how should I reveal him after everything that's been said, how should he make the entrance to his guests—this *thug, redneck, Bull Terrier, bruiser, rascal*, all covered in gold chains and cell phones? With these fat stubby fingers, a balding head, leathery skin, and a *boundless* butt? So, should he babble some nonsense as a greeting, spout some Menippean bullshit, or even better: should he read it off a piece of paper, stumbling comically on some of the letters and punctuation marks—about the heroes of business and the heroes of culture, *Stradivari's tambourines*, and all that jazz? Should he immediately address them informally, call all the guys (including the interwar Professor Doktor) *dude*, and all the gals—well, not refer to them at all? But then it wouldn't be him, it's not my hero.

Or should he feign being a golden boy, a former Komsomol apparatchik, an eternally youthful civic activist, with a neat part and a tie that has slid somewhat to one side, should he dazzle them all with his provincial polish, should he litter the air with dead turns of phrase intolerable to a normal human ear, something like *dear cultural activists, esteemed friends, at this economic moment that is so far from easy for our young state . . . we, patriotic businessmen of the manufacturing sector . . . will protect you with our warm care . . . Carpathian hospitality . . . Siberian longevity . . . creative inspiration . . .at the clear sources . . . may the force be with you . . . blah-blah . . . bathrooms and lounges . . . breakfasts and lunches . . . live long and prosper?*

But this is not him either, I beg your pardon.

In reality it might be good to reach for the *opposite*: may he be a sickly teenager with almost transparent pallor, a bespectacled nerd with the complexes of a baby genius, an evil computer genius, a virtuoso hacker, an asthma sufferer in a wheelchair, a maniac inventor whose clothes are spattered with green saliva, or a mean circus dwarf with a beard down to his knees! Or should he actually be a woman, a lady, a lady of easy virtue, a witch, a hawk-nosed crone who is capable of turning into a mysteriously seductive damsel, who could also turn into a wolf, a crow, a snake, a dream?

The possibilities are endless, but nothing will come of it: Ylko Vartsabych, the owner and sponsor, will not come out, will not reveal himself, will not bless them with his presence, and then the entire group of eight, after waiting hesitantly on the porch, or in the lobby, or in the fireplace-lit lounge, would finally make its way to the appointed floors and rooms, leaving for tomorrow the introductions, getting to know one another, and various topographical exercises.

3

The building to which they were brought tonight recently acquired the name “Tavern “On the Moon”—yes, it was written precisely like this, with asymmetrical quotation marks in the middle. Of course, here too a prehistory is impossible to avoid, in fact there were three different prehistories, each of which demands close attention.

Everything begins with a hopelessly spasmodic attack of gray louse-ridden infantrymen ordered to push the enemy off the mountain ridge and capture the strategically important Dzyndzul alpine meadow. It is 1915, it seems, and each operation concocted at the army headquarters smacks of recklessness and helplessness. This is precisely why almost all of them perish during their advance on enemy lines, methodically doused in shrapnel, their bodies senselessly rolled down the grassy mountainsides. Right there, in the grass sticky with blood, lies one of them—a gray-eyed volunteer with an incomplete university education—as he falls into the corridors of darkness and sighs ominously. The final atheist vision in his eyes that gradually get glassy consists of the sky torn into shreds and of the figure of the Angel of Cyclones, the one who brings the clouds together and scatters them back apart over this cursed place. However, the gray-eyed infantryman, as he falls into emptiness, already does not see this ethereal figure finally bend down to him.

Some ten years pass, and almost everything repeats itself: lying in the grass amidst scattered bullet shells, a rising star of the Warsaw meteorological school looks, just like back then, into the skies torn to shreds, until the same angelic palm closes the same gray eyes. In his sleep he sees his goal.

Do not ever come back to the place where you were dying once.

The ensuing years fly by under the sign of the struggle to realize his plan. Endless meetings of scholarly committees, fiery speeches and reports, travel from one conference to another, appeals to senior academics, exhausting examinations of the expense estimates, the gathering of letters of recommendation from Stockholm, Paris, and London, and finally, a private meeting with a very prominent and highly placed official. All of this in one way or another contributes to a final positive decision. Thus one fine spring the construction actually begins: timber, stone, and metal are brought by a special railway branch built through the forest. But only the incredibly tough and sturdy Hutsul horses could manage the final stage, where the slope became too steep, and they are used to bringing everything necessary, as well as everything unnecessary, up to the mountain ridge. What definitely saves the budget is the cheapness of the labor force: local men sell themselves just as easily and inconsiderately as their descendants would sell themselves some seventy years later at East European markets. Thus with the help of endlessly snapping whips, tightened muscles, and a few deaths from accidents and drinking along the way—not to mention countless shady deals and three or four reckless compromises—everything finally came to be: halls and offices; a semicircular tower with observation stations; labs; a radio station; an independent power station; a heating system that also supplied hot water for bathrooms and laundry rooms. Finally, the most cherished dream—a library, a dance floor with gramophones and jukeboxes, a pool hall, a winter garden, a screening room, and a small art gallery with decent copies of late-Romantic alpine landscapes. All of it, put together, was called a meteorological station—and precisely here that very gray-eyed enthusiast moved in at the beginning of one summer, and along with him a team of trouble-proof storm watchers. There were even wives, children, and several maids. The life on the mountain had to look normal, in no way different from that in Warsaw, Krakow, or even Lviv.

However, life on the mountain turned out first of all to be extremely windy, and many among them lost their hat to the wind that carried it to the Transylvanian abyss beyond the border while they took a stroll along the former military road. Interestingly, only their young boss from time to time picked up those bullet shells, rusted helmets, and half-rotten hats ridden with bullet holes. His wife, by contrast, knew no rivals for the picking of flowers and medicinal plants that added to the extensive herbarium collection. Here one could also add the idyll, every Sunday, with two loud kids and a maid that barely kept up with the others, carrying a picnic basket with milk and biscuits, but I am not sure whether they had kids. However, I am certain about something else: they must have been followed by the cries of birds that were also always blown away, just like the hats and ladies' shawls, in the same direction of Transylvania.

But as a matter of fact, were those cries only of birds?

I am equally certain this first summer he was entirely happy, living on one of the world's greatest peaks, seeing how truly sublime this country can be sometimes—the mountains, observing the sky and the rolling fog, making detailed notes and calculations, listening to the approaching thunderstorms, how mountains are pelted with hail, foreseeing that during one and the same day in August the weather would change eight times and all four seasons would manifest themselves in a somewhat jumbled order: summer, winter, fall, spring. This was the fulfillment of the duty, and the realization of a plan, and a dream come true. Wasn't it all too much for just one infantryman?

However, already early next spring one had to fulfill some agreements that weren't reflected in the budget: the realization of such expensive dreams could not have happened without substantial support of one of the most powerful international partners. This is actually what was plainly stated during that confidential meeting between the gray-eyed idealist and the prominent official. Soon thereafter the location was unofficially visited by a very responsible *representative of the government of the United Kingdom* (RGUK below), accompanied by a few experts surprisingly well tanned for early April. A week later, after dining at a certain villa in Chortopil well hidden from strangers' eyes, the polished RGUK for the umpteenth time dipped the end of his cigar into the glass of cognac and, taking the final pause for a hefty puff of smoke, told the Warsaw strategists who were sitting there frozen something like "*Well, you have convinced me, gentlemen,*" and proceeded to sign all the respective protocols.

Thereby already before summer came, the naïve gang of meteorologists was not really brutally, yet rather decisively pushed aside in their mountain residence. The number of the rooms halved, the number of residents doubled, and those new residents brought with them not only more modern radio equipment, exercise machines, countless safes, padlocks, training models, ammunition, and a very different kind of book (mostly textbooks on encryption and the Russian language, which they completely sincerely believed to be the language spoken by the local *Ruthenians*). They also brought with them something that could be called an *atmosphere*. This was first and foremost anxiety, a suffocating obsession with conspiracy that easily slipped into obligatory nervousness. All the personnel, family members, and domestic help were immediately forced to sign certain papers. Then a rather severe redistribution of space took place, as a result of which the meteorological station lost some of the essential sites, including the tower. During their morning jogs they shouted some indecipherable military slogans, and half the dance hall was taken over by the gym. It became clear as day the world was slipping toward something really bad, and all sorts of horrors could start at any moment.

The sensation that everything was going straight to hell did not immediately capture the meteorological genius. For a while he tried to squelch his despair and find some optimal *modus vivendi* for this unavoidable evil. Sometimes during his spare time he even liked sharing a bottle or two with the boss of the new inhabitants and practice his English (of the three major Western languages he, a former citizen of the Habsburg Empire, knew this one the worst). Or play a game of chess —the players' skills were roughly on the same level. Besides, it seemed to him the storms and winds remained just as they had been before, stars clawed their way through clouds moving swiftly across a nighttime sky, and the cries of birds rolled about just as relentlessly as before.

But one day he was simply shocked, irritated by yet another violation of the sovereignty of meteorologists he, recalling his original rights, and more precisely tormented by suspicions, broke onto forbidden territory where he found in one of the cubicles the two—the chief of spies and his own wife—in the state of *bodily entanglement* (thus our movie has just metamorphosed from scientific documentary into melodrama). After a few days (and most importantly nights) she finally left this place for good (four Hutsuls carried her belongings down the slope, then the white gauzy shawl flashed for the last time through the first trees down below like the top half of the lowered national flag). He did not succeed in challenging the seducer to a duel. However, he drunk himself into a stupor both then and the following night.

Between these evenings and the final descent of the Angel of Cyclones onto the Dzyndzul meadow he somehow got through another year. Everything was really going to hell, vodka was not giving strength but taking it away, Hitler annexed Bohemia and each new order from the bosses in Warsaw smelled of panic and dishonesty, plus he somehow caught syphilis from one of his rare gap-toothed lovers. This time the Angel of Cyclones did not have a chance, even though thirteen years later everything looked almost the same: the same Dzyndzul meadow, the same grass, the same glassy stare at the sky, but this time he turned out to be a much better *volunteer*, shooting himself skillfully and entirely voluntarily.

One is left thinking that after his *demission* the affairs of the meteorological station got even worse: the personnel scattering in all possible directions, exhausted by their complete uselessness, or perhaps simply by the nonstop howling of wind and the cries of birds. Surprisingly enough, in parallel to these events the neighboring institution also began pulling up stakes—it seemed the place was of interest to them only as long as one worked with the elements.

The final safes with secret archives and lists of informers were taken in the direction of Transylvania only a few days before September 17, 1939. Later, there was a big all-consuming fire: the furniture and the floors burned, walls melted, and with them went the victrolas, the radio receivers, countless herbariums and Russian language textbooks, although now at last these latter would have been of use.

And this way ends our first prehistory.

But for the second one to begin, the burnt shell of the meteorological station would have to stand untouched for nearly three decades. Although "untouched" is too strong a word—from time to time it was used by occasional travelers hiding from hail and snow under the remainder of the roof or by nearby residents who carried away for their needs various fragments and segments of what once had been whole. What else happened? Sometimes someone lit fires from the remaining furniture, someone made love on charred radiators, someone was ready to die from fear listening to the howling of wolves and, of course, the cries of birds.

In any case, one fine day at the end of the sixties, beginning of the seventies, a special *commission from the district* visited this place. This was the time of *intensification of work with the young and especially teenagers*; yet again the powers that be turned their utmost attention to the problems of leisure activities of the *children of the proletariat.* Sport and physical education were granted utmost importance. The Olympic movement was sweeping the whole country, thus everywhere a laborious and exhausting search for young talent for the Olympic reserve was under way. *Our* victories in sport testified to the general triumph of *our* ideas. Understandably, in winter sports *we* had no rivals. However, in some disciplines *a certain lag began manifesting itself*; a few *expanded plenary meetings* and conference calls were dedicated to solving it. The situation was the worst with ski jumpers, whom the inventive journalists nicknamed *flying skiers.* Thus, *in order to meet the demands*, etc., the commission from the district decreed a boarding school preparing young ski jumpers would come into existence—and it would become the nursery to sprout *our* inextinguishable victories. (A few reasons for such winged hopes did exist: traditionally, the local Hutsul children, starting at quite an early age were very comfortable with alpine skiing, their fancy ski tricks resulted in tips from various gullible visitors, immediately spent on beer and smokes.)

Although by then the local authorities had no Hutsul horses left, and two thirds of the railway line had been disassembled already in the first postwar years, one fine spring the Dzyndzul meadow saw everything start anew.

The picture now is a bit different from what happened in the preceding case: one sees for the first time some caterpillar-tracked monsters, the roar of motors for the first time rivaling the roar of winds above the mountain range, but the main engine propelling construction this time is vodka, amplified by the construction manager's guttural curses which, like everything else in this place, winds blow away to Transylvania.

The boarding school, its ski jumping hill not quite finished, was solemnly opened in time for the winter sport season. A few dozen of the most talented kids took their places in classrooms and dormitories, taking advantage of the autonomous heating system, the bathrooms, the sewer system, reanimated with considerable effort from the days of the meteorological station.

However, the *district leadership* committed an error that eventually led to truly fatal consequences for the whole project. But why call it an error? In fact, they had no other choice: no one among the *local inhabi-*

tants yielded to the pleas and threats; a few even openly made warning nods towards the *evil place.* Thus it was a certain Malafey who agreed to take the position of the boarding school principal: a rather pitiful looking guy about thirty years old, his face covered in freckles and pimples, graduate of a phys. ed. vocational school somewhere in the brotherly North-Central Region of Russia, a failed jumper who once placed something like seventy-ninth in a regional competition and since then made ends meet with the meager salary of gym teacher in secondary schools, living alone, unkempt and generally unnoticed, although every now and then getting wildly drunk on payday. "We Tatars don't give a fuck," said Malafey, accepting the command over a far-away mountain boarding school. "Good, at least it won't stink of Russkies here," thought the department head in response, shaking squeamishly Malafey's sweaty hand.

However, finding himself at a great distance and—most importantly—height from the hated gym teacher's existence, sensing besides the fullness and limitlessness of his power at least over the teenagers, the newly appointed principal of the boarding school shockingly quickly morphed into a new incarnation. After a month or two of sedentary existence, well fed and well heated, ruling over his tiny domain in the clouds, his former helpless shyness disappeared. His palms stopped getting sweaty, his ears stopped getting crimson. As for his nose which made one think of a chicken's beak, it did not become aquiline, but did acquire some weighty gloss. One could welcome all these metamorphoses were they not accompanied by an exuberant release of everything that for years sat unhappily deep inside this little man without any hope of ever spilling out. Malafey's time had come.

First and foremost he finally gained access to female genitalia. After working over, in the course of just a few weeks, the few unhappy and defenseless schoolteachers (Ukrainian language, geography, medieval history) who seemed to have been sent there specially for his ravenous appetite, he tried switching to the deaf-mute cook who was pushing sixty and whose body always smelled of cooking fat, and finally crossed the ultimate limit of the law, forcing a few of the students to conduct proscribed physical exercises. Impudent and aggressive, he concluded dictatorship was the best method of rule, and thus he kept his victims obedient and submissive, attaining his goal with the help of pinches, punches, and handcuffs brought over from God knows which prison camp, most often on the rug of his office, although sometimes also in the classrooms, on the exercise mats in the gym, or in subterranean corners of the showers.

Besides, thanks to his new post, he now had the opportunity to drink without any breaks and not only on paydays. For this he mostly used the male students, inventing an obligatory exercise of a long-distance run to the general store thirteen kilometers away and back, *cross-country race, go!*—and none of the students was advised to come back with a bottle later than two hours, thirty-four minutes, and sixteen and seven hundredths seconds. Later he invented for them a longer, *near-marathon* exercise, to the convenience store at the train station which sometimes carried popular brands of cologne (Was it Chypre? maybe Cypress? Oh, these childhood smells!). For some reason, Malafey couldn't stand local moonshine.

In all other respects he was doing well, and as a member of the Party he even sometimes, after a beauty nap and a soak, finally pulled himself together and came down to the valley to attend a meeting of the local cell.

His rule over the boarding school and the world would have continued for many more years were it not for a new female student who was transferred there mid-year due to her considerable success in alpine skiing. The girl, it turned out, came from a rather traditional upbringing. She was due to marry in a year or so and, as they say, she *protected herself*. Thus, for several weeks she managed to slip from Malafey's attacks and threats that were getting ever wilder (*I'll tear your womb out, you miserable bitch!*). Finally, one late evening after the night's all-clear, having completed her assignment in the cafeteria washing a pile of dirty dishes left from that morning's cream of wheat, cornered hopelessly near the cafeteria exit (the freckle-covered claws spread, the light switch clicks, the heavy odor of grub and cologne wafts), she finally yielded, but in the end succeeded in begging in a whisper for just one *favor*, and thus, according to the folk wisdom, remained a virgin.

The following morning she ran away, disappeared, dissolved in wind and fog, but in reality she turned up five days later in her native town (a separate saga involving hitchhiking, commuter trains, and the last bus of the night filled with drunken lumberjacks). Now we are left to imagine her testimony, tears on the bitten lips, a physical, bruises on the buttocks, an anal smear, photos of the injuries, gnashing teeth, phone calls, closed meetings of the *educational and law enforcement officials*, and finally, a *difficult decision* by the local executive powers.

Like the first time, everything ends very badly: late at night, during a snowstorm, a team of commandos enters the premises of the School of Olympic Reserve (how did they get there—by helicopter?). Actually, it was three or four heavy-set middle-aged guys. They walk through the hallways, offices, classrooms, but can't find him anywhere, although finally one of the children fearfully points towards the basement, some crying, half-dressed lass darts out from the shower room, streams of hot water flowing on the concrete floor, he barricades himself with lockers, they give him ten minutes to get dressed (*no nonsense, punk!*), but as he does not come out even after twenty minutes, they proceed to storm in. On the twenty-second minute they break inside and, making a way through dense steam and crushing empty cologne bottles under their feet, finally find him in the last stall where everything is by now completely red. A broken bottle came in handy for slitting both wrists, and I bet you his final words were a favorite phrase from a beloved movie of childhood days, "You won't get me, suckers!"

This is essentially the end of the second prehistory, for there is no need to recount in detail that the alpine boarding school with the never-finished ski jump hill was soon liquidated. The most experienced among us remember how that very season the country's leadership made a sharp turn from alpine skiing to kayaking and canoeing.

And thus again desolation, destruction, and dispersal in all possible direction of anything that could be of use for something.

As for the third and so far still unfinished prehistory, for it to begin another quarter century had to pass, although this is not simply a matter of time flying by. This third part would never be able to begin were it not for a whole chain of fantastic cataclysms, a consequence of which in the city of Berlin, very far from the Dzyndzul alpine meadow, a Wall came down, the map of Eastern Europe underwent a rather radical change of colors, and sometimes also contours, and in the young state of Ukraine there came into being a *new type of man.* In other words, an opportunity manifested itself, narrow as a needle's eye, of striking it rich really quickly and remorselessly. So, as soon as the first half of the nineties passed, everything again started swirling around: agreements, certificates, mortgages, stocks and bonds, a few ephemeral banks, trusts, holdings, and then a certain citizen Y.Y. Vartsabych, not known to anyone, suddenly grabbed all for a pittance, and truth be told, who gave a damn about this place? It's a good thing such a person popped up, and it's wonderful he grabbed it all—otherwise where would my heroes have ended up that night?

Thus, within two to three months the aforementioned edifice again rose from the ashes, including the tower and loggias on all three floors: Finnish metallic roof tiles, German drywall, bathroom tiles from Spain, parquet from Italy, bathroom fixtures from the Emirates—sorry, parquet from the Emirates and bathroom fixtures from Belgium—and, naturally, exclusive high-grade furnaces, copper pipes, water and fire, laminate, vinyl insulated windows, special mansard windows (three hundred bucks each)—all of it together christened the "Tavern "On the Moon" resort—yes, it was written precisely like this, with asymmetrical quotation marks in the middle.

As you can see, this third prehistory is really short, although it is still unfinished.

In the meantime, morning has come and it is time to wake Zumbrunnen. We will need him in order to have a look at the house from inside, while everyone is asleep. One should hope his nearsighted eyes are professionally more attentive than many other eyes present. Thus he is the one we should wake. But how?

Karl-Joseph Zumbrunnen woke because behind the wall someone and someone else were unambiguously and loudly—how shall I put it?—making love. The female voice reached such high audio frequencies that it is useless to try to visualize the immensity of its passion. From time to time it was joined by another voice, likewise on the verge of madness. As for a male voice, there was no certitude about it, although twice one could hear some satisfied throaty murmur. Besides, all the furniture in that room—and not just the bed that was turned into a trampoline—seemed to jump in unison to an ever-accelerating rhythm. Not sure what to do about his involuntary erection, Karl-Joseph remarked to himself that the room beyond this wall certainly could not belong to the Voronych-Pepas, which gave his soul a noticeable relief. Yes, he was quite certain that Ms. Roma and her husband got the room two doors down from him, and on the other side. What remained was to reach, after straining his memory, the not terribly realistic conclusion that the above-mentioned sound extravaganza arrived from the room of old Professor Doktor. Refusing to seek any explanations for this phenomenon, Karl-Joseph (his erection persisting) was just about to turn away from the wall when suddenly everything ended in a hurricane of orgasm, both voices for the last time rising in unison, and then everything settled dead calm once again, including the furniture.

But there was no chance of him going back to sleep. His inflamed imagination ordered Zumbrunnen to wake, carry out the necessary minimum of procedures (the excitement finally died only after a cold shower) and take a walk around the silent building. So, a dozen minutes later he entered the hallway and first of all stood for some time in front of the door to the neighboring room. But the silence—just like everywhere else—was so deep it led one to imagine the deathly sleep that embraced the unknown couple as soon it had reached the peak of their lovemaking enterprise. A similar occurrence is described in a poem by Antonych (see his "Ballad of a Blue Death") but Karl-Joseph did not know about this. He likewise did not know whether it was indeed a couple behind the door.

Everything Zumbrunnen saw while wandering floor to floor, moving from one wing to another, passing sections large and small, left the impression of a strange combination of times: entire fragments of past existence kept resurging, vividly penetrating the present—a fragment of exposed prewar SERAFINI bricks, a piece of Soviet mosaic with Sputnik and some cosmonauts. In an entirely unexpected niche there suddenly appeared, shameless in its innocence, a cast iron Austrian bathtub with noble green faucets, then a phosphorescent deer—the pinnacle of sixties decorating imagination, life-sized—shocked him from its pedestal decorated with river pebbles.

The second thing that struck him was the intense degree of clutter—everything he encountered in these rooms, hallways, and stairways bore the same stamp of coexistence of several strata of daily life simultaneously. Here one saw: computers, photocopy and fax machines, printers, simulators and synthesizers, and also stimulators and sublimators wrapped in electric wiring, some of them totally gutted. The digital/laser luxury goods included abandoned video cameras, home theater systems, antennas (regular and satellite), various generations of TVs, music systems with and without karaoke, vacuum cleaners, food processors. Here and there one saw various remotes and other small-fry modems, surge protectors, halogen lamps, radio transmitters, chargers, CD players, Tetris games, cell phones and various accessories for them. All this diversity slipped into depravity, for here and there one also saw various superfluous depilatories, vibrators, ejaculators, potency meters with electrode sticks, night vision goggles, rapid excitement machines, milking units, and then without any rhyme or reason: cocktail and sound mixers, toasters, boosters, a few hard drives, portable land-sky-land rocket launchers, special dryers for chest, armpit, and also for pubic hair—thus it would be hardly surprising if the nuclear football was also to be found there. However, all these things comprised barely a third of what one saw, since there were also large decorative platters (wood carved, metallic, ceramic; the colors: yellow, green, dark brown), traditional folk hatchets, forged metal plates, hats, rifles, and belts, lacquered wooden eagles, bears, wolves, boars' heads (both stuffed and plastic), embroidered shirts, pearl and ordinary necklaces, toy horses and unicorns, storks in nests, bats, flexible wooden snakes, mouth harps, rafts, alpenhorns, Hutsul stove tiles, tambourines, shoulder bags, reed pipes, pens with figurines of erect Hutsuls, pan flutes, boxes decorated with shells and river pebbles, corals, skirts, jackets, vests, Adidas track suits made in China, wooden shoes, scissors for shearing sheep and boars, Hutsul kilims (the colors: grey, black, and burgundy), Yeltsin matryoshka dolls, Easter eggs decorated with space exploration and Olympic motifs, cross-stitch portraits of St. George, the writers Yuri Fedkovych and Ivan Franko, and the current president, vases and pitchers already mentioned earlier as "ceramics," a group sculpture, *Commisar Rudnev and General Shukhevych Become Sworn Brothers*—in other words, it seemed the entire museum of Hutsul folk art together with the famous arts and crafts market from the town of Kosiv for some unknown reason had been moved here. However, in case this somehow didn't suffice, one could also find here and there samurai, Arab and Turkish swords, dragon teeth, a few canvases by Fragonard (originals) and approximately as many by Fraunhofer (copies), elephant and mammoth tusks, petrified Mesozoic-era mollusks from the days when this area was the bottom of a sea, antiquarian books on cabbala and ballistics in Gothic script, mandrake roots preserved in moonshine together with lacertines and salamanders, kidney and moon stones, Venetian mirrors and chandeliers, pendants, chalcedonies, firebird feathers, archaeopteryx eggs, a set of silver balls over which seven Catholic priests, seven Orthodox priests, and seven rabbis have recited the required prayers, Spanish Duende dueling pistols (each in a separate storage box), butcher knives, stilettos, bracelets (in both the literal and metaphoric senses), amulets, crossbows, tutus, plaster figurines of mourners, bathers, and fellators, Victorian-era oleographic pornography, urns with the remains for ladies and gentlemen burned God knows when and for what, a modest collection of skull goblets for red wine, scarecrows, fans, and ash boxes, King Kong's fur, angel hair, assorted chicken feet, also countless other objects of material culture from eras past.

Another circumstance that struck Karl-Joseph during examination of the building was connected to the doors, not so much their incredible number meant to witness a corresponding quantity of rooms and passageways, as the inscriptions *on* them. Moreover, there weren't even two door plaques in the whole building done in exactly the same style—it was as if they were torn from all over the place and brought to this strange site, thus a weirdly chaotic sensation grew, pushing Karl-Joseph, rather diffident to begin with, into a dead end of fruitless wandering and wondering.

A few plaques (TREATMENT ROOM, PROCTOLOGIST ON DUTY, DISSECTION ROOM) seemed somehow to refer to the present use of this building as a residential spa facility. Others seemed neutrally universal and did not signify anything in particular (ASSISTANT DIRECTOR, CAFETERIA, POULTRY PROCESSING, GENERATOR ROOM, COMPLAINTS AND FEEDBACK DEPARTMENT). Still others bore a touch of recommendation/injunction, rather common in this country (VIP WAITING ROOM, NO SMOKING, CLOSED ROOM, DO NOT ENTER). But if one could more or less make sense of those, the inscriptions SADNESS CABINET, FINAL COMMUNION and THIS WAY TO THE TUNNEL looked fully impossible to understand. One also came across fairly light-hearted ones: SPRINGTIME BILLIARD HALL, SILENCE OF THE LAMBS ROOM, HOUSE OF MIRRORS NO. 6.

Karl-Joseph was beginning to suspect that his puzzlement might be due to an insufficient command of the local language. This hypothesis might have been credible were it not for plaques in other, more familiar languages: FUCKING ROOM, RED ARMY OF THE UNIVERSE, DO NOT MASTURB' PLEASE, then EXQUISITE CORPSE, ETERNAL DAMNATION, HELLFIRE, KISS OF DEATH, TORTURE NEVER STOPS (he involuntarily recalled blood-red-and-black magazine covers of his high school days when he was a heavy metal fan; from the depths of memory almost automatically popped the image of some black-leather-and-chains-clad bitch with blood-red lips on a deathly pale face). Further on it was just as good: DANCE MACABRE, SUICIDE REHABILITATION, then simply THE DOORS,[4] for some reason in the plural, then in Russian, FIRST DEPARTMENT, HEAD OF PERSONNEL, VISAS AND REGISTRATION DEPARTMENT, followed by PIEPRZENIE NA ZIMNO, ACHTUNG—SCHEISSE, VAMPIRENTREFFPUNKT, the completely out-of-place LOKALBAHN NACH BADEN (with the arrow for some reason pointing to the basement) and the fully illogical DAMEN-PISSOIR . . .

All this made him want to get somewhere outdoors as soon as possible, and Karl-Joseph indeed found himself on the enclosed porch where he recognized still unpacked suitcases, duffle bags, and backpacks that were stacked there last night and, after spending some thirteen minutes fiddling with the lock on the front door, jumped out onto the still frozen slope underneath the entrance where he finally calmed himself with the thought that since he had left his room without eyeglasses, he must have simply hallucinated most of the above.

And now he decisively walks downhill, chopping the air with resolute arm movements, slows down on a slippery patch, looks around and searches amid the first thickets of juniper for a path to the valley devoid of cold wind and screaming birds, where it has already been spring for several weeks now. Karl-Joseph

4 These words and the preceding ones in this sentence were written in English in the original.

takes this path for the first, but not the last time.

And we must follow him if we indeed want to see the local surroundings. So, behind us the mountain range and the Transylvanian border, and ahead, that is downhill, springtime. With each hundred yards there's more and more of it. Now it wafts from shiny cobblestones of an old military road, then reminds you of itself with the smell of warmed-up juniper. Boulders, juniper, also dwarf mountain pines, then young freshly sprouted grass. In a week or two, following the tradition of St. George's Day, shepherds and their herds should come here—but they won't, since they never come to the Dzyndzul meadow. And for this reason its grass is probably the sweetest.

We are going to leave on the slope to our right, some two hundred yards away the crooked edifice of the unfinished ski jumping hill. Karl-Joseph will make a mental note of it as an object for his future Masochist album: the rusted steps, each other one missing, and the in-run with a completely destroyed surface.

Further below begins the primordial forest, planted not with a human hand but by the Anti-Spirit himself. That is, no Karl-Joseph Zumbrunnen, Sr., merited imperial forest ranger, had any connection to it, although he managed to spy after the Anti-Spirit (Nature?) in order to gather the know-how for planting trees in this area.

At the level of primordial forest, which some time

later Karl-Joseph Zumbrunnen, Jr. enters like an enormous train station building—so, at the level of primordial forest the road becomes less and less steep. In fact at times it is completely flat, yet filled with various obstacles: enormous puddles swarming with flies, fallen trees, stone-hard clay caterpillar tracks (something was going on here last year, wasn't it?), then a bit further the tractor itself, stuck without any hope of return—if over the course of the summer it became covered with grass, vines, flowers, it would make a decent postcard photo!—then suddenly barbed wire appears out of nowhere, along with remnants of poles, gates green with age, plywood billboards with warning and banning inscriptions, but here only we, and certainly not some photographer-spy, have a right to guess the proximity of abandoned missile silos, their wells saturated with the smell of mushrooms, urine, and deep mystery, along with smashed control panels and smashed beer bottles at the bottom.

But not only this: here, quite close, another network, in its time no less mysterious: underground bunkers. The last of them doused with grenades some time in the early fifties and nobody came out from it. Actually, the grenade version is much nicer than the other one, nerve gas.

And then on our and Zumbrunnen's path appears another ruin: a train track, rather, an absurd section of it leading from nowhere to nowhere, without beginning or end, ideally suited for vipers who crawl out onto sleepers April 7 and then live among them until late autumn. Karl-Joseph knows nothing about this serpentine habit, thus he riskily steps onto those very sleepers, not seeing anything beneath his feet. However, this time he will be forgiven as a foreign guest, thus he will walk without harm above the invisible reptiles, by lucky accident stepping exactly where he should and not hearing the unhappy hissing below.

This railway ruin, like everything else in this forest, now belongs to Vartsabych, but no one can tell why he would need it. Perhaps just for fun?

The tracks end at a stone mound, thus Zumbrunnen for some time needs to make his way through a thicket of hazelnuts, again in search of the road he lightheartedly abandoned. If he finds it, he would see a meadow by the river, completely suitable for grazing, in other words fresh and green, but still with deep traces of a recent flood, full of puddle traps with clay soil that makes chomping sounds beneath his boots.

It is thanks to these Salamander boots, and also thanks to a certain kind of clumsiness that is definitely not local that they recognize him—three or four teenagers in old sweaters with holes on the elbows, baggy flannel trousers tucked into rubber boots, dirty and loud; they cross his path having run out of their shack a little higher above the River, and will start pestering him, distant descendants of banished Brahmins with Indian rings in their ears and noses, they will plead with him in all the languages of this area (*gimme, gimme some money, sir, gimme some candy, gimme some cigarettes, gimme your palm, your soul, your body!*)—OK, not in English, that would be too much, but in all the other languages, that is, using many different words from many different languages, including Sanskrit. They follow him up to the bridge, since he does go in the direction of the bridge (that's where the forest road ends), and he thinks they are young enough to be his children, yet still he does not give them even a penny, just five hryvnias, in the end.

When he steps onto the bridge they immediately fall behind—for there, beyond the bridge, where they are not allowed, there begins the forbidden world: a paved, badly potholed highway, on the other side of which a ravine that in the summer becomes densely overgrown with burdocks, and at the bottom of this ravine dozens of old broken down cars. This is a car pit, the end of ends, dozens of car bodies, rusty Rolls Royces, Mercedeses and Volkswagens, let alone Ladas and Škodas—all of this also belongs to Vartsabych, although nobody knows why his people keep bringing all this scrap here. So, a ravine, and then, shortly after the bridge, another road branches off the highway. Not even a road but a path, or rather a Path, that is, some kind of lumberjacks' path that winds along the course of the stream, rising higher and higher, but one shouldn't, one shouldn't go that way, for there is the end of all ends, the thirteenth kilometer, a dead end with the last pub in this world for those very lumberjacks or sleepwalkers.

So, the teens fall behind and remain at their meadow by the river. They are not allowed onto the other bank of the river, nor are they allowed into the forest. And this is how they exist, between two forbidden areas on a narrow strip between fear of the past and fear of the future.

4

Only when he hit thirty-seven did Artur Pepa realize he in fact had a heart. Everything began with nighttime awakenings, where he found himself all alone against a viscous black desert, half-immersed in the scattered remnants of dream. The other half of him was fully conscious of being suspended in the here-and-now, yet this didn't make things easier. He decided to blame it all on alcohol. Indeed, the damn irregular heartbeat usually manifested itself soon after especially long-lasting *carnivals* and *jam sessions* that included walks on one's head and shuffling abysses. It was enough to start, in the afternoon (*two hundred-gram glasses of strong stuff, some tomato juice, and something else to chase it all*), reaching higher elevation later in the evening (*oh show me the way to the next whisky bar*), and finally getting stuck at the very first stop until sunrise, downing at full speed whatever remained in all the bottles and emptying all the cigarette packs (*who runs from one 24/7 shop to another like I?*)—yes, it sufficed to pass yet one more time all these 24/7 stages for *it* to return the following day with iron-clad inevitability. Someone once saw him faint in a coffeehouse, his cigarette falling into the coffee cup, and the chair making a horrible screeching noise sliding sideways with its metal leg on the slippery floor. He did not see it himself, having fallen for a few minutes into loneliness and isolation, at the bottom of a murky chasm with monotonous ringing (could it be *there* too it would be the same, is it really only a murky chasm and monotonous ringing?). Yes, then it became apparent, just like the sweat that poured over him once he came to his senses.

Frankly speaking, the incident at the coffeehouse wasn't the first time. Indeed, at a certain point Artur Pepa started getting used to these states and even liking them—with the same selflessness as when he rushed towards changes in emotional states at the shifts from sobriety to drunkenness. There was something in this sudden rupture of the crazed heart, its fluttering rush somewhere right under the throat, in this iron fist that liked, with all the skill of a bird catcher, to grab him and not let go. "It's good it happened precisely like this," he would sometimes persuade himself. "Now I know at least what's in my cards. Sudden cardiac arrest is not that bad a version compared with something slower and more destructive." In the meantime, he mentally went though other *options*: a growth inside his body of some amoeba-like amorphous tumors, changes in the immune system, a frightful and shameful withering away of muscles, or an inexorable slide into the vegetative abyss of Alzheimers—no, his fate carried with it a much better prospect. Although, recognizing in the middle of the night, between two and four o'clock, the unavoidable return of arrhythmia, he still was afraid. Afraid that at some point his heart wouldn't be able to handle it and burst—not because it had to be unable to handle it and burst, but out of fear that it *might*. In other words, he was scared of being scared.

Thoughts about death are a definite sign of a life crisis, that's clear. Artur's crisis could be explained first and foremost by that dangerous life stage he was approaching. However, that stage does not come on its own; on its own it doesn't even mean anything.

Instead, there were several shocking publishing flops—something that happens to all crowd favorites at the moment their free and joyful floating stops being only their own personal matter. The awareness that something is expected of you all the time, this lovingly impatient and incessant external pressure makes you hesitate and lose your cool. In Artur Pepa's case the worst thing was not even the record number of negative reviews he had received in recent years in response to each new published gesture (and for him creativity was, generally speaking, a form of gesticulation). All this is nothing, superficial stuff, short-lived froth; all this is ultimately just a manifestation of a strange love from naïve or envious characters, fans of petty intrigue—this way Artur (as it seemed to him) put them in their place. However, there was also something else: the loss of the joy of writing. The simplest explanation would be, like all narcissists, he desperately needed admiration and recognition.

Without them Artur Pepa lost his easygoing nature. He no longer liked himself, and this was reflected in his writing. In other words, once he hit thirty-seven Artur Pepa suddenly felt he didn't like to write, that he actually hated this occupation, that his writing desk was turning into a site of horrific psychological torture and a burning shame about all that finally remained on paper. Sometimes he stumbled on the second phrase, sometimes even the first, unable to move forward and somehow rid himself of this, to chase away this demon of tongue-tiedness. Sometimes the result of his exhausting three-hour war with a phrase was something like "In springtime, women's skin health temporarily worsens." Although he did feel satisfied in the end, after writing "His foolish brain splattered in all directions like bird poop." Perhaps—he retained a glimmer of hope—writing has become more difficult for me because I now write better? Perhaps the writing of true literature is indeed an immersion in torture, he thought, as he squirmed from the inappropriate stupid rhyme. If I were able to not write, I would work the land, he said, not so much quoting as mocking someone else, and the entire gang burst into laughter. They were into quotations. They were also into him, Artur Pepa.

Undoubtedly, he exaggerated the public's attention to his persona and their interest in it. In reality, few people cared what this sonofabitch was writing out there, and Artur Pepa not so much felt as imagined all this energetic external pressure. Actually, who the hell cares about this world of literature and its petty infighting! Shut the fuck up about serving the Word! The things at stake were graver and more real.

Once he hit thirty-seven, Artur Pepa noticed death waltzing around him in circles. This happened in the closest circle, at the distance of reaching out with one's hand: relatives, friends, friends of friends died or disappeared. Thus the obligation to attend funerals, be a pall bearer, lay wreaths, cross himself at wakes arose as often as twice a month, and it couldn't help paralyzing some important nodes of his—and let us forgive him after all!—cranky and impressionable ego. It was especially nasty on death's behalf because it looked like blatant revenge for Artur Pepa's freethinking younger days. Once, in the middle of a particularly stunning spring, when it still did not know how to ruin women's skin, Artur wrote almost unconsciously the irresponsibly pathos-charged lines, "Not a word about death. It is only a form / whose eternal content is life, bumblebees, and dew." And death did not forget about it, throwing him, like a notch on a tree, its "you'll have to answer for this."

Thus it gave him the thirty-seventh year, crowned by the murder of his close friend, an investigative newspaper reporter, always open to any and all breakneck (literally) adventure, who was thrown at full speed from a train somewhere between Zdolbuniv and Kyiv (drinking in the compartment, smoking between the train cars, accidental fellow-traveler buddies, a flight among sparks, broken neck). Artur Pepa knew almost nothing about his late friend's *investigations*, but could guess from time to time the degree of risk he faced. Thus when in a month or two a *law enforcement representative* calmed down the *public* present at the press-conference saying that *this murder had nothing in common with the professional activity of the victim, excuse me, of the deceased*, Artur Pepa also signed a loud protest letter, two thirds of which was written in all caps. But more than the various letters or drunkenly signed declarations, what was essential was his internal cup running over. From the moment the risk-taking buddy flew forever beyond the train car into the night crisscrossed by poles and rails, Artur Pepa realized: something had passed irrevocably, the Golden Age would never come, ahead of him was only thickening darkness and cold.

But these circumstances could not be considered his crisis either. All of these were consequences: sluggish writing most often suggests feeling morally drained, death always peeking in where there is not enough love. Thus no one except Artur Pepa himself could know that all of this was happening precisely because of the loss of love. Or—if that phrase seems too bombastic—due to the increasing indifference towards once beloved women. Or—and this Pepa feared the most—due to complete loss of a capacity to love. Yes, this was first and foremost the waning of his sexuality, although sometimes a sudden notice of various hips and buttocks flashing by in the street could still awaken in him the former spermatosaur. The one who so recently, during far better days, attracted to his heart's content during the day-long free-floating so many electric gazes, waves, burns, breathed in fully all the spring, wine, perfume, the secrets of secretions, who could that very night give it all back so generously that Roma Voronych, his wife and greatest lover, was on the verge of fainting.

She was almost five years older, but this couldn't have any importance whatsoever for him, back then, during the moment of their first convergence.

Everything began with an exhibition of antique prints at the History Museum. Luckily they lived in a city where such events are simply a requirement in order from time to time to shake the depressing stasis of the environment. Artur Pepa wasn't much of a connoisseur of antique prints, especially colored ones (and this was an exhibition of colored prints), but he also couldn't avoid attending—at the very least because of drinks inevitably to be had later in the company of an army of *wandering comedians*. ("You know, sometimes I completely freeze on the inside when I think I might not have come that evening," he would tell her a few years later, in bed, happily exhausted, a barely calm palm of his hand on her stomach, still slippery from lovemaking. She would understand he meant that very exhibition, for she would answer,

"And I was only planning to pop in for five minutes—a few of my acquaintances were there."

Perhaps this wasn't an exhibition of prints at the History Museum. Perhaps it was an exhibition of antique clocks at the Anatomy Museum? Or a performance art piece with a Plastic Fish and quicksilver thermometers? Now this is of no importance to us. Now this is of almost no importance to them either.

But then, passing a young woman in a raincoat on narrow wooden stairs and trying not to step on the feet of the little girl she was holding by the hand, Artur Pepa had to slow down to grab this woman by the elbow. The story of a heel broken on the stairs had to find its continuation: feeling himself a somewhat parodic page of a queen neglected by the rabble and casually breathing in her face a whimsical mixture of beer, coffee, and brandy consumed earlier, Artur Pepa set out in search of the main hero of the exhibition ("Don't leave, please, I'll be right back . . ."—this to her, while he dove down the stairs into the crowd at the opening, from which he finally procured his dearest friend Furman, with golden cufflinks on his golden hands). That evening Furman, who was hosting the event, dressed in a tuxedo borrowed from the opera, which did not prevent him, being a hero and also slightly drunk, from arming himself with a museum hammer and some nails and restoring the broken heel on—so let it be!—the golden shoe of the unknown Ms. Clumsy. "There you have it," said Furman solemnly, spitting out the spare nail cobbler-style with a somewhat bossy attitude. For this he got a kiss on the cheek, and Pepa, not to lose the initiative, courteously asked for permission to put the little shoe on the little foot (a history museum! harpsichords! a courtly festival! rococo! oh-oh-oh!). Of course, it was her little foot he had in mind, although he did not permit himself to say, "Allow me to shod you," no matter how much he wanted to. "And this is Kolya," she said for some reason, pointing to the girl and smiling nervously. "Kolomea Voronych," corrected her the little one solemnly, emphasizing the "r" in the middle of her surname so strongly it came out as "rrr." Both wore raincoats of the same style (differing, naturally, in size) and had very similar hairstyles. Thus inebriated Artur Pepa thought her a magic fairy with her disciple. "Still, I wouldn't mind drinking champagne from it," he nodded towards the little shoe. "All right, they are waiting for me down there," declared Furman who wisely and quickly disappeared, the golden one.

And when some ten minutes later they were walking through Market Square in search of their shamanic champagne (the times weren't favorable for this: it was right during the agony of communism, plus a sleet storm, especially dreadful because it was April), so when another gust of frenetically fatal wind tore the umbrella from her hands, and for some reason she rushed to try to catch it, walking in a heron-like way on those very heels over the square's cobblestones, without any hope of success, since the umbrella was hopelessly broken—so, at that very moment Artur Pepa suddenly felt that this magic fairy had long been on the bad side of all the higher powers, that her life wasn't going as well as it usually does for fairies, that it was in fact going rather badly, and that he desperately wanted to do something for her, otherwise he too would be screwed.

This is what, broadly speaking, he had in mind when a couple years later he whispered the typical words of a lover, "You know, sometimes I completely freeze on the inside when I think I might have not come that evening." Because that evening he did come.

Roma Voronych taught German language classes and was a young widow. She had once married a certain ethnographer from the Kolomyia region. Much older than her, right at the time he was looking for a woman from Lviv to bring some kind of order to his personal life, his extensive collection of folk jackets and papercutting, and also the stomach ulcer that was increasingly bothering his bachelor way of life. "Mr. Voronych, you will destroy yourself," various female enthusiasts kept telling this custodian of the *unclouded sources of folk beauty.* "You require regular permanent womanly care!" But all of them bit their tongues when one day Mr. Voronych declared he was getting married. Indeed, it was a very *unequal* marriage, even the female fans of his drooping wheat-colored mustache recognized this. What pushed Roma to tie her life (indeed, have her life tied up, exactly!) with this unkempt aging man, with his coughing, his yellow teeth and long johns, his outstanding educator award, his folk ditties noted in pencil in student notebooks, his (although it's no sin) unpleasantly-smelling socks—no one was able to say. One is left to believe the more than doubtful and typically Lvivian rumor that this ethnography enthusiast was in fact a Carpathian sorcerer who used the entire arsenal of his secret recipes to subjugate the will of an inexperienced, fantasy-prone idealist.

Whatever the case, after a year of family life they had a daughter, closing for Roma any possibilities of retreat and fully cementing the family status quo. The times that followed (yet another eternity) were spent washing diapers and those very long johns, and standing in pre-dawn lines for baby food. I am not even going to talk about the various dietetic experiments and pharmaceutical tricks she needed in order to mollify the husband's capricious ulcer. One morning Roma Voronych woke as if from a dream, looked at herself in the mirror, and thought, "I am twenty-eight. My skin is sallow. Life is over." And it turned out this was enough—just to think, to formulate, to plea. It was enough for *him* to not be there anymore. Someone higher than him simply blew, and dandelion fluff circled like snow over old Lviv, two KGB men dressed like drunken blue-collar guys grabbed him by the arms at a tram stop and threw him face down onto the tracks. The tram didn't have enough time to brake: the old man probably was no sorcerer after all.

He left behind, in their crammed two-room apartment, an enormous collection, which Roma, having been overcome during the first months by piercing emptiness, tried to distribute to various museums. Even without those folk jackets she was not very good at dealing with the material world. However, up until a new, more liberal era finally arrived, the museum leadership was still not terribly willing to meet her offers with open arms, always citing *problems with museum funds.* Only in the late eighties did everything finally thaw out, the name of Voronych the *collector of folk treasures* was even solemnly given to an applied research center devoted to Easter egg decoration, but remnants of the rarities he had accumulated—various inlaid boxes, hatchets, stove tiles—long and maddeningly reminded Artur Pepa that in this home once lived another *proprietor*, even *master*, that here he had walked, coughed, applied a water bottle to his stomach, relieved himself, and—unavoidably—slept in this very bed with this very woman. Although this thought added to his and Roma's mutual sexual satiation a certain element of illicitness, even sinfulness, making their relations more passionate, the pleasures more intense, and the falls sweeter. It was as if *that guy* could return any minute and catch them in *flagrante delicto.* It was as if they had not much time and had to manage to do it all.

However, as years flew by, this *hot* stage of their relationship certainly had to pass, yielding to family routine and inertia. The sorcerer's threat irrevocably retreated into the deepest reaches of the unconscious. In the meantime, his daughter was growing up, developing a somewhat precocious interest in sexual matters. For Artur Pepa, all of this gradually became entangled in a rather insufferable ball: balance and steadiness; regular, muffled, ever more formal *healthy* sex; falling asleep and waking up in the same (boring) bed; getting used to once resolutely ignored nighties, pajamas, and bathrobes; morning and evening sighs; plunging into his own, separate dreams—and, in fact, the *springtime worsening of skin health.* No, one cannot say there was no longer anything between them. Occasionally *it* did happen, but indeed *between them* and, frankly speaking, somewhere beyond them.

The passage of time mocked Artur to his heart's content, discovering in him some previously unknown horrible feature. Approaching his thirty-seventh year, Artur Pepa noticed not only an accumulation of exhaustion, which manifested in shameful and earlier impermissible snoring, not only in the dense growth of unseen-before nasty hair in nostrils and ears (*what other gifts do you have in store for me, Lord, my Friend—dandruff, loss of teeth, prostate inflammation?*—rebelled from inside the alcoholic agnostic), but first and foremost he noticed his increasing propensity to notice stuff, and this was the worst. He noticed occasionally he did not want to touch her. He did not really want to look at her body when she was getting dressed in the morning. All these slips, stumbles, spills of hers now irritated him—while earlier they provoked in him a most sincere desire to defend, save, and heal.

The passage of time slipped him another nasty surprise in the form of Kolya's growing up. The unbearably crammed *everyday conditions* couldn't help but provoke even unintentional collisions and gazes (we won't talk about intentional ones). The girl grew to be incredibly long-legged and, undoubtedly aware of this fact, knew no restraint in shortening her skirts. For the last year-and-a-half to two years he preferred, just in case, to not enter her room decorated with photos of Jim Morrison and Janis Joplin. Truth be told, at her age he also listened a lot to those two. For her eighteenth birthday he and Roma gave her eighteen CDs of 1970s music. Having seen off a large crowd of guests, the rather drunk Artur Pepa locked himself in the bathroom and, opening the hot water faucet, thought to himself, "Can one really have sex with a woman whose daughter is a legal adult?"

It was right then that he noticed for the first time he terribly regretted his past ("*You know, sometimes I completely freeze on the inside when I think I might have not come that evening*") madness. It would have been enough, he thought, to stay put for another half hour, Bomchyk was just ordering a third round of shots. It would have been enough not to hurry—she told him herself she planned to stop by for only five minutes looking for acquaintances. It would have been enough to miss each other—let someone else catch her by the elbow, let someone else get this *luck*, but today I would have been my true self and not someone else. I would have lived my own life, flirted with women right and left, and probably seduced fresh lasses like this one, shivered with excitement in springtime just like twenty years ago, rather than gradually turning into a potentially patented impotent. Thus pun, although not terribly recherché, came from his penchant for phonetic drollery. Even remaining one-on-one with his streams and monologues, Artur Pepa never stopped being a professional man of letters.

This meant nothing but that he had to count on his literary income to make ends meet. Once he thought of writing a bestseller (just at that time, the topic "where are our bestsellers? and why don't we have bestsellers? and who would write a bestseller for us?" was discussed with a paranoiac persistence in the ghetto of domestic literary milieu; it seemed everyone had gone nuts about this topic, from authoritative egghead ideologists to the eternally misinformed and actively gossipy newspaper parvenus). Thus he got a desire to stick out his forearm, his tongue, or whatever else at all this cabal. Naturally, it had to be a novel. That it had to be signed with a made-up name was also without doubt. A narrative about a man who kills his own wife—in a moment (or rather, in a burst) of exhaustion and hatred that accumulated for years. After the murder began tribulations with the corpse. He wants to get rid of it in such a way that no one would ever come across the remains. Tie to it two large stones and drown it in a black lake in the woods. A black lake with white asphodels, he thought. For that the body had to be put into the trunk of a car and taken far outside the city. In fact, this had to be the story of one night. How he drives around with the murdered wife's corpse in the trunk and more and more obstacles appear on his way (the police, acquaintances, friends, prostitutes, gangsters, etc.) and thus he becomes increasingly and fatally distant from his goal. The action-packed story should alternate with lyrical fragments. They would shed light on their previous life and shock the reader by their almost brutal frankness, especially in the details pertaining to the physiology of a woman's aging, all these autumnal smells, wrinkles and folds, the rustling of dry leaves, the coldness of the womb. In general, it was supposed to be a somewhat improbable mix of a thriller, a confession, a black comedy. It was supposed to be, but it wasn't: in the end, Artur Pepa buried the idea, suddenly realizing the temptation to have this horror come true was becoming more and more real. Thus he stopped, just in time, leaving it to others to produce the *long-awaited potboiler* that was supposed to save national literature from readerly oblivion.

But what was supposed to save Artur Pepa himself? A brutal divorce? Burn the bridges and flee beyond the borders of the visible world? A nightclub for forty-year-olds? Would the foolish heart finally give out during yet another hangover-time coffee and cigarette?

He thought to himself that the only counterweight to everything that was happening to him lay on the boundary of alcohol and creativity. Somewhere there an immaterial territory was still to be found, where he could seek joy or at least a reminiscence of joy, a hint of its possibility. The rest bore the name of *future infinite coldness* and pointed to the only possible direction of movement and complete absence of the right to choose.

Up till then he was known to a thousand or two admirers primarily as the person directly responsible for the appearance and disappearance of two books (he himself called them *projects*), none of which could claim to be *authentic* literature. Moreover, both of them boasted so openly their *inauthenticity, artificiality, and bookishness* that those very domestic literary milieus immediately proclaimed Artur Pepa a player not without talent, yet empty—a sated and occasionally elegant gourmand (dandy-brandy, blah-blah-blah) who had never even sniffed the cruel bloodiness of reality.

The first book was titled *Artur's Brothers* and looked like a poetry anthology supposedly compiled by Artur Pepa. In reality, the crude mystification was evident to the naked eye: having invented nine poets *not known to the broad reading public*, their biographies and personalities, he then *compiled* fifteen poems by each, hinting in his preface about the symbolism of the Round Table and the Holy Grail, yet doing so in such a mocking way that his publisher, a zealous neophyte, canceled the original title, *Artur's Knights*. The texts by each of the invented poets differed so radically from one another that this also could not help but point to the obviousness of the mystification. The first of them supposedly wrote surrealist prose poems; the second, bawdy rhyming couplets balancing between softcore and hardcore pornography; the third, free verse miniatures, notes of a completely marginal climatologist or philosopher of nature. The fourth, according to the legend, was gay and an admirer of all things Western; the fifth a neo-populist of the soil (his contribution was not separate small texts, but a long poem titled "Trypillia and Trident, or, the Bucket of Renaissance"[5]). The sixth, apparently, had an obsession with Rimbaud's "Drunken Boat": his contributions were all variations on this text. The seventh and the eighth were, respectively, an unabashed anarchist advocate of a drug-infused free-for-all (his section

---

5 A reference to the Cucuteni-Trypillian culture, a Neolithic culture that existed on the territory of Ukraine, Romania, and Moldova approximately between 4800 and 3000 B.C.; it is viewed by some circles in Ukraine as a direct ancestor of modern Ukrainians.

was titled "PropaganJah") and a conscientiously sonnet-focused neoclassicist, mama's boy and straight-A student. The ninth, the most interesting, was a serial killer; each of his poems a story of yet another murder and each dedicated to its own victim.

Artur's Brothers, naturally, was panned unanimously by the critics and received enthusiastically by the readers. The book sold out within two or three months, first and foremost because of a few lawsuits brought against the *editor*. Artur Pepa resoundingly lost all these suits, but without any grave consequences. However, PEN International included his name in a list of writers *potentially in danger of persecution*. Ill-wishers even alleged that this agile *self-promoter* organized all the legal scandals himself. Someone especially envious even published a satirical column about *black PR* (this term was just then becoming fashionable in the local media). Although, in this case, it was Pe-Ar.

His second and last book, *Literature Could Have Been Different* (with the subtitle *Ukrainian Classics, Reread and Augmented*), came out next year. In his preface, Artur Pepa noted bitterly that *the unwillingness of the younger generation of our readers to immerse themselves in the treasures of national classics should be overcome through a radical gesture*. With this in mind, he proposed *new possibilities of developing canonical plots familiar from the days of secondary school*, rewriting them with a more-or-less respectful preservation of the authors' poetics and *changing their problematics with an eye towards making them more modern.* Thus *Kaidash's Family* in his version became a settling of scores within a mafia clan, the struggling seminarians in *The Clouds* to the point of nausea and hallucination smoked the hash they procured from southern sugar refineries, and "The Horses Are Not to Blame" ended with a gang rape of Arkady Petrovych Malyna, a liberal landowner, by the squadron of Cossacks he had summoned to his estate.[6]

Understandably, this brought about a new round of curses. In a few secondary schools in Lviv and elsewhere in Galicia, *Literature Could Have Been Different* was even publicly burned during the opening convocation of the new school year. Awarded the honorable appellation of one of the *fathers of spiritual poison* and one of the implementers of the alleged *Harvard Project,*[7] Artur Pepa fell silent for a long while, irremediably sliding towards his thirty-seventh year, already mentioned above.

It was right then he started thinking about a completely different novel. But what does "started thinking" mean? In reality it so happened that one day a

6 Two novels by Ivan Nechui-Levytsky (1838–1918) and a story by Mykhailo Kotsiubynsky (1864–1913) (author's note).

7 Some conservative Ukrainian intellectuals believe that there exists an American, Harvard-based neocolonial project aiming to subject Ukraine to intellectual revisionism aimed at destroying Ukraine's traditional values, especially in regards to its literary classics (author's note).

friend invited him to his house in the foothills of the Carpathians to help finish picking a harvest of apples, so bountiful that year that the *Savior had to be saved.*[8] Artur liked the pun. Besides, the desire to run away somewhere, at least for a couple of days, was potent. So was the unambiguous prospect of soothing his soul of an alcoholic *in the great outdoors.* Thus, as a consequence of his own personal depression and the aberration of railway schedules, Artur Pepa found himself on board a terribly early commuter train that with great effort moved in the direction of the mountains, its speed barely exceeding that of pedestrians. At approximately half past seven Artur Pepa yet again shuddered, half-conscious and half-asleep, his cheek and temple peeling away from the dirty train car window. The train had stopped at a small station in the foothills of the mountains. Outside, the fall red-and-yellow bloom of forests, cobwebs flying in the air, an intensely blue sky, the kind that only happens in October. All of this lasted for no more than a minute—this eternal quiet, the voice of a rooster at its very bottom, a neglected station house, a well into which red maple leaves were falling, the smell of coals. Two figures were moving away from the station, apparently having just exited this very train: a woman in black, a walking stick in one hand and a wooden suitcase

8 The Savior of the Apple feast is a traditional East Slavic holiday of pre-Christian origin, now conflated with and celebrated on the same day as the feast of Transfiguration. It is associated with the harvesting of ripe fruit, especially apples.

in the other, and a man with his legs missing, on a wheeled platform who advanced convulsively, pushing against the ground with his enormously long (as it seemed) arms wrapped in black cloth. Artur Pepa saw them only from behind, but it was enough. Less than a minute later the train departed, and the novel began.

It was to be a story of an old Hutsul theater (or choir—Artur Pepa wasn't sure yet), told in a breathless stream-of-consciousness. He had once read or heard something like that: back in 1949 in Moscow they decided to mark Stalin's seventieth birthday with the greatest possible pomp. On this occasion, they summoned, from all over, legions of various folk performers who were to take part in the Festival of Gratitude to the Great Teacher. In this enormous crowd, next to the Yakuts, the Karelians, the Mingrelians, the Chechens, and the Ingush, the West Ukrainians newly joined to the USSR certainly shouldn't be absent. Of those, the choice of the high-placed organizers without any hesitation fell on the Hutsuls, dazzlingly exotic, in tight red pants and feathers in their caps. Immortal Joseph's Empire was just then entering its late-Roman, somewhat Hellenistic stage: primordial communard asceticism, now thoroughly discredited (not least by the recently ended exhausting war), gave way to an entirely hedonist fashion for brightness and splendor. The victors indeed weren't judged; on the contrary, they judged the others, making abundant use of trophy fragments of the world of the vanquished. Thus the pinnacle of the Pyramid got used to canvases by Rubens, plush chaises, chocolate, and fine lingerie. Things were sliding inexorably towards grandiose orgies of grape-and-cognac abuse and sexual perversion. Therefore, a state-organized entertainment provided by costumed *dances of small peoples* couldn't help but tickle the taste buds of these first postmodernists.

A Hutsul theater (or choir?) had existed in Chortopil since the days of Austrian rule. None of the later powers-that-be had the wherewithal or the time to liquidate it—it is probably not necessary to explain here why it did not really offend anyone. The majority of its members weren't comprised by authentically autochthonous talent of *the common people*; no, these were mostly the usual small-town characters, local intelligentsia one might say, but the kind that were still considered working-class, that *had not yet torn themselves from the roots.* In other words, using the somewhat trite imagery of Artur's predecessors, their blood still smelled of the smoke of mountain taverns' hearths, yet their thoughts were already nearing the understanding of the True Meaning of History.

Naturally, the moment the sluggish commuter train departed from the above-mentioned little station, Artur Pepa did not yet see all of this. The only thing that stuck inside him for many long weeks was a presentiment of a novel, materialized by two handicapped figures and the morning stillness enveloped in red fall foliage. Only some time later all this was joined by another story, its serpentine head peeking from another memory vault—the story of the Hutsuls' great journey to the Imperial Capital.

Attractive to the point of swooning, it carried with it the possibility of mythmaking and poetry, the tension of an eternal drama of *the artist and power.* Chronologically, it was in the middle of the century, allowing one to build bridges across time in all directions, sending the descendants and the ancestors into one wild dance, killing the living and resurrecting the dead, to make a temporal and likewise a spatial collage, turning mountains and abysses upside down. It contained a possibility of getting at the proximity of death. In fact, it smelled strongly of death—and Artur Pepa hoped to be fit for the task. All of his novelistic presentiments suggested the contours of Márquez. Yes, exactly him—a variety of *magic realism*, long and hypnotic sentences almost completely without dialogue, density and saturation of detail, with very elliptic hints. Precisely because he saw and understood it in this way, he kept procrastinating: he didn't want it to turn into Márquez.

Another delay factor was his never having mastered how to narrate full-fledged stories. The surrounding brocade came to him much easier than the guiding line. For instance, he still did not know what actually happened to this theater (choir?) after the performance in Moscow and whether there was indeed a performance. Was there, for example, an attempt to assassinate the Big Kahuna, for which the author had to prepare the reader over the course of the book through the protagonist's fragmentary monologues of, undoubtedly connected with the underground? Should the hero randomly shoot his flintlock pistol from the stage in the direction of a black theater box? Should he serve the Great Father a silver goblet with poisoned wine? Or perhaps there should be several heroes and several assassination attempts, none of them successful? Should there be betrayal? And if so, should there also be love? And how would love fit this whole story?

In any case, he kept reminding himself, documentary style should be avoided. This couldn't be a retelling of the events that actually happened in 1949. It should be subtler, yet much broader. In order to avoid paraphrasing events, one actually should get to know those events as thoroughly as possible. For as the old Dr. Dutka, a grammar school professor emeritus had taught Artur Pepa, only he who *knows something* rather than knows *about* something does actually know. This is why Artur Pepa did not dare: he *didn't* know.

He didn't know their itinerary. He had to see it in detail: undoubtedly they were taken by train in a clear northeasterly direction, but in no way suffice it to say *Northeast*. One had to see in the most vivid fashion how the landscape gradually became increasingly northern as well as increasingly eastern, to see clearly this emptiness of autumnal fields, sudden transition from fall to winter, rain to snow, thus also the various hellish train stations overrun by various freezing escapees, stations rebuilt by German POWs, humiliated and cold. One had to move past echelons of prisoners and deportees, surreptitiously slip them bread and cigarettes, recognize among them friends and relatives, grow pale and faint. Geography was hiding mysterious traps and intrigues of which he had no inkling.

He also did not know any of the labyrinths of limitless power—what was signified by these nighttime interrogations in the dungeons, bullets in the back of heads, confrontations, identifications of corpses, and other devices of the secret police. One had to live though this fear, be investigated, provoked, or at least suspected, torn between death and duty, to remember in detail each of the thousands of tortures, ever improved in order to procure necessary testimonies or, more likely, to force you to crawl and squirm. One had to transform at least temporarily into a woman and truly feel what rape actually is, especially when you are raped by a gang of ten, two at a time, one had to know the *zone*, and not from the stories of others.

He also did not know anything about resistance. But a novel like this had to find lots of space for resistance, otherwise it lost any sense. Hence one had to understand all the advantages of guerrilla warfare:

the absence of morning roll calls and drilling; remote underground hideouts, secret apartments and bunkers. One had to learn to give whistle signals, plant mines, learn to get rid of lice, fleas, and syphilis, navigate through nighttime forests, pass encoded messages sown into the lining of hats. Also to carve victory signs on tree bark and human skin. But most difficult was having to learn that any guerrilla warfare was hopeless and doomed, that everyone betrays everyone else, and there would be the last ambush, the last siege, the last bullet into oneself, even though He does not admit heroes like that into his Heavenly Garden.

Finally, the God problem—what to do with it? Should one give Him a chance and start believing?

Artur Pepa didn't know. He also didn't know what to do with Hutsul country. There existed a whole branch of scholarship about it, scattered across hundreds of books and therefore dispersed, diminished, thus he didn't know what to start with and whether to start at all. Should he begin with Shukhevych, with Vincenz? With Hnatiuk, Kolberg, Żegota Pauli?[9] With dozens of other homegrown ethnographers? Perhaps with the oilcloth-bound student notebooks of Roma's first husband? For no one had ever created the one Book that would comprise everything: the vernacular,

9 Volodymyr Shukhevych (1849–1915), Stanisław Vincenz (1888–1971), Volodymyr Hnatiuk (1871–1926), Oskar Kolberg (1814–1890), Żegota Pauli (1814–1895), noted Ukrainian and Polish scholars and writers who had studied the Hutsuls (author's note).

the lambswool, the seven traditional ways of cheese-making, shots into the air next to churches, the first wedding blood, the evil circles of ritual dance, the rafting techniques. Thus he had to learn many odd words and phrases (*katuna*, he repeated, why they call soldiers *katuna*; why *fras*; why *hia*?), check countless details of mountain sheepherding, as well as of extra-marital if not otherworldly lovemaking. Therefore, he needed to know the smell of herbs with which they rubbed shoulders and chests before sex, what they called each decoration on their bodies and clothing, all the details of traditional ornaments put together and taken separately, and what they used to make belts and boot laces, which type of leather worked best for them, what they call eyelets by which to put laces through footwear (for even they had a specific name, but a different one for each different kind of footwear), and once again: how sweat smelled *before* and *after*, and what ointment was best for the hair, the penis, the lips, and how to get your lover drunk, what you should drink yourself—but even knowing all this he wouldn't have known even a tenth of what he should know: words, customs, crafts, herbs. Yes, you needed to know hundreds of plants (not only some *Potentilla erecta*), their names, features, the entire hidden esoteric biology, so that somewhere on one of the novel's pages a mention is made in passing, one, just one—for example, that very *Potentilla erecta*.

And also: how a witch groaned in the throes of death.

And also: statistics of tuberculosis cases in the upper Carpathians in the late 1940s.

And also: the history of all musical instruments except the *trembita*, the Carpathian alpenhorn.

For in reality his novel had to turn out extremely fragmentary, only some hundred typewritten pages long, and nothing listed above needed to be there, but there had to be the knowledge of all of the above—otherwise a novel like this simply couldn't be written. Thus realizing this, Artur Pepa grimaced from the thought that he had to buy various note pads and voice recorders, old books, military maps, digital cameras, go on endless expeditions and not come back from them, systematize and classify everything collected, absorb it with his whole self, become a part of this collection, merge with it, in other words, be Flaubert. But he didn't want to be Flaubert, thus the novel writing wasn't progressing.

Besides, he didn't even know what it was all for. Having buried the obsessive idea of the novel a thousand times, just like he had buried thousands of other ideas of novels, he still couldn't free himself from it. It seems to me that such a split had to be related to his crisis-related fears and despair. He could consciously postpone the moment of materialization of the novelistic text, having convinced himself this novel had to be exhaustive. It would, that is, exhaust his present-day predestination, and therefore, as soon as all is written, the roads to death would be cleared *from above*. Hence he invented many obstacles in order to not even begin. On the thirty-seventh year of his life, Artur Pepa's superstition knew no limit: he was sure such novels do not pass without punishment. Having stepped once on this murderous path he was, as it were, accepting an *all-or-nothing* agreement.

At the same time, he was convinced it was unavoidable, that he couldn't escape this novel, this writing, this old Hutsul theater (choir?). Therefore, one way or another it all had to end with a sudden cardiac arrest (as if it could somehow end otherwise). "Probably already after Easter," he thought for some reason. The main thing: not right away, not immediately, not here-and-now. The main thing was to live through one more spring. Starting at a certain moment, springs began passing by almost unnoticed, without the former rustling of moist wings and vitamin-deficient high. This had to be remedied.

Thus he fairly easily agreed to go to the mountains during Holy Week together with Roma and her daughter. A business owner whom he did not know, but for whom from time to time he invented advertising slogans, invited them to visit his residential spa at the Dzyndzul alpine meadow. Official invitation sent by mail opened with a somewhat garbled quote from Antonych, with the words *have a few drinks* highlighted, as if specially for Artur Pepa. The invitation, in the worst traditions of the transition era, bespoke Christian charity, and also the *heroes of business*, who even in extremely challenging conditions of tax burdens and government corruption managed not to forget the *heroes of culture* and, to the extent their modest means allowed, support them in their *initiatives* (this word was also highlighted—on purpose, as it turned out later). Then it spoke of spending a few days at the "Tavern "On the Moon" resort (meals, Jacuzzi, busy hands, private bedrooms, this and that, blah-blah-blah). Then for some reason followed a passage about Antonych whom, as it turned out, participants of the event were to celebrate. Not a word though on how they were to celebrate him. Everything ended in a rather nonsensical call to support with their votes a certain Carpathian *Initiative* Political Bloc (there's this word "Initiative"; it popped up again!), and again a poem, this time not at all by Antonych:

> They'll warm you all over; all others they will outstrip
> in everything fully as well,
> the heroes of entrepreneurship.
> At the "Tavern "On the Moon" you'll feel swell.

Artur Pepa agreed even without taking into account this final couplet. The fact that Roma's Austrian buddy for whom she served as an interpreter was also going to join them in the mountains, even in spite of that. Artur occasionally ran into this somewhat dimwitted photographer, although at those occasions they both remained silent. "You'd better learn Ukrainian if you've become so intent on traveling here, buddy," reproached him Artur in his thoughts, having no idea how much the other was *interested* in his "interpreter".

That Kolya was also present in their company did not help things much, but we won't talk about this. Suffice it to say, Artur Pepa easily made peace with all these inconveniences, since there, deep inside him, still he hoped for a moment in the spotlight as the poet, Artur's Brother, and he wished so passionately for nothing else than to finally wake on the thirty-seventh year of his life.

II.

Of Stone and Dreams

5

In the end, all of them did wake up that morning—naturally, in different ways and with different baggage.

Artur Pepa was torn from dreams almost by force. He wanted to stay a little longer, bring the story at least to some kind of conclusion, however the noise created by Roma Voronych in the bathroom (entire avalanches of various cosmetics, jars, and spray bottles knocked into the bathroom sink) brought a decisive halt to his otherworldly wanderings. Now he was lying on his back, on his side of the bed, next to the untouched line of demarcation between his and his wife's territory, engaged in sadness-tinged reconstructions of everything just experienced. Artur Pepa enjoyed this melancholy overview of his own dreams.

This time, half the night was spent trying and ultimately not succeeding in picking up a young woman of uncertain appearance, most likely a university student. In other words, it was one of his most boring dreams ever. He recalled that in some large company she suddenly very suggestively winked at him (in the end, he now understood, this was nothing but animal curiosity)—however, this was enough for him, the old fool, to decide to make a pass at her. Later, they talked for several hours of this and that, having found a quiet nook far from the crowd. During this, each time the conversation reached a hopeless dead end, he kept surprising himself with succeeding, in finding, with a somewhat naïve ingenuity, a last-ditch way to keep it going. Besides, they kept smoking various crap, and Pepa with a slight fear thought unavoidably about getting close to their *first kisses.* The student turned out to be not terribly educated. She had heard that her interlocutor was an *interesting person* yet had very foggy ideas about his occupation, and thus she talked mainly about her own life—parents, siblings, relatives who lived in Poland, in Piotrków Trybunalski, about some Bagheera who bore four kittens, how many girlfriends she had, how many were true friends, for in reality they were such bitches (here she became a broken record, repeating emphatically ten times "bitches, bitches, bitches"). Finally, she jumped to talking about her classes at school (she even shared her entire school schedule, Monday through Friday; memory preserved in particular a class on *latent cyclomechanics* that met Thursdays), how they copied each other's class notes, skipped recitations, went to aerobics classes because the swim coach *constantly made passes* at them. Then she talked about their life at the dorms, about sealing windows in winter with insulating tape, including the shared bathroom, and that in the bathroom the *greater half* of the sinks were broken. Also, how they made macaroni with ground beef and watched the TV show *Big Laundry.* Saying something completely inappropriate in response to her question about the ending of yesterday's episode of *St. Petersburg Gangsters* which she had skipped because of (note: a dream) a *meteorite shower*, he smoothly shifted the conversation to her pantyhose, and had to listen to her go on about some *Slavik from the flea market* who advised her to wear *a size smaller.* She meant, of course, the jeans into which her slit miniskirt managed to transform, who knows when and how. Then came her instructors at school: all of them marched across the stage in front of Artur's feigned interest, completely non-charismatic ladies and gentlemen, some twenty of them, each described in detail and not without sarcasm ("And Yakiv Markovych, the chemistry prof, always *farts*!" she concluded joyfully). Taking advantage of the girl's unexpected chattiness, Artur Pepa considered his next steps. He also remembered the need to find a key to lock the room from inside and move to concrete lovemaking. Thus, while the girl methodically pushed his hand off her knee (she no longer wearing jeans), told him about her prospect of failing *taxonometry*, he managed to examine the surroundings and decide that the key had to be inside the toilet, which for some reason was placed right in the middle of the room's parquet floor. The key indeed turned out to be stored there, and so having thoroughly wiped it with *Tempo* paper tissue, he casually danced toward the door and managed to lock it just as some unknown moose of a fellow began banging from the outside, presumably with horns. The girl, in the meantime, sat on the toilet and did her *pee-pee*, as she put it, which turned out to be sufficient for the moose on the other side of the door to calm and fall silent. Artur Pepa told her he loved her very much, but the girl kept shaking her head and forbade him to touch her breasts, although she did allow him to hold her by the hand. Hence, he had to persuade her in a more active fashion, and come up with truly amazing resources for his lover's discourse (all these courtly cascades stayed in the dream, but he remembered he totally aced it). He told her he'd waited for her all of his life, he was the kind of person who fell in love only once, that tonight was a true miracle, it was enough for him to feel she was near in order to be completely happy (the funniest thing was, totally carried away, he even called her *my little swallow*, which made him feel especially ashamed once he woke). In the meantime, he kept kissing her arms and shoulders, becoming more and more enflamed. He must have radiated love and tenderness, for in the end she said coquettishly, "All right, I will believe you tonight," and proceeded to lie down on her stomach, completely naked. Then, while he was trying to enter her from behind, Artur understood he actually did not really want to do it that badly. The stupidest thing was that he had spent so much time and effort for all this, that now he had to apologize for the trouble—and at that moment when the final hope for an erection waved good-bye, someone started banging heavily at the door, this time with jars and spray bottles. Water noisily poured from all the faucets opened by his wife, and Artur Pepa unglued his eyes.

Now he was lying face up, thinking whether such a dream could be considered erotic, or yet another testimony to the passage of time, life slipping away, and most importantly, whether it portended something bad.

"What a fool; my God, what a fool" thought Ms. Roma. "Such a fool, fool, fool," she continued thinking as she sat down into the just drawn bath in an eccentrically shaped acrylic tub.

The water seemed too hot to her, and she opened the cold faucet thinking the water was too hot and that he was a fool. He was aging so badly. It was like a natural disaster. If only all these foolish tarts who tried to seduce him, whom he tried to seduce, only knew how limp, talentless, and uninteresting he had become, how *indifferent* he had grown to be! Would they still beg him for autographs?

"But he is simply a fool and nothing more," she concluded, stretching blissfully in the bathtub.

She enjoyed washing her fairly broad, rounded shoulders in this greenish lightly foaming water. Shoulders, her best attributes. "I should wear open-shouldered cocktail dresses as much as possible," she thought and imagined herself in the nineteenth century. Breathing heavily and drenched in sweat, Honoré de Balzac made his way through a crowd of vile-looking aristocrats and cast a telling glance down her cleavage. "The Balzac Age, what is it exactly?" she thought. "When does it begin," she clarified, opening her eyes. "When did my skin start *blooming*? Good that I still have a few springs left ahead of me."

It is good that one can stay like this in this green water. Most importantly, it is plentiful, both hot and cold. This is not Lviv, thank you very much. It is not rationed by the hour. These millionaires can have it all! When is he going to come and meet us, I wonder? What might he look like? Probably balding, with a big stomach and narrow slits for eyes. Five foot tall. Skin folds on the back of his neck and elsewhere. They are usually former athletes, fighters, wrestlers. It's hard to imagine yourself in bed with a wrestler. Always pinned down. Unless he's a fighter for independence."

"This is my body," she thought, standing up in the bathtub and lathering herself thoroughly.

"Why is my body actually mine," she moved to her favorite sophism. "It is so strange: to think of your own *I*. What is *I*, why I am *I*? Something's hidden here; some ultimate thing concealed from us. This body could have been someone else's. Why is it mine?"

As years passed, her body put on weight, but not too much. She remained attractive: this was without doubt; the slightly fogged mirror wouldn't lie (in reality, the mirror, like most of the fragments of the distorted Antiworld, did lie a bit: it stretched figures out and made them look thinner—this time exactly to the extent necessary for Ms. Roma to stay satisfied with her body).

"Fool," she thought. "Hopeless idiot and utter fool."

She not only remained attractive: she was sexy. Sexiness is first and foremost self-confidence. She had read something to this extent a week ago in *ELLE Ukraine*. She liked this formulation a lot for its grace and precision: "Sexiness is self-confidence." And really, damn it, reflected Ms. Roma, what else could sexiness be if not self-confidence? Could one ever imagine a person who wasn't self-confident yet sexy?! From that day on she decided to be self-confident. She spent so many years not being confident that now what remained was the will to grab everything that remained. "Why do such life-changing truths come to us so late?" she grimaced in the mirror and actually stuck her tongue out to herself. The tongue seemed to associate itself with scoops of ever-present ice cream, that had to be licked slowly and passionately from all sides. "This is the influence of television," she rightly concluded.

Then she felt like standing on one foot, doing physical exercises, for example, the *swallow*. She hadn't done the *swallow* for years. The lines of her neck, shoulders, back, buttocks, and legs formed wonderful curves, semicircles, and convexities. She discovered her total plasticity. Since childhood, people tried to convince her she was clumsy. Who was the first person to come up with that nonsense, she wondered? Beloved daddy with his decrepitude? Hated mommy with her miasma? Or perhaps it was *him* who brought it about to keep her on a short leash, the old yellow-toothed sorcerer?

Ms. Roma was unable to remember whether they had begun considering her clumsy before Kolya, or after. Was it before the marriage, or after? Was it before she started school, or after? Was it already before she was born? Perhaps someone decided for her, and that was that?

He followed her every move, forbade her to dance with others, didn't know how to dance himself. And this was precisely why *he*, shitty old dog, told everyone his wife didn't dance, she—would you believe it!—was ashamed of her own movements. And now look, you croaked old sorcerer, look—would you believe it!—I'm doing the *swallow*!

Inevitably, she slipped and fell into the tub, producing a lot of foamy spray and spilling a good third of the bathwater onto the mat that bore the inscription "Glory to Jesus!" "Idiot," she thought. "My God, what an idiot, blockhead, fool!"

A little later, massaging under the shower a slightly bruised but still no less attractive spot, she added, "I stand between the two of them." She wanted to continue this thought, but it was as if she was hypnotized.

I stand between the two of them. I stand. Between. The two of them. Ice. Tand. Be. Tween. Twoofthem.

Later, when she was drying herself with all the five towels provided, her thought advanced. "I am in love with one of them; I *like* the other one."

But something was lacking here. "One of them loves me," she knew for sure. About the other there was no certainty, hence silence as far as he was concerned. I am in love with one of them. One of them loves me. I, oneofthem. Oneofthem, me. The body became dry and warm. This was undoubtedly *her* body. It was good this body was *hers*.

She again stood in front of the mirror, this time having climbed out of the bathtub. She was applying her favorite anti-wrinkle cream.

"You have a grownup daughter," someone said nasally behind her.

O Scheisse, she cursed in German. *He* was here again. She already knew that now he was going to make a pass at her and breathe down the back of her neck, tickling it with his drooping blond mustache. You couldn't see *him* in the mirror, but *he* was here. She decided not to look back.

"You have a grownup daughter," the voice hummed one more time. "Think about your age. You are mine."

"Take your arms away," she thought in response, shuddering from the cold pressure on her waist. "Go away, disappear. You don't exist."

But the voice repeated imperiously,

"You are mine."

"No, not this!" she thought, sensing how *he* was bending her forward. She tried to resist, but he had a thousand times more strength in his cold arms, and these machine-like arms closed over her breasts, and then one of them pressed her head to the ebony top of the makeup table in front of the mirror. "No, don't," she thought pleadingly, sensing something even colder than his arms, some icy probe with a rough round head was trying to enter her from behind. In a moment she understood that any resistance was in vain, that now was going to happen what had happened to her in dreams many a time before, ending with her shameful surrendering orgasm. But as soon as she realized this, sensing deep inside her the first merciless thrusts of the hated and sweet piston, she immediately realized something else: this was only a dream, and she could wake from it at any moment—she only needed to wish for it very much.

Thus she quietly freed her right hand from the deathly cold weight pressing on her and blindly searched for the curtain to the right of the mirror, to chase *him* away with a spray of daylight. She heard numerous jars, spray bottles, other such things, mostly from Vienna, tumble from shelves she had accidentally brushed, how all this stuff fell in a noisy avalanche into the bathroom sink and onto the tiled floor, then a white light hit her eyes, the icy piston suddenly softening, weakening, painlessly slipping out of her.

The water in the tub had grown cold in the meantime. Ms. Roma again opened the hot water faucet, slowly coming to her senses, no longer surprised to see everywhere, on the floor and in the sink, traces of her recent struggle, about which that fool, fool, fool that complete idiot in the bedroom next door didn't have even the foggiest idea.

Yarchyk Volshebnik, director, was rereading that morning's versions of a script for the video he had come to shoot. It was going to be an extended commercial, several minutes long, for *Vartsabych's Miraculous Balsam*, a surprisingly vile concoction unlikely to be harmless to the consumers' health that recently had appeared on the local hard liquor market and had had a lot of trouble staking its share next to more recognized and better-known competitors. Neither the ridiculously small price of six hryvnias sixty-five kopecks, nor the dark swampy color of the stuff, which in the producer's opinion had to signify Carpathian longevity, nor even the cute slogan "Once and Forever" inscribed in a fake old Slavic script was to be of any help. The situation could be saved by a loud and intrusive advertising campaign. The *product* Volshebnik had been commissioned to make was destined for all the TV channels in the country, although—and the *client's representative* did not hide this—their ultimate goal was to reach NTV, STS, TVN, RTL, and even MTV.

"You know, grab a *chick*, or better two of them," said the *client's representative*, a thick-necked stocky guy missing the index finger on his right hand and the thumb on his left, conveying His wishes. "Grab two *chicks*, dress them up, you know, as Hutsuls, take them into an alpine meadow and . . ."

Then the client's representative fell silent and kept pouring *Ballantine's* into his glass, popping hazelnuts into his shark's maw with his four-fingered hand and crushing them with all four rows of teeth simultaneously. Whatever came after the ambiguous "and" was up to the director. They trusted him as a professional cultural producer, and the *client's representative* did not forget to emphasize this. This happened in Lviv seven and a half weeks ago.

Now Yarchyk Volshebnik read the following in proposed script no. 1: "Alpine meadow on a sunny morning. Two girls dressed in the brightest kind of Hutsul folk clothes run around in the grass. Butterflies circle them. The girls laugh cheerfully. They wear beautiful low-cut boots. One of them picks beautiful flowers. The other weaves beautiful wreaths out of them. When both wreaths are ready, the girls put them on their heads. One of them puts her hands on the other's shoulders, the other puts her hands on her friend's waist. They start spinning in a whirlwind Hutsulochka dance. Close-up on the knees. The dance is becoming faster and faster. The girls spin in one direction, then the other. Again, close-up on the knees. The music becomes faster and faster. Finally they fall, hugging each other, and their lips meet in a kiss. They kiss more and more passionately. Voice-over, 'Once and forever: the land of work, the land of song.' A bottle of *Vartsabych's Balsam* appears, covering half the screen. On the other half, the girls keep kissing. Voiceover: '*Vartsabych's Balsam* is like a kiss from a mountain girl. Let your lips get wet.'"

"I wonder how much they pay these shitasses to write such crap?" thought Yarchyk Volshebnik, disgusted, pushing away script proposal no. 1 and immersing himself in script proposal no. 2.

There it was written: "Alpine meadow on a sunny morning. Two girls dressed in cheerful yellow-and-black striped skirts with transparent wings behind their backs cheerfully fly from one flower to another. On one of the flowers they start spinning in a whirlwind of the Hutsulochka dance. Close-up on their hips. The dance becomes faster and faster. The girls spin first in one direction, then the other. Extra close-up on the hips. Finally they fall, hugging each other, and their proboscises meet in a kiss. They suck more and more passionately. A bottle of *Vartsabych's Balsam* appears, covering half the screen. On the other half, the girls keep working their proboscises. Voiceover: '*Vartsabych's Balsam* is like the honey of your fatherland. Listen to the hum of lively bees.'"

"They couldn't help hinting at politics," grimaced Yarchyk Volshebnik. However, he admitted in spite of himself, the second version looks better. "But how am I going to make these stupid bitches fly?" he asked. A perfectly justified technical question.

(And here a clarification needs to be made. The budget included funds that allowed him to hire fairly high-level performers from a well-reputed modeling agency in Kyiv, or at least a fairly decent agency in Lviv. However, Yarchyk Volshebnik, experienced in fulfilling orders for a creative product of this kind, taught himself to approach budgets creatively as well, freely maneuvering between different categories of expense. Thus a buddy, active in the business, formerly an employee of the Department of Culture of the city of Chortopil, supplied him with two local strippers, one a blond dyed black, the other brunette dyed blond, "Lilya" and "Marlena" respectively, as he called them. Those two were ready to jump at any opportunity to make even meager money, since for the past month and a half they had had no income whatsoever because of Lent. It was those two he had just called stupid bitches in his thoughts.)

Last in the folder was script proposal no. 3: "Alpine meadow on a dark night. Bikers performing one of their secret rituals somewhere in the charmed Carpathian Mountains. They circle an enormous bonfire, then jump off their bikes and start dancing, passing each other various bottles (*Jim Beam*, *Courvoisier*, *Acapulco*, *Smirnoff*) and taking turns swigging them. A kaleidoscope of faces, the bonfire's reflections on stones and the grass, varicolored liquids set on fire. Two girls are chosen. One raven-haired, the other blond as a dove. They stay in the center of the round dance almost licked by the flames, then start casting off their leather bikers' gear. The bearded guys freeze in tense expectation, mouths gaping on their lustful mugs. A moment later the two girls are dancing the Hutsulochka, dressed in the brightest of Hutsul folk clothes. Everybody starts dancing around them, but the bottle they pass to one another is new one, a *well-recognized* one. The remaining liquid is poured into the fire, a large column of light rises above it, suddenly the ground starts moving beneath their feet. The girls keep dancing, and a giant skeleton rises from the ground. In just seconds it is covered with flesh, hair, clothes, with a lightning speed it passes in reverse order all the stages of human physiology, gradually transforming from a dead man into an old one, then a mature one, and so forth—now in front of us is a strapping young lad who spins both girls, the blond and raven-haired, in an impossibly wild whirlwind, the Hutsulochka, holding them tight right beneath their waists. The music becomes faster and faster. Voiceover: 'Once and forever: let us not be ashamed of what's rightfully ours.' A bottle of *Vartsabych's Balsam* appears, covering half the screen. On the other half of the screen, the smiling young man hugs the two girls in bed. Voiceover: '*Vartsabych's Balsam* is like living water. It will even raise the non-embalmed.'"

"This is cool," thought Yarchyk Volshebnik. "Here I would have fun. Enya, Marilyn Manson, Katya Chilly. Stanley Kubrick. Steven Spielberg. Freddy Krueger. Special effects, computer graphics, animation, Photoshop, CorelDraw. To find some twenty decent motorcycles won't be a problem, same for a few decent unshaven bikers' mugs. I can find a cool stiff, an old fart too. But where would I find this strapping young lad? This handsome son-of-a-gun?"

The male of the species, around him, corresponded less and less to the mythological standard. There were, true, a few decent-looking actors, but lately they had been invited to appear in commercials, so frequently and indiscriminately that their old-news faces simply stopped working, annoying the hell out of the whole world, or at least one country in particular.

Thus Yarchyk Volshebnik had good reason to become lost in thought. The problem of the male hero. Scratching his hairy chest, he set out in search of the kitchen and the breakfast that had been promised in the contract, part of the full room and board clause.

"Not bad," said Lilya, a non-pedigree but rather nice-looking kitten, stretching in bed.

"Sure, it works," agreed Marlena, kitten number two, the black one, crawling from under the side table where she had just found the lost golden earring.

They were best friends and never quarreled, for they loved each other like sisters. And more.

"Just like the Czech Republic," added Lilya. "Hotel rooms are similar: the layout, the furniture."

Some time ago she did indeed travel to the Czech Republic, where she had been promised a place, the recruiters told her, in *the main variety show in Prague.* However, she never succeeded in crossing the Slovak-Czech border, and for more than half a year she languished as a so-called dishwasher (*a hundred bucks a month and everybody fucks you*) in some crappy inn at the outskirts of Liptovský Mikuláš. But only she knew about that.

"Was it cool in the Czech Republic?" asked Marlena, putting the newly found earring back on in front of a mirror.

"Like Germany," sighed Lilya. "Almost."

She heard this comparison once before, on board a train. There, a lady traveling, knowledgeable about everything, announced to the whole car that *in the Czech Republic life's almost as good as in Germany.*

"Poland it's not so bad either," added Marlena. "You can earn three hundred bucks a month."

"And you did too?" asked Lilya, not without some doubt.

"Sure I did," said Marlena, firmly, feigning disinterest in her friend's doubts. "Although sometimes a bit less than that."

"There you also danced?" Lilya continued setting her trap.

"Sure I did," repeated Marina her favorite phrase.

"It was a cool hard-currency bar. That's what it was called in their language, *Bar Walutowy*. Solid customers. Various business types would drop by and hang out."

"So, why did Ruslan say you hung out at train stations?" Lilya's trap closed its teeth.

"Ruslan?" asked Marlena, nervously grabbing her toiletry bag.

"That he found you at some train station," clarified Lilya, with a sigh.

"He bullshits a lot," Marlena found an answer. "And you believe him? He's so stupid!"

"Stupid or not, he's getting a third car already," argued Lilya.

"Big deal: he changes cars!" retorted Marlena, emptying her toiletry bag onto the side table. "Let him tell you how he lost a thousand bucks on a shipment of herring."

Lilya stretched once more in cat-like fashion and sat up on the bed.

"Pani Walewska?" she asked in a minute, seeing Marlena now do up her lashes.

"Estée Lauder," replied Marlena, deciding to disagree with her friend about everything.

"I like Max Factor more. Or Revlon," Lilya started pulling her skimpy nightshirt over her head. "Here, Estée Lauder stuff is usually counterfeit," she added, as if in passing.

"And I didn't buy it *here*," Marina said condescendingly. "I got it as a gift. A guy from Benelux, a businessman."

"I'm telling you it doesn't matter how you make money abroad," Lilya returned to her topic, finding on the floor next to the head of the bed her barely-there undies. "As long as pay is decent."

"There's a fold on your stomach," noted Marlena. "You should work on your abs."

"Well, tastes differ," Lilya waved her hand.

"Soon you won't look good enough for the stage," continued Marlena, pursuing her revenge.

"I don't care," Lilya started to boil. "In any case, I don't plan to strip to music in front of some guys for the rest of my life."

"You're such a fool!" Marlena shrugged her shoulders, finishing her eyelashes and moving to the lipstick. "You don't know anything else! Oriflame," she said a minute later, showing Lilya her lipstick.

"Big deal!" Lilya didn't give up, resolutely now up from the bed and fastening her bra in abrupt gestures. "Do you remember Leska from group 32 at the vocational school? A bad dye job, nothing special. She's in Italy now, in . . . what's the name of that city on water, Venice or something, you know? She's an attendant at a paid toilet—just sits there all day. The pay is quite good, and she also found a guy, Armenian or Greek or something. . . And she couldn't do anything right, even strip . . ."

"A paid toilet? Just sit there?" Marlena even briefly

stopped working her lips.

"Just sit there!" Lilya continued her attack, putting her hands on her hips in a primordially feminine gesture. "Well, she has to keep it neat and orderly, sell the tokens . . ."

"This is still work," the stubborn Marlena shook her head.

"And ours isn't? No, tell me, is our work real work?" Lilya, shook her short white mane, not letting her hands leave her sides. "Dancing they say! Ballroom dancing! Not ballroom but bedroom! We know their dancing—they all want to cop a good feel for nothing, or even get screwed without paying. And all the bucks go to the big guys . . . You know how much of it is left for us?"

"Sure I do," said Marlena.

"You don't know anything, you stupid Hutsul," retorted Lilya. "We get six and a half percent, got it? Six point five!"

"You're a Hutsul yourself!" Marlena couldn't resist and threw the empty toiletry bag at Lilya. "Xenia the Hutsul girl!" she added the final insult.[10]

But Lilya only showed her the middle finger—a gesture she had learned from Pasha at the tax office—and disappeared behind the bathroom door.

"Don't forget to brush your teeth!" Marlena shouted.

---

10 An allusion to "Hutsulka Ksenia" ['Xenia the Hutsul Girl'], a popular Western Ukrainian song from the 1930s.

She did not see the middle finger that Lilya showed her once again from behind the door, but she did hear the loud flushing of a toilet.

The young Kolomea Voronych, or simply Kolya if you like, had long been feeling seriously hungry, and since no signs of attention were coming from the old ones' room, decided to go looking for an adventure on her own. Fortunately, the search for the kitchen didn't last that long—having slipped past the door with the sign DEFLORATION and paying almost no attention to another door with the inscription LASCIATE OGNI SPERANZA, she finally found herself in the corner pantry room where she dashed towards the worm-eaten old cupboards. Kolya thought she badly wanted some cheesecake—and immediately found it. The cheesecake was quite fresh, someone had already cut a few slices, but most of it still remained on the tray. Kolya also wanted to have some milk, but in this respect her desires weren't listened to, so she had to make do with a jar of greenish pine honey which also didn't look that bad.

Kolya sat at the table by the window and, cutting pieces of the cheesecake, dipped them right into the honey jar. While doing so she looked at the mountains outside the window, the grass wet from melting snow, the almost nonstop wind rustling in the juniper bushes. The day was sunny, the cheesecake and honey very tasty. Kolya was trying not to chomp, although she was frightfully hungry and badly wanted to. "Cheesecake," she thought. "Cheesecake is cool, it's simply super!"

However the flight of her thought was interrupted by the unceremonious appearance into the pantry of the old stocky Mr. Doktor. He entered, wiping his interwar eyeglasses and happily squinting into the sunlight.

"What beauty!" said Doktor. "My respects to the dear young miss. Is the cheesecake good?"

Kolya had just filled her mouth with the sweet and dense mass and could only respond with an inexpressive "aha."

"Morning and youth," Doktor wouldn't let go, sitting down at the table right next to her. "Everything that shapes the breathing of true poetry. At your age poetry determines each movement of the soul. You like poetry?" (He spoke with a bit of a lisp, but she had no trouble understanding.)

"Yes," answered Kolya after swallowing.

"Yes!" nodded Doktor decisively. "The period which you, dear miss, now have the pleasure of enjoying, one young poet once called 'salutations to life.' You of course know which poet I am talking about?"

Doktor glanced at Kolya above his glasses, in the manner of a well-intentioned professor at an examination.

"Yes," answered Kolya, but not without hesitation.

"I knew it; I knew you knew!" Doktor beamed

wholeheartedly. "Sadly, of late our young people do not orient themselves very well among these figures. You are not like that, I am sure about this. Please eat, please continue, the cheesecake must be very tasty, let alone this wonderful mountain honey." (Kolya continued eating, now rather in spite of herself.)

"Bohdan-Ihor Antonych," the professor spoke a minute later, openly admiring her youthful appetite, "was and remains in our consciousness foremost as a poet of springtime and youth. Poet of springtime intoxication—that's how he called himself, and one couldn't put it any better."

Kolya didn't know how to respond. Besides, the word "intoxication," due to her stepfather's interpretation, had for her a somewhat different meaning. Fortunately for her, Doktor continued,

"You, young people, do not notice the coming of spring. It seems to you spring is something ever-present in this world and you perceive and accept it calmly, without reflection. It is later, much later that a realization will come that all our springs, like our summers, are finite. 'My laughter is young, my soul still green'—that's how the poet Antonych suddenly sees this light. Please think about it *some more*. Isn't this a beginning of the essentially tragic discovery that we were given with our mortality?"

The professor, smiling, looked at Kolya. This suddenly made the mountain honey taste bitter. She feverishly thought how to respond, for she became somewhat sorry for the old hobbit. Finally she asked,

"Would you like to have some cheesecake? There is still plenty more . . ."

"Oh, hearty thanks," Doktor waved his hands. "I'm not allowed sweet things. Diabetes, you know. Once I loved sweets very much, especially my aunt's poppy seed cakes. But look there, out the window. How beautiful these mountains! Sunshine! Mountains and sunshine—two things gifted to us for the full-blooded enjoyment of fleeting existence. In the mountains the sun is closest—that's how Antonych put it. And he also said spring was like a merry-go-round."

They stayed silent for a little while. Kolya pretended to chew the cheesecake. But the professor apparently couldn't stay silent for long.

"It is also interesting," he declared a minute later, "how impervious to reason are the images the poet finds when writing about spring. For example, the twelve circles of spring. Yes, exactly: twelve circles of spring! Have you even counted to twelve, dear miss?"

Kolya shrugged her shoulders and thought she'd never before encountered such a dimwitted interlocutor. But for the sake of politeness, she pulled herself together and answered,

"Yes, I have."

"Wonderful!" The Professor almost jumped out of his chair, as if this was what he had been waiting for. "Could you count all the twelve circles of spring about which the poet Antonych spoke?"

Kolya thought "yeah, right" and said the first thing that came into her head,

"Well, the first circle—that's probably . . . chastity belts on girls."

She had no idea why she said this.

"Wonderful!" Doktor again jumped like a figurine of a Chinese deity. "And the second?"

"The second . . . The second—that's probably . . . a kind of dance, when they dance in a circle. Well, they put a hankie on the floor and everyone kisses everyone else."

"Phenomenal! Third, fourth?" Doktor said encouragingly.

Kolya concentrated and said,

"I must think about it some more."

"Then let this be a kind of homework assignment for you, dear miss," the professor rubbed his hands. "Promise by the end of vacation you'll be able to list all twelve circles? But no, don't promise anything; forgive me, this is odious professorial methods popping their blooming heads. Don't promise anything—just look and enjoy!"

Not to disappoint the funny old man, Kolya gave a concentrated look to the world beyond the window. It seemed to her she was circling on a dizzy merry-go-round somewhere up in the sky. An entire realm with forests, rivers, and tiny railway stations spread in front of her. But the humid scent of the blooming snowdrops passed quickly—almost simultaneously.

There remained only a small figure of an unknown man who slowly climbed the increasingly steep slope, making way from forest to resort.

"Or, for example, the smells," the professor guessed her hallucination. "Springtime in the mountains gives us such an unusual, moving array! Do you know the scent of juniper? Pine needles? Wet pinecones? Of those very snowdrops? Or, for example, the Potentilla? Or simply the smell of clay, ordinary clay, from which we all came and into which we shall return? All of this is not given to us separately, piecemeal, but all together, in one breathing substance! It is interesting Antonych employs the same epithet to describe it all: 'intoxicating.' But one wouldn't be able to put it more precisely than this. One couldn't, isn't that right?"

"Right," said Kolya, for some reason pushing away the honey jar, slow dribbles on its sides, now a third empty.

"Or let's take sounds," the professor slightly rolled his eyes. "Gusts of wind, the nonstop hum of trees and water, the bleating of sheep, cowbells—you never see these invisible cows, yet you hear them ringing their cowbells. Add to this the human voice and bird cries brought by wind. You, dear miss, probably like birds?"

"I do," said Kolya. "Some of them."

"You should like *all* birds," Doktor remarked softly. "And which birds do you like the most?"

"Eagles," said Kolya after thinking for a minute.

She didn't want to offend the old man with an impolite answer. Although she badly wanted to say "penguins."

"Antonych mentions penguins as well," the professor replied in unison. "I think it's in the poem 'Polaria,' although perhaps not. 'Polaria' or 'Arctica.' Do you remember by any chance? Is it penguins or seals?"

"I forgot," Kolya shrugged her shoulders apologetically.

"I should ask Pepa some more about this Antonych," she thought. Usually she obeyed her mother's wishes and called her stepfather dad when speaking aloud. But in her soul she preserved her freedom: no other name fit this good-for-nothing as well as his actual surname. Pepa.

The professor observed her with a smile. She looked away several times, but suddenly decided not to give up and cast a long, brave, even insolent gaze into his eyeglasses—the kind she usually practiced with her girlfriend when about to go downtown in the evening. She knew hobbits were a bit fearful. After some ten seconds that stretched unbearably into eternity, the professor blinked and grew shy, his smile slightly quivered, became crooked, and he capitulated. It even seemed to Kolya he blushed a little.

"Funny old man," she thought.

Outside the window everything was just as beautiful as before, only the figure on the slope came much closer, and Kolya could bet her bottom dollar this was her mother's Austrian acquaintance with something yellow and white in his hands. (Karl-Joseph was indeed returning from his morning scouting trip carrying a bouquet of still moist crocuses—guess for whom.)

"Well," Doktor finally muttered, casting a fleeting and shy secret glance at Kolya's uncovered legs and rising rather clumsily from his chair. "Thank you, dear miss, for your wonderful company. It was extremely interesting for me to have a talk with you."

"You are welcome," said Kolya somewhat inappropriately.

The professor bowed, also a bit clumsily, and behaving in an even more uncertain fashion, as if he had been caught in a sack of his own clothing, made his way sideways and backwards through the door.

"I will give you as a gift my monograph concerning the poet Antonych when the opportunity presents itself," he assured her from the hallway.

"Give it to your aunt, you old codger!" retorted Kolya and immediately felt so cheerful she reached again for the honey jar. "What weird morons hang out here," she added good-naturedly.

After which something completely unexpected burst out of her:

"And the third circle is the embrace of my faraway sweetheart . . ."

Only after that she heard on the porch the heavy Salamander boot steps of Zumbrunnen, full of spring and flowers.

6

Rumors concerning the imminent arrival of Bohdan-Ihor Antonych to Lviv first capture the attention of the *local milieu*, it seems, in 1928—in fact, almost a year before the poet actually makes his home in this realm of stone lions. There's nothing extraordinary about this game of anticipation: there *was* a foreboding of Antonych in Lviv; the city badly lacked a figure of this kind, and in the meantime alarming, mind-bending news about the latest escapades of this enfant terrible of Galicia's alternative scene kept systematically arriving from Przemysl, Sianok, and Drohobych. In Bruno Schulz's well-known letter to Antoinette Spandauer, dated exactly March 1928, we find, for instance, a rather expressive passage: "on several occasions, Drohobych has already been shocked by his [Antonych's] wild exploits. All the salons worth any attention now gossip mostly about his latest performance with a severed pig's head and impaled Małgoska . . . Despite all the eccentricities he remains a rather pure phenomenon in respect to lyrical self-expression. And given that he is not yet nineteen, entire bunches of exotic flowers of hope are now generated by him, albeit somewhat frostbitten in this slush of provincial routine . . . No further than yesterday he and I organized a rather whimsical entertainment at the Red Lamp, resolutely ignoring the small-town views on decency and, most importantly, the resolute disapproving mutterings of my rigorous Adela. I don't want to go into details. Soon, dear lady, you will learn everything yourself from the scandal chronicle. Suffice it to hint, the ballet leotard fit me like a glove this time, and the clanking of shackles and whistle of the whip couldn't help producing an entirely Acmeist impression. And there you have it—today the entire town is shaken, and our so-called *establishment* simply shitting itself out of angry powerlessness."

This mention, the only reference to Antonych currently known in the letters of the famous Drohobych creator of dummies, is quite telling in regards to the role the homeless young man consciously chose for himself in the far from simple situation of a morality theater daily performed by the so-called *progressive Galician citizenry*. His role, first identified as that of a *bad boy* and an entirely appealing daredevil (NB: secretly loved by many!), with years (although what years—Antonych's life speed was so lightning-like, his evolution so rapid, one must speak not of years but of months, sometimes even of weeks!). . . So, as months passed, his role acquired an increasingly serious, indeed tragic dimension, finally revealing to the most attentive among us the catastrophe of a personality that fully belonged to the global fraternity of *poètes maudits*. One should look for traces of Antonych's presence precisely there, among them, in their illegal nightclub where Baudelaire still gets stoned on opium, Stefan George hallucinates beautiful youths, Rimbaud pukes his own precociousness, Trakl sniffs vertiginous bittersweet ether from his bandages, and Jim Morrison avidly and inconsiderately lets his Indian death enter him. Precisely, where one talks about *expanding consciousness* to the point of entirely losing it, precisely among all of them, lost and bisexual, should be the place for Antonych, between a counter stained with flammable and strong cocktails and the worn-out podium of a mercilessly noseless stripper. "Accept, accept into your house this eternal wanderer and vagabond, accept, accept the poet of rebellion, luxury, and despair," addresses Antonych their Club Owner and, having drawn his personal secret sign at the entrance, he crosses its threshold forever.

Thus he arrives in Lviv not in 1928, as rumor had it in quasi-bohemian circles, but in 1929, a year later. There exists a large folder of contradictory memoirs as to by whom, when, and in what circumstance he was first seen and—what insolence!—*welcomed.* No need to believe any, especially those that come from university classrooms and corridors. All these attempts (dated decades later) to describe Antonych as a *star student*, ready with a well-thought-through answer, never missing a single lecture on comparative linguistics, are nothing else but naïve and spasmodic attempts of that very Galician *theater* to defend its habitual values, according to which a great poet should undoubtedly be a star student—otherwise, where would his poetic greatness come from? Yes, it is precisely this hypocritically philistine view of what a poet—*the spokesman and maître of the spirit of the people*—should be like that we can attribute legends circulating later about a timid and tongue-tied virgin, cozy slippers and bathrobes, easy propensity for migraines and therefore the head always wrapped in a towel, about his chubbiness and clumsiness, and most importantly, the almost animal fear of everything—dogs, girls, cars, bacteria, drafts, and especially the despotic *aunt* in whose house at 50 Horodotska St. he was supposedly forced to live.

This version is especially telling because of the unceremoniousness of later post-Antonych falsifications; in reality no aunt ever appeared on the horizon. The person in whose house on Horodotska St. he boarded was his long-term (1929–1933) mistress, widow of an imperial post office inspector, insatiable in her bodily amusements and culinary inventions, queen of turn-of-the-century New Year's balls and charitable lotteries whose final surge of desire was honored by the sleepless nighttime service provided by the green and passionate Lemko.[11] That her attraction to the young boarder was more than carnal is testified already by

11 The Lemkos are an ethnographic subgroup of the Ukrainians who until the mid-twentieth century forced resettlement lived in the present-day southeastern Poland; Antonych was of Lemko background (author's note).

the fact that Antonych was allowed to stay even after the gradual waning of their sexual relationship. Besides the shared affection for absinthe and strong hand-rolled cigarettes, they preserved many other platonic reciprocities. Sometimes he played violin for her. Sometimes, when her grave hereditary illness manifested, he served her coffee and cream in bed. Following the conspiratorial custom of many secret liaisons, he did in fact call this femme fatale his *auntie*, just like she called him her *tomcat*—and not because she knew his father's real last name.[12] Only Yaroslav Kurdydyk, one of the fellow vagabonds and a close friend of the poet, dared hint vaguely in his as yet unpublished memoirs that once, about a year before his death, having had a lot to drink, Antonych confessed about his *auntie*, "There does not exist a thing in this world that she and I didn't try." Then added, "Existence is the most mysterious of all phenomena."

It is his, Kurdydyk's memoirs in regards to Antonych where one probably trusts the most, although not without some caution, since they too contain exaggerations and falsifications. But most importantly they are brimming with life and describe animated drunken discussions, nighttime parties in clubs with a mostly criminal and proletarian clientele, as well as an incredibly juicy scene of Antonych's improvised reading of *Rotations* on 11 June 1936 (Lviv's first jazz

12 Antonych's father's original last name, which he changed later, was Kit, which means 'tomcat' in Ukrainian. (Author's note.)

café "Beyond the Wall," clarinet solo by Alphonse "the Negro" Kaifman), and an incredibly heart-rendering episode where, hanging at the doorstep of the first morning streetcar, bowing and jestering, he says goodbye to a friendly gang of actresses and chimney-sweeps with words they don't quite understand, even if now they sound prophetic: "I am departing. Here I was only a fortuitous guest." The streetcar departs, and the meaning of those words they would understand a few weeks later when the poet's light body is entombed at Yaniv Cemetery. Although this is not the only thing we find in the memoirs of one of the Kurdydyk brothers: there is also the tension of a frantic intellectual search, mountains of devoured dictionaries, eternal struggle with normative word stress, a quiet hunt for the rarest of esoteric manuscripts in the obscure nooks of the Ossolineum Library.

And what is no less important—there is Lviv. Of the kind it was in the 1930s, a city that in essence no longer exists. If it does exist after all, it is somewhere in an unreachable realm, separated from the present-day by an unbridgeable gulf whose name is Dream.

So, Lviv and Antonych. Was it love or its opposite? No one would dare give an immediate answer to this question. Whatever you say, it was here the poet spent the final and most important eight years of his life. These are eight years that made him who he was. According to later analytical discourse (yes, *discourse* is a good word here) he had to feel bad, however. Stones and asphalt depressed him, as did humongous human crowds, *churches, candy stores, the stock market.* Many among the learned poetry scholars, mostly wise foxes by nature, see Antonych first and foremost as a kind of Lemko Mowgli, immersing body and soul in deep, root-bound, ethnographic green. Some even try to prove with the help of his very texts that the appearance and unfolding in the poet's urbanist picture of the world increasingly leads, his salutary vital spirit to a deadening, and the wild celebration of the *bios* yields its place to gray-and-black rituals of *thanatos*, marked by an overtly menacing *technos*, therefore, of *chaos*.

One could generally accept such an interpretation as a basis (as those analytical circles would put it) were it not for the certitude that in reality it is applied by force to the model of Antonych that has very little in common with his real (and surreal) personality. This is already because this model, although in part already existent during his lifetime, mostly develops as a posthumous trap set for the poet by that very *theater of Galician citizenry.*

For in reality nothing attracted him with such a harsh and irresistible force as Lviv. (By the way, the hints of many analysts regarding Vienna, Paris, London, or New York only testify to the complexity: the poet was in the midst of preparing himself for the Grand Tour, writing and mailing increasingly despairing letters to the Metropolitan, Count Sheptytsky, with requests for financial support for future wanderings.)

Yes, Lviv, a city of police brass orchestras, provincial public gatherings, popular coffeehouses and social teahouses, a city with a giant prison on its main street, quite close to the poet's raffish shelter. It would not be difficult to identify two main segments that held Antonych's attraction within this same city.

The first of them is the underground Lviv, buried and flooded, with dead-end subterranean tunnels and corridors, secret labyrinths half filled-in, and the enclosed river against the banks of which schools of blinded fish kept rubbing themselves, pressing from below at buildings and at cracking eggshell asphalt pavement.

The second is proletarian Lviv, perhaps even lumpenproletarian, that is, all its outskirts, terribly lit and impossible to pass through in spring and fall, with all the various distilleries, tanneries, butteries, breweries, omnipresent dirty flea markets and trailers, also broken-down limos forever stuck in mud, street vendors peddling dog meat pies, poppy seed, counterfeit liquor, girls. Clearly, with countless dark and warm caverns where day and night, drowning in the merciless din of music and eating sunflower seeds, sit some clean-shaven men and their girlfriends, heavily made up with hair dyed blue.

Let us note in passing that this Lviv, in many respects, defined Antonych's existential behavior and led to persistent overtures toward him, by the era's local communist enclave, to get him somehow involved in their publications, both legal and underground, lavishing him with signs of attention as well as compassionate interest, ably alternating compliments with reproaches yet still not succeeding toward their ultimate goal.

Now we are left to trust the testimony of the earlier-mentioned elder Kurdydyk, which stands out in a particularly telling scene at a bordello in Levandivka which had to take place at the end of 1936—beginning of 1937, most likely December, shortly before Christmas. "That day," writes Kurdydyk, "was exceptionally gloomy and gray, it started growing dark already at three in the afternoon. We met Bohdan at the Hetman Ramparts and grabbed one warmed beer each, then slowly set down Pidvalna St. in the direction of Riznia Square, then to the intersection of Vuhliarska and Kotelna Streets where at that time the Omana Movie Theater was located, popular among pickpockets. Bohdan loved cinema, especially newsreels concerning various foreign countries. Along the way we bought a bottle of rather vile berry wine, only because of its laughable price. Sitting in the dark movie hall we passed the bottle to each other, taking slow sips. The white screen showed the first episodes of the Spanish Civil War. Some exceptionally badly trained division for the entire forty days tried to storm the enemy's fortress. Alcazar—that's what its name was, I think, although many years have passed and I cannot recall it with certitude. We sat in the front row because of Bohdan's weak eyesight. He went to the movies often, and always sat in the front row. We sipped wine and laughed now and then. The clumsy humpbacked tanks were funny, and the thieves behind us spoke loudly in Polish until Bohdan turned around and told them to shut up. 'Write it on your forehead,' muttered the fattest among the bandits, warning that their paths would cross after the show. Those thieves had a large gang at and around the Krakow Farmer's Market. Bohdan stayed silent, but I would never suggest that this was out of fear. Then next was shown another newsreel, this time from Abyssinia, where the Italian army could not overcome armed African tribes. As soon as they showed Black warriors shooting arrows at Italian airplanes, the gang behind us started giggling. Then Bohdan in one gulp finished the berry wine and, turning around, smashed the empty bottle on the foolish Polish head of the big guy, making sparks fly out of it. While the thieves were coming to their senses, Bohdan and I ran out into the street and through some gates and passages that only he knew reached the beginning of Yanivska St. where we confirmed no one was chasing us. Afterwards we sat down at our buddy Fedio's pub 'The Babylon Saint' where we usually ordered dark Bock beer and a large shot of Bon-Gut alcohol. Inside it was packed to the gills with drunkards, and a boy from the street brought in the evening newspaper and shouted across the entire pub that the Japanese minister had just declared war. 'Slavko, Slavko,' said Bohdan wiping his sweaty brow, 'something bad is happening in the world—Spain, Abyssinia, Japan.' And repeated from time to time, 'Rome, Berlin, Tokyo.' I can't recall how long we sat there or whether we ordered another round of shots. But I do recall how late at night we found ourselves at a certain club in Levandivka. Mostly railroad workers frequented it; there were a couple of engineers as well, but from the railroad. Gals with funny cockades on their butts came down the stairs to greet us. I chose, as usual, the tall and thin Oryska, for I do not like taking time to get used to a new ass, and bought her a cordial. As for Bohdan, he kept repeating his 'Rome, Berlin, Tokyo' and was unable to choose anyone; even the engineer Povoroznyk started teasing him, 'Is Mr. Poet looking for his muse here?' Upset, Bohdan took the small and bony Louise, daughter of the Levandivka notary, an alcoholic; she was not even fifteen years old then. Louise was very stupid and always sucking her thumb. Usually no one took her, for they said she was epileptic. We had a friendly chat with the railway guys about this and that, and when the time came to go with the girls to the bedrooms, Bohdan bought for Louise a lollipop so she would stop sucking her thumb. Thus we scattered, and Bohdan kept saying his 'Rome, Berlin, Tokyo.' In my young days I was very quick; thus some half an hour later I came downstairs in the best of moods to wait for Bohdan, since we agreed we were not going to stay there long. I sat for an hour—he's not there; I sit for another, then I think to myself, 'Eh, something's not right,' and go back upstairs to Louise's bedroom. This was the kind of establishment where the clients were occasionally robbed or even poisoned if things went "well". I stood by the door, and inside Bohdan was reciting, 'On the heaps of black arms and black legs, red blood and yellow foam /the slippery foam of death on lips opened by a gun's kiss.' Knocking on the door, I enter, concerned, and he continues, 'The tulips of subsoil—mines explode like burning bushes /invincible echoing greetings of fireworks come from earth's bosom.' And what do I see when I enter? Bohdan stands in the middle of the room on a stool and recites a freshly composed poem, and little Louise like an angel, is lying in bed, her blanket carefully tucked in, sucks on a lollipop and listens to him attentively and with great respect. This was, as I now know, 'The Lay of the Black Regiment,' which I too had to listen to till the end. Then came 'The Lay of Alcazar'—Bohdan had composed both these poems that night. And we did not leave until he finished them. At the end my unforgettable colleague came down from the stool and, bending over the child, kissed her on the forehead. He didn't say goodbye, only asked of the *beautiful nymph* to pray for him and for us all. Later I heard somewhere she was gunned down in the street during the war by a German. And Bohdan and I somehow made it on foot under persistent sleet to Horodotska Street around four o'clock in the morning. 'You know,' he told me while we shared a last cigarette at his entryway, the number 50, 'sometimes it seems that someone simply whispers these poems into my ear. Really, whispers.' I felt shivers running down my shoulders, and he said one more time this 'Rome, Berlin, Tokyo' of his and went inside up the stairs, stooping somewhat, probably in anticipation of his auntie's scene."

Interestingly, Antonych said the same regarding the *whispering* of poems at least to two other persons. We find them in memoirs of another friend of his, the artist Volodymyr Lassovsky, and of his fiancée Olha Oliynyk.

Volodymyr Lassovsky, the author of the essay "Antonych's Two Faces," exceptionally precise in its detail and particularly convincing, was no less close to the poet during his lifetime than the two Kurdydyk brothers. Suffice it to recall that it was him—Lassovsky—Antonych had asked to do graphic design for his published collections. It is therefore strange that his—Lassovsky's—writings produce the image of a clearly different person—that very star student with straight-A's, auntie's disciplined nephew, a typical Galician son of a priest with an unambiguous predilection for academic lamentation, cozy slippers, bathrobes, and plumpness.

If one compares the behavioral characterizations of Antonych provided by Lassovsky and Kurdydyk, one cannot rid oneself of the exciting impression they are talking about two different people, so distant from each other in their real lives that their trajectories could scarcely have ever intersected even by accident. (However, Lassovsky does seem to hint about the presence of a mystery, using the image of "the two faces".)

Indeed, if Lassovsky portrays Antonych as sluggish and even apathetic, Kurdydyk portrays him as energetic, almost to the point of burning on the inside with a secret thirst. ". . . He suddenly grabbed the fiddle and bow from the hands of Ferenz, the Gypsy virtuoso, and started playing 'The Devil's Game of Bridge,' then immediately the arkan, to the point that the company present jumped from their seats to congratulate him," writes Kurdydyk about this improvised performance at the Hotel Georges restaurant in the spring of 1936.

If in Lassovsky's text Antonych comes across as stodgy and incommunicative, unable to start a conversation or maintain it, Kurdydyk portrays him as incredibly inventive and often very quick-witted: "All of us rolled on the floor with laughter when Bohdan jumped out on the circus arena in baggy clown pants of red-and-green checks, and later these pants even fell down. That evening he made a bet with Havryliuk and Tudor he would appear in public pantsless. And, clearly, he won."

Lassovsky describes Antonych as unnaturally fearful (suffice it to imagine how almost paralyzed by fear he walks in small steps down Lviv sidewalks, focusing his last effort on staying as far as possible from cars, thus literally pressing his body against the houses!). However, in Kurdydyk's writings we deal with a person who is rather recklessly brazen. The above-quoted episode with a bottle smashed on the head of a criminal could serve as an excellent confirmation of that. Although no, there is a confirmation even more telling—here he is the first to climb the roof of a building engulfed in flames, saving a four-year-old girl clutching a kitten to her chest (the hot summer of 1935, environs of Kaiserwald).

Lassowsky wrote that Antonych had the reputation of a somewhat stingy person, so when someone managed to drag him, along with a group of people, to a café, Antonych created lots of problems when it was time to pay. He hesitated, blushed, mumbled something hard to understand—not to mention he always ordered the cheapest thing on the menu, usually weak tea, and even without lemon. Kurdydyk not only emphasizes Antonych's hypertrophied profligacy—his memoir reveals rivers of beer ordered and paid for by Antonych, along with streams of vodka, schnapps, punch, cognac, and brandy. Antonych scatters coins in all directions, buying the fanciest Paris clothing, the most expensive tarts from Teatralna Street, or for example, Iranian hashish from a colonial goods store in Zamarstyniv.

And if on the pages of Lassovsky's text Antonych generally comes across as a prematurely old-behaving and very sedentary *plump guy in glasses*, Kurdydyk gives us someone undoubtedly popular with the ladies, indeed a lady-killer, a wandering musician and carpenter, who leaves behind in each village and town trampled flowerbeds, sleepless nights, eyes crying out, and children out of wedlock. Actually, the poet himself put it best, "Young women and girls sizzled in drunken happiness /Oh many among them lost their precious wreaths!"

On the other hand, Lassovsky tactfully balances his rather unsympathetic portrait with the help of one yet decisive opposition. His Antonych is simultaneously a poet. Not simply a poet but a nighttime visionary, whose true life unfolds in dreams. "In the morning sleepy Antonych put on his glasses, got up from bed and immediately sat at his rickety desk to hastily compose the poetry that had ripened in his dream," writes Lassovsky, not avoiding a certain, to put it mildly, excessive literariness (why, or why must this desk be rickety!), yet also projecting a succession of facts in a completely dignified manner. As for Kurdydyk, we find almost no deeper insights into the poet's metaphysics—for him Antonych is an excellent companion, perfect for drinking partnerships and wandering the city, getting into fights, fleeing police, but nothing beyond that. From time to time, truth be told, there appear colorful scenes involving the reciting of poetry—if not in a bordello, then a pub—yet all of them do not fit the real chronology of the poet's creativity, throwing up doubt in the minds of anyone familiar with the topic on a more than superficial level.

In search of an arbiter let us turn to the memoir of yet another person, Olha Oliynyk, the poet's fiancée. This round-faced and (for that era) fashionably coiffed young lady outwardly resembled—judging by the photo—bit-part movie actresses whose names are now hopelessly forgotten even by film historians. She was to become the *principal companion* of Antonych's life. Their wedding was planned for the fall of 1937, and were it not for the poet's death in July, things would have ended in their *happy marriage*. Antonych dedicated several two-stanza poems in the "First Lyrical Intermezzo" section of *The Green Gospel* to her, most notably "Nuptials," where eroticism, as if on purpose, is entirely absent—unless one takes as erotic hint the words "Curly moon has braided with your hair, my beloved" or "why is your palm shaking?"

It seems one could boldly and safely assume the poet had no premarital sexual contact with his fiancée. Such were the demands of that era's morality, these unbearably prudish rules introduced by gray-haired superintendents from the *theater of Galician citizenry*. Thus Antonych, this *beastly bad boy*, couldn't come up with anything to oppose it. All his attempts to seduce the young lady of firm convictions with early intimacy were shattered by her good breeding and decency which bordered on frigidity. One can assume Olha never allowed the circumstances to develop in such a way so that she and her fiancé would find themselves alone. No, it was always in someone's presence—girlfriends, teachers, Basilian nuns, and last but not least, her parents. All of them had the nasty habit of staring at Antonych and judging him unkindly, as if before them stood some Minotaur or Fantômas who intended to drag their foolish child into his secret den of iniquity. "And how does he make a living?" asked Mrs. Oliynyk on numerous occasions, staring holes through her daughter with her lorgnette, never satisfied by the answer regarding some ephemeral prize from the Writers and Journalists Society or the deeply symbolic stipend from His Eminence the Metropolitan, Count Andrew.

Thus it is in no way surprising that in the memoir of his fiancée Antonych comes across as someone not very special. She wishes to emphasize his softness, kindness, dreaminess. For example, how diligent he was in his studies, how he would not leave libraries for days or even weeks (obviously, a different hypothesis about true motives and his constant absence invites itself in here). Of all the vague and ambiguous phrases allegedly uttered by Antonych in her presence only one sticks in our memory—perhaps because she read it in the memoir of Kurdydyk: "You know, I have an impression someone was whispering in my ear. Yes, literally whispering."

It goes without saying Antonych experienced this sort of relationship as a painful drama. Clearly aware of his special place in a metaphysical society of the *poètes maudits*, he was broken to pieces by the demons of rebellion and destruction, which he far too clearly saw in the closest prospects of his life: marriage, everyday routine and boredom, refusal of the most important, capitulation, and therefore—a disgraceful spending of the rest of his days surrounded by a completely foreign and demanding family while serving as schoolteacher somewhere near Kolomyia. It's precisely these moods of his that call out to the most attentive among us when we read among his writings, "In my skull the marriage bed of two vipers," or even more telling, "The flowery décor of dens of honorable families /a canary, a bed, a puppy, and standard love." And most importantly—here the drama outgrows itself—absence of options, that is the full realization that this was how it was going to be. Other paths simply weren't available.

Summer of 1937 was going to be the final summer of his freedom. Time was mercilessly pushing towards the wedding. He no longer could break out of this dependency—the theater of human relationships we know so well would never forgive him this desertion and not let him out, and even if it did, he would still have no air to breathe. The situation was markedly complicated by his new passionate interest which promised to become even bigger than simply an *interest*. Antonych encountered it in the depths of the old city, among ghostly stone mansions and stuffy courtyards with narrow and wet stairs, either on Virmenska or on Serbska St.

The name of his new passion was Fanny. She was slightly over thirty, and had two kids whom she chased into the courtyard from her apartment cluttered with artificial flowers whenever one of her steady clients would visit (these were a neighborhood policeman, the always drunk delivery man from the Halytsky Market, a few medical school students, and the choir regent of the Church of the Assumption, his butt hopelessly sagging). When Antonych appeared in her life she stopped receiving them all, resulting in furious anger, especially coming from the policeman, the only one using her services free of charge given his special work duties. Fanny had long legs like streams of milk, a silky and warm stomach, a velvety clean vagina. Her skin was so white that in a medieval romance they would have written she drank red wine and one could see it flow down her esophagus. Back in the day they tried to convince her to become a dancer at The Golden Goat, but Fanny rejected the proposal as too indecent.

As weeks and months flew by Antonych discovered in her ever-new secret fonts. It is doubtful, though, they ever spoke about poetry—they themselves *were* poetry, and that was enough. Making love on heaps of artificial flowers they reached that lost wholeness of the two halves which many religious and medical treatises unsuccessfully strove to describe. For each of them this was happening for the first time in their lives, that is, earlier they had only heard of something like this. But what is more important, each of them — and almost simultaneously—came to the realization this was a great exception and that they would never again be able to experience this for a second time with anyone else. "When is your wedding?" Fanny asked once in early June, on one of those nights that morph into dawn without ever starting in earnest. Or, more precisely, in the middle of the day, for she never chased her kids out into the yard in the middle of the night, thus she and Antonych only met during the day.

"In three and a half months," answered Antonych and immediately he felt breathless. It seems it was then his *intention* took root.

At the end of June he came to her at the agreed hour and they closed all windows and doors. Undressing, they didn't utter a single word. Antonych wrote on the wall with a piece of coal his final words which in the depth of their meaning surpass stanzas of his mysticism: "No one is to blame, do not seek the culprit!" After this they opened the gas faucets and lay on the bed. No, there was also a record: Fanny put on the victrola *Blue Angel*, their favorite jazz piece with the clarinet solo of Alphonse "the Negro" Kaifman. They knew how to make love so selflessly and also with such concentration that death—or perhaps the eternal void—was to reach them after the final sob of the clarinet and its ultimate languorous explosion. He'd already described all of this in his "Ballad of a Blue Death"—about which she probably had no inkling.

Everything had already been described—except the finale, which even he could not foretell in visions from several years earlier. Thus when they were losing consciousness—either from love or from the poisoning—they still heard outside, from the almost nonexistent world, the noise of the door being broken down. Already a minute later, when they did not care anymore, a gang of tense and drunken *rescuers* burst into Fanny's apartment, led by the noisy neighborhood policeman. Even his horrifying barks and shouts could not bring Fanny back—it was now hopeless to call out to her.

Antonych was hastily taken to the clinic in Kulparkiv (the ambulance honking frenetically in midst the city filled with pedestrians, villagers' carts, streetcars), where an assembly of the most authoritative and thus the most cynical doctors, after a brief consultation, resolved to start fighting for the life of the victim. This action had to consist first and foremost of *detoxification*, that is, of a full changing of his poisoned blood for good. Antonych spent the next day and a half in a barely lit corridor between two worlds, the hopelessly thorough medical supervision and an unwieldy and fragile assemblage of glass vessels.

News of his hospitalization immediately captured Lviv. However, the *theater's leadership* could not agree on the true version of the catastrophe: suicide attempts in no way belonged to plots established in the realm of national literature. On the other hand, the fact of a *grave illness* could not be expunged or hidden. Consciously creating their own model of Antonych, the *theater activists* launched the first thing that came into the head of one of them and appeared fairly innocent, that is, neutral: an acute appendicitis followed by later surgery. They expected that after the successful blood transfusion the *patient* would spend the same amount of time at the hospital that it took to recuperate from any surgery. There was, however, no certainty as to how the patient himself was going to behave once he left the hospital—first of all, would he start *disseminating* right and left the true reason for balancing between light and darkness? The most decisive of the manipulators were ready to handle this as well. On the third day after the unfortunate event they dispatched to the clinic a delegation which, after examining Antonych's bed and covering it in peonies and oranges, managed to extract from him a forced nod to signify his submission.

"He has lost a lot of weight, and his skin has a bit of an earthy tint to it, but his spirit is vigorous and will continue serving great civic causes for a long time"—this is how members of the delegation reported their impressions, and most periodicals picked up their formulation. In the meantime, already the following night, Antonych suddenly felt much worse and again slipped into unconsciousness. His body did not want to make peace with the foreignness inside himself—perhaps during the transfusion there was a blood type error. One shouldn't neglect the possibility of conscious abuse: those were years when the entire city was saturated by rumors of black market donors and various machinations to procure internal organs.

Already the next day the bravura assurances of the doctors yielded their place to panic statements about the sudden deterioration of the situation. The *theater* almost immediately responded with a new twist of thought: the appendectomy was indeed successful, the poet's health relentlessly improved, yet a new trial befell his exhausted organism: pneumonia. The authors did not worry too much about this being a rather atypical illness for early July. Like all mediocre scribblers and liars, they were forced to pad and develop the story with extraneous exculpatory circumstances, quickly deforming its not terribly elegant structure. Hence the idea of drafty hospital wards in which the poet supposedly spent several days, the cause of the complications. This was where the co-conspirators, the doctors, started protesting: the image of a nonstop draft that ran through the hallways and wards of the clinic did not compute with expectations regarding the personnel's thoroughness and their own hygienic standards. The story-spinners had to continue their inventions: no, the treatment conditions were entirely good, but everyone knew how much a sensitive, easily wilting creature this Antonych was. In Lviv, even the sparrows knew he was morbidly afraid of drafts. It was then that the testimonies appeared about Antonych's chronic colds, runny nose, weak heart, and—this was supposed to be the pinnacle of image-making—the habit of wrapping his migraine-tormented head in a towel. And all this fussing, entirely devoid of sense, over the poet's dying body, intended to serve the extremely important (so thought its participants) cause of saving his *moral* image.

Antonych was alone in his dying. In an ultimate sense, he was already out of reach of all rescuers in this world. None of their vain attempts could return him to where he felt he had been *only* a guest, understanding that his true home was *elsewhere*. A few years earlier, in a poem ironically titled "Ars Poetica," he also foresaw these final hours: "and as always, you will be alone in order to forget it all." Most importantly, forget about those who spent so much effort tying him fussily and clumsily down to earth, to entangle and tame him.

His death came during the night of July 7th. Someone saw in this another trick of signs gone crazy: the dance of the primordial forest, Kupala lights around his final resting bed, an invitation to the seething maelstrom of green. The *green* came for him in order to take him and dissolve him inside itself.[13]

In reality there was six hours of agony, beyond whose limits we are not allowed to peer, for we can observe only the lowest steps of this metamorphosis, linked to fully palpable matters such as blood circulation, heart, brain, kidneys, the beginning of decomposition.

The following day he was taken home, to Horodotska St., where thanks to the *theater's* efforts a procedure was organized, appropriate for such cases and very strictly censored. A good half of those present could not fathom that *this* actually happened. Some of them came to *say farewell* convinced this was only a performance—perhaps cynical, but still typical for this self-sacrificing jester. It seemed that in a moment he would rise from the coffin and start reciting his best iambic stanzas and then lead everyone to The Babylonian Saint or someplace like that—to celebrate his second birthday. This is how he lay, dressed in black-and-white, that is, fit for a holiday, lightly made up, a bit artificial in his gradually waxy turn, yet this too belonged to his arsenal—all these tricks with

13 Kupala is a pre-Christian Slavic midsummer holiday, later conflated with the feast of St. John the Baptist and celebrated on the night between July 6 and 7 according to the Gregorian calendar (which is June 23-24 according to the Julian calendar, used in many Eastern Christian traditions). Traditional beliefs (reflected in the writing of Gogol, among others) speak of the spirits of the netherworld coming out on that night (author's note).

makeup, dressing up, and pantomime. Only the presence of close and distant relatives, the conversations hushed to semi-whisper, busy manipulations with wreaths, candles, sheets of paper, prayer services, and above all the *auntie* frozen in the furthest room (from that day until her own death she would not utter a single word) convinced that *this* really did happen, for no joke would have gone this far.

His funeral was, also, accompanied by strange phenomena. Oksana Kerch mentions Olha Oliynyk's long and fruitless search for his final manuscripts. The fiancée remembered that up till the last moment Antonych was working on two collections. The first of them, *The Green Gospel*, was essentially complete, the second, *Rotations*, more than a third ready. But she couldn't find either of them! The repeated and increasingly impatient rifling through drawers and bookcases only produced detritus: old bills, newspaper ads, and most frustratingly, some too risqué photos taken with street beauties. Biting her lips and almost in tears, Olha was ready to believe that no manuscripts existed and everything he tried reciting for her from time to time, casting sideways glances on the vigilant ears of her chaperones, was only a fiction, a dream. An hour before his body was supposed to be taken she suddenly yielded to an internal call (the shadow of a tulip? the rustling of a shroud? the flight of a bumblebee?) and brusquely approached his desk (the *rickety* one, according to Lassovsky) where in the most visible spot, pedantically stacked page by page, sat the two manuscripts, the finished and the unfinished. How did they turn up there? She already looked at the desk a thousand times and they weren't there earlier! "This is him," she said to Oksana Kerch. "Someone he left behind just placed his manuscripts on the table."

The poet Havryliuk remembers another surprising thing. On the way to Yaniv Cemetery, where he was going not with the main procession but on the sidewalk, dropping in at watering holes along the way to fortify himself, several times he thought he saw Bohdan—if not in the midst of a crowd, then standing at the entry to a house, and once even at the head of the procession, as if the old friend was indeed leading them all. "From that day on I started thinking about our reflections," noted Havryliuk in his diary a few months (!) later. "When I was rereading his *Three Signet Rings*, I stumbled upon the lines, 'and again from the portrait, from the silvery frame /painted on canvas /my double calls to me,' I understood there is nothing more real than poetry."

They decided to bury his violin with him, thereby—so the funeral organizers thought—responding to his lines from five years earlier: "God has put me like a violin in a case." So, it was placed, together with the bow, in the case—numerous witnesses observed this ritual—which was then placed inside the coffin. How could this violin reappear at the apartment on

Horodotska St. when the tear-stained and hushed company returned there for the wake, featuring mostly *tea*? Did they really bury an empty violin case?

These and other unexplainable things, sown into the fertile ground of the Lviv *milieu*, couldn't help but find further development. During the months and years that followed the city was captivated again and again by stories of Antonych *seen* here and there. He appeared, for the most part, in the dense human crowd and dissolved in it when one got closer. Often people spoke of seeing him from the back, a few succeeded in seeing for a moment the turn of his head, but then everything melted away. Only once Sviatoslav Hordynsky saw him not in a crowd but all alone, from a distance of no less than three hundred steps: he stood on a hill near the woodlands, a bit north of Pidholosko, stooping from the cold, his hat pushed over his forehead, his hands in the pocket of his fully buttoned jacket. The day was wet and windy. It was September 13. Having stood in this pose without movement, he then pulled hands from pockets and waved his arms a few times as if they were wings. Hordynsky, when writing this, asserts the gesture had to be intended for him, the only observer attendant to that situation. He felt a sudden desire to call from below to this *indubitable Antonych*, when the latter suddenly turned around and, walking in steps that were somehow weightless, set out in the direction of the forest where he disappeared among tree trunks, shreds of fog, and gray snow hanging from branches.

The conversations gradually died down at the end of 1939 when the new powers-that-be started decisively purging the heads of local citizenry of various metaphysical nonsense. Many of those who knew him departed Lviv forever, both in the westerly and, sadly, easterly direction. The *theater of Galician citizenry* was almost completely destroyed. What remained were various small groupings scattered around the world that never succeeded at full-blooded rebirth. The years that followed, with their nightmares of war and repression, weren't conducive to his return, even in dreams or apparitions. There was, however, a collection of poems published in Krakow, but its respected editor, a literature professor, included in it only the primary texts. Still later, during the times of *thoughtless destruction of historical memory*, brigades of anonymous persons in padded jackets set out rehabilitating Yaniv Cemetery. His grave, along with those of hundreds of other undesirables, was leveled.

Thus when, in the early 1960s, the unexpected company of his new twenty-year-old adepts, using the cemetery records and inscriptions on surviving gravestones determined his place of burial and erected there a new gravestone for him, none had any idea they were thereby acting contrary to the lost legend whereby he had not actually died but continued living all those years, in Lviv, and that he was supposedly still living and that one of these days this secret would be revealed.

7

Either that very morning or the following one the guests all gathered together in the larger dining room. It was located in the northeastern wing of the resort, the second floor, its window opening onto the alpine meadow. It was the wing with walls decorated with Flemish still lives, deer antlers, as well as platters—of various kinds and intended uses, both ceramic and metal, mementos from an unknown brass orchestra.

It is probably worth visualizing who was sitting where. At the two heads of a refectory table sat, naturally, the esteemed Professor Doktor and, for some reason, Yarchyk the video maker. On the professor's left (correspondingly, on Volshebnik's right) sat the family: Ms. Roma, Artur Pepa, their daughter Kolomea. On the professor's right was everyone else, that is, Karl-Joseph Zumbrunnen (face-to-face with Ms. Roma, as it happened), and Lilya the raven-haired and Marlena the blonde.

Also, two guys from the staff—naturally, with buzz cuts, wearing black turtlenecks, cell phones tucked into their belts. We can more or less neglect them, since they remained completely silent, taking turns to bring from the kitchen platters of food, as well as tea and coffee, only to disappear again with trays full of empty dishes.

As always, the host wasn't present; however, those present no longer appeared surprised by this. One of them, truth be told, did inquire feebly, but the answer from a taciturn server was exhaustive: "They will come later." Thus the topic was exhausted.

The invitees unconsciously absorbed the house's silent atmosphere. Karl-Joseph, who would prefer not to speak due to the language barrier, caught Ms. Roma's glances and, unnoticed by others, trembled when taking from vis-à-vis another platter or bowl, touched for a moment the palm of her hand, her wrist, her sleeve. Ms. Roma, feeling sufficiently self-confident and because of this, full of inexpressible sensuality, her hair still wet after her morning bath, occasionally performed her interpreter duties, time and again announcing specially for Zumbrunnen: "*Wurst!*"—or "*Käse!*"—or "*Frühlingssalat!*"—as if he did not see that himself. Lilya, outstripping her BFF, quickly took the seat next to the *foreign photographer.* Now she concentrated on working out how best to start seducing him. Marlena was not thinking anything, quietly rejoicing in her girlfriend, S.O.L. with her plan. Kolya secretly studied these two, in her head mercilessly criticizing their horrible makeup jobs. Soon, though, she got bored with this and withdrew deep into herself, the way girls of her age can do so well. Volshebnik the director ate a lot. Artur Pepa strained to hide his inebriation, as a result of which he bore a very ironic expression, his knife repeatedly sliding off the head of a pickled mushroom, making painful noises as it scratched the plate—which led Ms. Roma to cast an irritated side glance. And only Professor Doktor, smiling amicably, occasionally interrupted this laconic meal with out loud thinking, for instance:

"I beg the esteemed company to direct attention to the objects present here. What a surprising and thoroughgoing sophistication! Yes, *our* grandparents still had their 'home,' their 'well,' a familiar castle nearby—yes, even their own clothing, their overcoats. Almost each and every thing served as a vessel from which they took something human and in which they stored something human for the rainy day. And now from America there come empty things invading our space, ghost things, a window-dressing of life. Things we brought to life, things which shared our fates now vanish and cannot be replaced. We are probably the last ones to know such things."

Or:

"Nietzsche's recourse to the pre-Iranian prophet Zarathustra is not accidental in this respect. The creative personalities of Rudyard Kipling and Joseph Conrad brought into being a surge of so-called 'culture of the exotic' in Great Britain. A very special case of Symbolist exoticism is offered by the prominent Ibero-American poet Rubén Darío, whose work is a curious interweaving of ancient, Medieval, and native—that is, Amerindian and Afro-American—motifs."

Or suddenly:

"Bohdan-Ihor Antonych—and this is fully understandable—also could not stay away from such quests, symptomatic for his time. When one reads some of his lines, the imagination involuntarily produces ancient seafaring maps, where depths and waves covering the vast oceans suddenly disgorge abject, chimerical creatures, terrifying monsters and freaks, echidnas, dragons, and "sea bishops"—all that aquatic bestiary that becomes a prologue not only for the phantasms of Surrealist painting from his contemporaries, but also the Hollywood horror film."

"Fuck it, then," suddenly said Pepa reacting to this and chuckling into his plate.

"Already?"—Roma darted at him a condemning glance. She suddenly felt quite embarrassed by her husband.

"Already what?" shot the unmasked Artur in response. "What do you mean, sweet chickadee?"

"Already loaded first thing in the morning," explained Ms. Roma. The comparison with a chickadee did not convince her in the least—on the contrary, it made her all the more concerned.

"Come on! I haven't had any chance at all to get loaded!" declared Pepa with an air of Hamletesque irony (or so it seemed to him) and gave a wink at Lilya—as it happened, she was sitting right across from him.

Lilya, without losing her countenance, remarked

to herself *this dude is also good pickings.*

"You are entirely correct," said the professor, now smiling personally to Pepa, "when you negate my preceding thesis. I resorted to it purposefully, to create a kind of intellectual provocation. Your reaction is precisely what I need to radicalize our discussion. However, can one really dispute the fact that Antonych utilizes oceanic imagery with a surprising frequency?"

"But no one negated anything, sir," retorted Pepa with all the irony he was capable of at the moment. "You two are probably sisters?" he asked Lilya and Marlena.

"*Banusch*," announced a bit too loudly Ms. Roma, "*ist eine typisch huzulische Speise, eine Spezialität sozusagen, etwas wie italienische Polenta . . .*"

"She is speaking Spanish," commented Pepa in a nasal voice.

"I know banush," assured Karl-Joseph hastily. He occasionally succeeded processing a few phrases in Ukrainian.

"Sisters?" repeated Lilya.

"Yea, something like that," acquiesced Marlena.

Pepa caught her by the hand as she was reaching across the table for the coffee pot, and with a whistle produced an exclamation that almost sounded like a hiccup:

"Wow, those are some nails! Why do you need such black nails, sweet chickadee?"

"Artur!" his wife shouted authoritatively, knocking

a juice glass with her sleeve—an empty one this time.

"Artur?" retorted Pepa. "Yes, I am Artur. I have now been Artur for thirty-seven years."

"An old fart, but still sort of cool," thought Lilya and Marlena simultaneously; the latter also succeeded in freeing her hand.

"Give no attention," said Roma to her, coldly, instead of offering an apology that would have been appropriate here.

"Pay no attention," corrected her Pepa. "In this case, 'pay' is more correct. Nice girls, aren't they?"

Ms. Roma pretended the question was not addressed to her and noisily began rising from the table. Really, why should one take so much time to have breakfast? She came to the window. Behind it on that exceptionally transparent day one could see a rather large chunk of mountainous region and several snow-capped peaks on the Ukrainian side of the border.

The two girlfriends exchanged knowing glances, and Professor Doktor again stayed on top of things:

"It's wonderful you take words so seriously, Mr. Pepa," he said excitedly. "This testifies to your poetic talent being far from ordinary. Remember these lines of Antonych, 'And then I cross with thunder /My spear-like sharp and simple words'?"

"You are being too kind, dear sir," Pepa modestly rejected the compliments. "Far from it! What thunder? Although I must admit, the idea of crossing does fascinate me at times . . ."

But this time he failed to catch the eyes of either Lilya or Marlena: having figured out this *loaded dude* was only a poet, they thought in unison, "*dismissed*." Poets were guys whose writings they had to memorize back in school, and it wasn't cool. "And may you too go where the sun don't shine, stupid hicks," thought Pepa in response, and lit up a Prylutska, a rather brutal brand of cigarette, expecting it to make him even giddier—in other words, *expand his consciousness*.

Karl-Joseph stared in the direction of the window. Above all else he wanted to come close to Roma and see something that only she was capable of seeing.

"*Es ist heute so unglaublich sonnig, dass wir dort auf der Terrasse sitzen konnten*," declared Ms. Roma without thinking of the consequences.

But others also heard the word "terrace." For Lilya and Marlena it was associated with their extremely revealing swimsuits. Artur Pepa thought it would be great to stretch out in an easy chair and finish the half bottle of walnut schnapps he hid under the bathtub. Kolya barely restrained herself from saying, "And the fourth circle's the embrace of warm wind, a whirlpool of energy." Yarchyk Volshebnik, the professional, having made for himself his seventh sandwich with cold roasted veal, cheese, sliced tomatoes, lettuce, mayo, sardines, and ketchup, suddenly asked Professor Doktor:

"And you . . . how shall I say . . . did I hear you say you do watch Hollywood's product? I have here a tape with my new . . . video. It's about this guy of yours . . . The title is 'Old Antonych' . . . Shall we go watch it?"

"I only said each picture must reflect a profound feeling," answered the professor with a good-natured smile, "and 'profound' implies 'strange,' while 'strange' means 'unknown' and 'unknowable.' For a work of art to be immortal, it must reach beyond human experience."

"Aha," nodded the director. "That's right. And you, Mr. Pepa? Your thoughts too . . . you know . . . so to speak . . ."

"Call me Artur, old man," said Pepa magnanimously.

And then again everyone fell silent, even Professor Doktor—probably in order to not irritate the gloomy guys from staff nor distract them from the slow-paced, indifferent clearing of everything that half an hour earlier could be called a breakfast.

On the screen of an enormous and flat Telefunken TV flashed black-and-white—mostly sepia-toned—frames that were supposed to invoke several stylistic trends simultaneously, especially *retro* and *underground.* In and of itself this technical trick was in no way something new; in fact, it had been used long and hard by everyone from Bergman and Tarkovsky to, most recently, the makers of *Moulin Rouge.* The new thing was that all of it took place in Lviv: each second yet another background image of some hidden nook—an old courtyard; a dumpster; an underground labyrinth. At one moment the tower of city hall leaned and almost fell on top of the viewer, complete with a trumpeter in it. At another, the Gunpowder Tower blew into bits. Then some guy in a hang-glider fell crashing into the industrial ruins of Pidzamche, with pieces tearing off his artificial wings, raining on the factory chimneys and construction cranes. One was supposed to understand all this as a sign: a spirit of impending catastrophe ruled over this world. The end of all ends. A foretaste of apocalypse.

Yarchyk Volshebnik's *apo-video* was made for the song "Old Antonych" by the rock band Queen Rabbit—a purely local hit with a patina of typically Lvivian *independence* at the margins of all possible *trends* and *waves* from the recent decade. Thus first and foremost it was the band members themselves that filled the flashing screen, led by an androgynous front man wearing a plastic crown of thorns. The musicians made their appearance sometimes with instruments, sometimes without. Sometimes in the dilapidated rooms of some abandoned villa, sometimes at the steps leading to the ruins of a church, sometimes by a medieval stone wall covered with graffiti full of English-language curses. The song went something like:

old antonych is still alive
he still isn't dead, he has a bad heart
he loves jazz, he drinks a lot
his loooooove is as sweet as a girl of the night

This was followed by the refrain, entirely composed of two words, "old antonych!"—repeated sixteen times. On the screen one saw all sorts of freakish-looking types kissing, heavily-powdered prostitutes entering mysterious dark limousines, champagne exploding, someone shooting up on the filthy floor of a public restroom, and at one point the façade of the Grand Hotel flashed by, covered by improbable-looking cracks and vines, as a crowd of homeless men danced around a bonfire in front of the Opera. This last frame especially amused Artur Pepa, who during the interval between breakfast and the screening did partake of the walnut schnapps and now energetically stomped his feet to the music, catching only a few random phrases describing how

> old antonych creeps through the night
> from one bar to another he cannot sleep
> for three hundred years owls and owlets
> fly above him who doesn't know him

So, here indeed this alleged Antonych—a tall old-looking guy in a hat and trench coat, earrings in both ears, looking like some kind of urban phantom. He walked the city, opening the doors of basement bars with his foot, immersing himself in their hellish atmosphere, as if making his personal rounds ("And this actor, what is his name?" asked Ms. Roma in a hushed voice in response to a request from Karl-Joseph), and then he made love, without taking off either hat or even trench coat, to some half-dead heavily tattooed beauty; around her hovered the inscription "MY NAME IS FANNY—I'M REALLY FUNNY". Occasional bits of color in the black-and-white picture made for a relatively interesting find by crafty Volshebnik. Thus, when Antonych drank wine from a large goblet, the liquid was red. It was equally red when it flowed through the throat of his transparent lover. There were also yellow flowers on a smoky trash heap next to an unknown and draped monument. Golden stardust fell onto the city like snow—but that happened later, when the now-solitary Antonych disappeared in a moonbeam ("You wouldn't know him, he's an amateur," answered the video maker, likewise in a hushed voice).

In the meantime the action was nearing the end—streams of underground waters rushed in from all directions, the city with all its sinners, male and female, sank to dark depths, in whirlpools it created circled dead birds, condoms, syringes, old records. Only the musicians remained, on the stage of either an abandoned club or an opera house, the front man tore his temporary crown off his head into the water, the camera rapidly retreated, creating an entirely metaphysical spatial perspective with a small dot of a stage above the global flood. The remaining words were sung in complete darkness, accompanied by a muffled cello—as if from a half-flooded room or from damaged tape:

old antonych wanders the ground
of the old city this cursed ruin
his girls are still so small
and death still gazes at the moon

That was the end. Everyone present at the screening breathed a sigh of relief. Artur Pepa couldn't help speaking up, since it was he who first felt the itch to on his tongue.

"You know, Yarchyk, everything would be great if not for the final semi-rhyme. What's with this '*ruin—moon*'? It would have been better to have something classy, like '*missy—pissy*.'"

Instead of belly laughs from the group, he got only Roma's remark, "How witty!"

"Here on this tape there is also . . . you know . . . some explanation . . . commentary, so to speak," answered Volshebnik, and after fast forwarding a bit, he stopped at the scene where he himself, lounging in a cushy chair in the midst of a studio, recounted to the TV audience his idea.

". . . thing else. It took me several years to reach this vision," said Yarchyk's on-screen double, scrubbed of all the "well's" and "you know's" through editing. "I was attracted to the universal story of an immortal idol—say, a poet. Now producers from both NTV and MTV are expressing interest in our work. I'm really glad that Queen Rabbit . . . how should I say (here the unknown editors cut themselves some slack) . . .

delivered this image to me."

Then Queen Rabbit's front man appeared on the screen. He turned out to be a girl with a beer in her hands, smoking a cigarette. They filmed her somewhere in the old city, against the background of a very graffiti-covered wall.

"All of us heard scary stories about old Antonych back when we were kids," she said, taking pauses to sip and smoke. "I remember how my parents, when they thought I behaved badly, told me, 'Just you wait, old Antonych will come and take you to his dark cellar.' Apparently, this person was once buried in our city but started appearing in various places. He lived in gross cellars, gathered empty bottles and waste paper for recycling, wore a long trench coat. And spoke a clearly prewar language, with all the characteristic phrases. Sometimes I was afraid of him, sometimes not so much. One day I was drawing secret signs in the sandbox near our house, I invented signs and then destroyed them, that is, wiped them away. I drew one such sign and was getting ready to erase it when I sensed above me someone's presence. It was the man in the long trench coat. At first I got scared, because he said, "You summoned me with this sign. What do you need?" Then I started apologizing, babbling all sorts of nonsense that it was accidental, I did not know, et cetera, and he sighed and went on his way. Now I think I only saw it all in a dream. But still I can't forget. The title of our second al . . ."

Here the recording cut off, and the screen was filled with a greyish-whitish hissing mass, however, they all stayed in their seats—in part because Ms. Roma was still in the middle of translating for Zumbrunnen the gist of the just-told story, skipping around a bit. Although the story didn't hold any meaning for him—the main thing was that she, Roma, was speaking to him. That was enough.

"That's some cool chick," thought Artur about the girl with the beer. "Didn't even bat an eye. I must . . ."—but here he grew too lazy to go on fantasizing how they were going to acquaint themselves, smoke, drink, talk poetry, music, mysticism, sex, and so on and so forth—to hell with her, she wasn't *that* interesting.

"So what did you . . . professor . . . sir . . . you know . . . think of it?" Volshebnik reminded about his existence, ejecting the tape from the VCR.

"In my modest opinion, here we have a generally tactful penetration of the realm of archetypes," eagerly spoke Professor Doktor, making Volshebnik regret bothering him. "It is they who, according to Jung, create the contents of the so-called collective unconscious. Their immediate expressions come to us in dreams and hallucinations often containing much that is individualized, incomprehensible, even naïve. The archetype essentially reveals an irrational content which is supplanted, as it develops, by a rational and sensual content, and entirely fitting that specific personal consciousness where it arises."

"Thank you very much," Volshebnik nodded eagerly his long-haired head.

"This secret lunar lover," the professor continued, "this mysterious stranger in a trench coat is undoubtedly an archetype, always present at the border between consciousness and the unconscious in a fantasy world of each teenage girl who is beginning to blossom, who finds herself at the stage of her most personal passionate expectations."

Professor Doktor spoke these last words while glancing smilingly at Kolomea's rather boldly revealed legs and stopped his eyes on her flushed face. And this time it was she who couldn't help herself.

"Shouldn't we continue this on the terrace?" asked Ms. Roma energetically; something was making her really uneasy about it all.

However, at the terrace no one continued any other discussion—everyone was overcome by invincible incommensurable laziness that happens only in springtime sun. A slow slide into sleep, springtime sleepy softness of bodies and souls, the blissful suspension in nirvana that starts somewhere deep inside the finest fibers of your bones, captures all your tissues without exception, slows your blood, heart, yet mobilizes the receptors: the surging sensitivity of skin and nostrils makes us warm animals—so many touches, so many scents, *and none of them has a name*!

What was happening to the weather? Why this place, known mostly for its storm systems, unstoppable piercing wind, elements and fronts battling one another, why today so warm, clear, calm, and lucid? Why the temperature in the sun pushing 72 degrees? Why wasn't wind the *wind* in true alpine meadow sense, but rather a gentle breeze, to use a too-pretty expression of which our local poets are so fond? Why was everything present—the sharp teeth of the main mountain range, the snow-capped tall peaks, the rocky smaller outcrops—so expressive, clearly outlined, so wonderfully visible? Why of all possible sounds and hums stored at the bottom of this silence remained the quiet steady drip and gurgle of snowmelt? And not a single scream of a bird? How could this have happened? How could it happen that even Professor Doktor did not say, "Silence is the language God uses to speak to us humans"?

Whatever it may have been, it couldn't last forever. The world's silence was broken by the noisy run down steps by a male body formed from its own devices—Artur Pepa appeared with a large chess board in his hands.

"Aha, everyone's here!" he shouted, judging with a quick glance the scattered human configuration. "And everyone feels good! What about communication, recreation? Did you come here to die?"

"Artur!" called out the half-asleep Ms. Roma.

She was sitting in a deck chair, and she badly wanted to pull over her head her coarse-knit linen blouse, baring her shoulders. "Why, why didn't I bring a swimsuit with me?" she lamented in her half-sleep up until this fool, fool, fool interrupted her.

"Yes, it's me," answered the fool. "Care for a game of chess?"

"What chess?" muttered Roma without opening her eyes. "Why chess?"

With these words semi-sleep again overcame her, and she saw herself from approximately the same distance Karl-Joseph would have had, sitting on the railing, playing with his camera. With a decisive gesture, she pulled the blouse radiating troubling scents of deodorant and sweat over her head, and with a beautiful gesture threw it somewhere far away. The camera clicked the very moment she managed to cover her large breasts with her hands, but all of this in a half-dream, a dream, a dream (she dreamt her breasts were much larger than they were, in reality).

"Old man, you perhaps?" Artur collared Volshebnik. "Bishop, rook, queen?"

"Well . . . you know . . . it's . . ." the long-haired guy mumbled from his sun lounger, but Pepa was already heading towards the two bikini-clad kittens who warmed themselves far off to the side on a couple of air mattresses.

"Wow, what athleticism!" Pepa gave a whistle. "Shall we play a game for three?"

Lilya and Marlena raised their heads, visibly annoyed, turning over with the same air of annoyance, and continued sunbathing, now on their stomachs. They believed this *always-plastered shithead* got in the way of the *foreigner* who was dying to take their *swimsuit pictures.*

"Aren't you afraid of sunburn?" Pepa kept pestering. "Shall I put some lotion on you? Did you bring sunscreen?"

"Dismissed," answered one of them, likewise in half-sleep.

"Understood," reassured Pepa; he appeared wimped out, but only for a couple of minutes.

Truth be told, he did not bother the professor, making a wide detour around his wicker chair. He likewise did not propose a game to Kolomea—first of all, because he generally did not seek to find himself alone with her, and second, because she was protected by the fifth circle of spring, her green innocence. There remained the Austrian at the railing, and Artur, shaking the chessboard in the air so that all the wooden pieces rattled inside it, inquired,

"*Schachspielen? Eine kleine schachspielen*, eh?"

Karl-Joseph put his camera down and jumped off the railing.

"All right, agweed," he uttered the simplest phrase he could muster, because formulating a refusal, including some polite way of getting out of the situation, was impossible. Besides, he suddenly felt some pity for this inebriated man needed by no one.

"*Jawohl?*" double-checked Artur, and thought to himself: "Why the hell have I picked chess? I really can't play very well after all."

In a couple of minutes they were sitting on top of two stools, arranging pieces on the board. And then the game began, which could be judged only by Artur's not always pertinent exclamations ("Knight! Pawn! Gardez! Bishop! Check! Zeitnot! Zugzwang! Queen! *Verstehen*, queen?). But Zumbrunnen was silent. He had to play the Whites—his opponent insisted on this, since "you are our guest, understand?" Essentially, Zumbrunnen did not care which side to play—back in the day he used to play chess a lot, won many a city tournament, corresponded with students quite similar to him, at Viktor Korchnoi's private school, and easily solved problems from the specialized magazines. On the fourth minute of the game Artur Pepa said, "Endgame! Kaput!" and offered to play another game, "But this time I play Whites, is it clear?"

Clearly, Pepa lost this game too, and then four more over the next half an hour, and only then did he pull out his secret weapon—the last "Prylutska," which for diversity's sake was stuffed with a hemp-derived mixture of rather high quality. After his very first puff the game acquired a slow-motion meaningfulness, and Karl-Joseph, briskly moving his nostrils, asked,

"*Hasch?*"

"*Wollen?*" Pepa winked at him and passed the cigarette.

"*Nicht schlecht!*" appreciated Karl-Joseph after the first puff.

"And what did you expect?" confirmed Artur.

Over a brief period of time, he came to the conclusion that the future development of the events on the chessboard was clear to him well in advance. For one hundred future games. There was no sense in moving chess pieces—everything was already marching on its own towards the victorious end. He could, without stumbling, list all the future moves for the next one hundred years. Both his own and those of his opponent. For he had transformed into one giant Brain Center—that's what he now was, Artur Pepa. This was a double Brain Center: one sat inside him, and the other was simply Artur Pepa, that was its name. This thought made him somewhat scared.

"Listen, what have we done here?" Pepa said worriedly. "Earth is burning beneath our feet!"

He looked at the sky and saw the sun was about to disappear behind the paravent of tall mountain peaks. Artur Pepa did not have a clear notion of what a *paravent* was, but he was certain the sun was disappearing precisely *behind a paravent*. He also saw heads around him: a whole crowd had gathered around the chessboard, animatedly discussing the situation and sticking their fingers, as thick as logs, at the chess pieces still standing.

"*Schlechtersmeinkopfbleiben! Streichmalwiederzurück und Bruchsleifenwandernzusammen!*" said

Karl-Joseph aggressively.

In response, Artur Pepa smiled knowingly and, with a decisive gesture, swept all the pieces off the chessboard.

However, that very afternoon, or perhaps the next one, the duel continued. This happened not at the terrace, but higher—at the tower located on the southwestern side of the resort, where everyone had shifted following the movement of the sun. At the top of the tower a circular observation deck, from which you could see all the ends of the world, including Transylvania—and here it suddenly became clear this world is composed mostly of mountains. It also became clear there was nothing more captivating in this world than watching the shadows cast by clouds move across half-snow-capped peaks. For in the afternoon clouds appeared.

And looking at them through the dark lenses of his Armani sunglasses, Yarchyk Volshebnik the director, was thinking through how he was going to do it all: "I will sit him in this . . . in one of the armchairs . . . they have some really cool ones . . . just like . . . eh . . . a throne, you know. With a very expensive-looking background—various fancy wall coverings, tapestries and the like . . . One of them on her knees in front of him . . . or maybe doggie-style? . . . well, that's still on her knees . . . we'll see. The other behind . . . back of that, you know . . . throne. What can she be doing? . .

. Is she hugging him? . . . Perhaps not from the back? . . . But then the vertical won't work . . . A neat vertical: body one—then he—then body two . . ."

Truth be told, Yarchyk Volshebnik was not the only one *deep in thought* at that moment. Observing mountains and clouds encouraged introspection. After exchanging initial excited exclamations regarding the view, everyone grew quiet, perhaps dreaming of rediscovering the nirvana that had been lost at the terrace.

The new apparition of Artur Pepa tossed them from the clouds onto the ground, or at least onto the tower.

"Aha!" cried Pepa. "I'm here again, oh pittance for the jackals!"

On his head was an improbable crazy beret, but the point was not the beret: in each hand he was holding a sword, and these were real fighting swords, a bit blunt and chipped, but each at least a meter long (in reality, one meter seven centimeters—at least that's the impression everyone had), and these swords were already dangerous in and of themselves, but it was even more dangerous that Pepa spoke in iambic pentameter:

"So hold your sword, oh wanton son of Vienna! I know, you trounced me while playing chess; but now let's see how good you are with swords. While chess is but a royal . . . entertainment—can you defend your honor as a knight? So hold your sword!"

With these words he threw one of the swords—fortunately, with the blade aimed down—in the direction of Karl-Joseph, who had nothing left to do but to catch it, which he did, skillfully, by the handle.

"I see you accept the challenge!" rejoiced Pepa, waving his sword in the air.

"Artur!" Ms. Roma was reminded once again of her existence by the sound of a parched voice.

"The fair Ophelia!—Nymph, in thy orisons be all my sins remembered," said Artur to her. "And you, oh Austrian guest, defend yourself!"

He began attacking Karl-Joseph, right away pressing him to the metal railing, behind which there was nothing but an abyss. Only then did Zumbrunnen understand he wasn't joking.

"Can anyone stop this?" Ms. Roma grew, rapidly, extremely pale. "I beg you, please do something . . ."

Her pleas could only be addressed to Volshebnik—the only one present who could be classified as belonging to the category "men." Professor Doktor so far did not count, since all signs pointed to him in the opposite category—"women, children, and elderly"—to which also belonged Lilya+Marlena, fascinated by this new attraction ("is he, like, for real?"), and also Princess Kolomea I, torn out of her Tolkienesque stupefaction ("the sixth circle is the iron ring of dueling giants"), as well as Roma Voronych herself ("my God, they'll kill themselves!").

Volshebnik did not rush to jump with his bare

hands between the two rivals—the situation attracted him first and foremost visually, so he only stepped a little closer, adjusting the camera ("nice pic!").

Having accepted the challenge, Zumbrunnen with two or three hits—sparks flew from the swords—repelled the attack of his adversary. Back in the day, he was a big fan of fencing and even took classes in this noble sport at the Teutonia academic fraternity, but had to quit due to his worsening eyesight. As far as technique was concerned, his body retained quite a bit in its cellular memory. Having handled in a flash Pepa's clumsy attack (the beret, a bit too large for Artur, kept sliding over his eye), he switched to an advance and, so that this would end as soon as possible, confidently hit the adversary's handle from below. Artur's sword flew out of the palm of his hand and, drawing a deadly arc above the heads of those present, clanked on the concrete floor behind their backs. But Karl-Joseph slightly miscalculated the strength of his blow: by inertia continuing its upward motion; his blade stumbled at his adversary's recklessly placed head, scratching the forehead and immediately producing a bleeding line, something like another furrow for life's experiences.

"'Tis now my end—the Austrian has won!" cried Pepa and theatrically fell down.

Karl-Joseph carefully put his sword aside and was the first to lean over the bleeding Pepa. Roma the second, saying over and over "fool, fool, what an absurd fool, and what if it had hit the eye" and tried to stop the bleeding—first with the unfortunate beret, then with her own shawl, and finally (when Kolya, just as pale as her mother, arrived with a first aid kit) with cotton wool.

"All the details of this picture," assured Professor Doktor judiciously, "create an extraordinary density of meaning and artistic realism."

"So I shan't die? My life will continue?" asked Artur Pepa, obediently letting his wife bandage his foolish dome.

"Shut up, you stupid idiot," replied Roma through clenched teeth and suddenly started laughing nonstop (or perhaps maniacally?).

Karl-Joseph, just in case, again moved back to the railing—this is how a boxer, after knocking down his adversary, must wait for the outcome or continuation in his—for example, blue—corner. From there he followed Roma guiltily—her efforts at first aid, her shawl stained with red, and her laughter (all the others were also laughing). He felt terribly uncomfortable, and he finally uttered, "I beg your pardon."

"It's nothing," said Roma hurriedly and again burst into laughter.

"What do you mean, nothing?" replied Pepa, somewhat offended, standing up. "Something *did* happen. What needed to happen, happened. Let four captains bear Pepa like a soldier to the stage," he doggedly demanded, in iambics.

But no captain approached him, so he left without honor guard, whistling the tune "I wish I lived in the Carpathians."

"Really, let's get out of here," offered Ms. Roma. "It's getting colder."

"*And beeches madly rush at one another like Stone-Age bulls /the moment sun, that crimson rag, inflames their blood*," quoted the professor quite àpropos while moving to the exit.

"Are you *also* going to shoot us?" asked Lilya in an intimate tone while everyone was descending the tight spiral staircase, so close to one another, when Karl-Joseph, the dispirited winner of the audience award found himself between her and Marlena.

"Pics of us? Will you?" clarified Marlena, as if in competition with her girlfriend.

"He won't," promised Ms. Roma between women, firmly.

No, it couldn't end well—later that evening (or perhaps the next one), when the company gathered for tea in the small dining room, Artur Pepa came up with a new bet.

"Translate to him," he ordered Roma, "that I can drink a bottle of *horilka*.[14] By myself!"

"No I won't," she riposted. "He already knows that himself."

"Translate that I want to bet him a bottle of *horilka* that I can drink a bottle of *horilka* by myself," repeat-

14 Horilka—Ukrainian vodka. Here used in the generic sense of hard liquor.

ed Pepa. "In one sitting!"

"Come down and stop it," Roma refused to yield.

"All right, I'll do it myself," the bandaged fighter replied, waving his hand. "Charlie, do you hear me? I. Drink. Bottle. *Flasche.* Vodka."

"*Warum denn?*" asked Karl-Joseph.

He was feeling increasingly lonely. The longer he stayed here, the less he understood what was happening. And it wasn't only the matter of words in a language he understood poorly. This was also the matter of her, the woman to whom over the last year he thrice proposed to abandon everything and come join him in Vienna. "You can teach Russian and German in Saturday school," he thrice tried to convince her. "We have lots of Russians now, they buy property in the First District and pay big money for lessons. I will publish my large book of photos. I will make enough money for both of us. Why can't we always be together? Why can't we tell him all as it really is?" Roma thrice asked him to wait and said something he didn't understand. Although she said it in German. Now, when everything was to be decided, Karl-Joseph was falling into some sort of dead-end burrow insulated on all sides with 100% sun-blocking felt, a burrow of incomprehension and incertitude. It was as if he was suddenly covered with something heavy and suffocating, and in this terrifyingly narrowed sack-like trap he only heard the annoying outside nagging of her husband.

"See? *Das ist eine Flasche.* I say: I will drink it. *Trinken*, see? You say: *nein.* I say I'll drink it. You again: *nein.* A bet!"

"*Wie so?*" asked Karl-Joseph.

"Zo-zo," said Pepa. "Or not zo. Not like that. Come look!"

He put in front of him two water glasses and filled them to the brim with the dark walnut schnapps. This was the last bottle brought from home, and Pepa went for broke. Roma clutched her head in her hands.

Kolya was the first to leave the dining room. Behind her, shrugging his shoulders and smiling sadly, trudged Professor Doktor.

"Don't know about you, but for me it's time," he said.

But as he was leaving, he couldn't help giving yet another quote:

"*The two of us today make one too many. And both of us are stubborn.*"

"Tomorrow you will be agonizing, with your heart condition," warned Roma.

"Agonizing?" Pepa rolled his eyes. "That's an imperfective form. Charlie!"

He gave his hand to Zumbrunnen. Not understanding anything, the other gave his own hand in response. Pepa clasped it tightly, and they froze—holding each other's hands, their eyes meeting."

"Break it up," said Pepa to Volshebnik.

"No need," Roma stopped the hairy shadow that

hung over the table and did it herself.

"Thank you, chickadee," Pepa winked at her and rose up. "Charlie! And all of you! Watch!"

Then he did the thing for which he had trained for half his life and which he practiced with and without an appropriate occasion. The glass, placed on the arm bent at the elbow, was picked up with his teeth, the head (this time bandaged) violently jerked back—and the dark brown liquid freely flowed in. The only thing working was his Adam's apple, that masculine decoration. But this was far from the end: having emptied the glass, Pepa no less violently (this time the lower jaw working) threw it up into the air and flawlessly caught it on his left arm bent at the elbow.

"Wow!" Lilya and Marlena broke into applause.

Roma again held her head in her hands. In minutes like this she did feel a little proud of her husband, but did not show it.

"Now it will blow up," she said.

However, Artur Pepa did not believe so. Breathing deeply several times, he observed conscientiously how the walnut-flavored warmth spread inside him, then he demanded, "count aloud, gals!"—and then quite lithely did a somersault and stood on his hands. And only after both *gals* stumbled in their count, well over seventy, Artur Pepa returned himself to a proper pose, standing on his feet. This was his triumph: Lilya and Marlena shouted bravo and squealed, Yarchyk Volshebnik drummed on the table with the palms of his hands, and Ms. Roma finally stopped grabbing her head in her hands—she only watched him silently, that's all.

And Karl-Joseph only now realized he was supposed to repeat it all, exactly as the other did it, otherwise he would be defeated. Only now did he realize this was a challenge he could not leave unanswered. Imprisoned in his felt-padded cell, he suddenly got restless, bobbed back and forth—and then took the second filled glass in his hand.

"*Aber du sollst das nicht, Karl!*" the woman for whose sake all of this was happening tried to stop him. "*Sei kluger, du bist doch kein Idiot, Karl!*"

But he didn't listen and took off his glasses, and then, having shrunk to the size of his awkward smile, at some thirty-third attempt managed to balance the glass on his arm. "Have I not drunk from glasses like this before?" he assured himself and reached the burning and slimy edge with his teeth. Already with the second gulp, when the word "Zumbrunnen" came to mean "tongue, palate, throat," he was pierced with revelation: "this will be the night when I die in Ukraine from liquor." Thus not willing to die before the right time, his body rebelled, blocked the suicidal pour, pushed the remnants of the pungent stuff out, and as that happened, his eyes got watery, and his jaws weak and opened—the glass, only a third of which had been consumed, slipped out into the felt-padded space and then—a miracle!—smashed into bits on the floor. Suddenly it smelled of alcohol and walnuts, only one of the girlfriends uttered a silly giggle, and then came silence, and in this silence Karl-Joseph thought that doing a handstand no longer made any sense.

He now felt even lonelier. Somewhere, outside the sack into which he had been plunged head first, wandered, stumbling, their guttural voices reciting an ode to *horilka*—all except one, for her voice wasn't there: she was silent. And Karl-Joseph didn't have the strength to look at her.

"Fuck!" said Karl-Joseph and rose up from the table. "I'm going. I'm buying. *Noch eine Flasche.* Votka for you!"

And he stuck his finger in front of him—where Artur Pepa should have been sitting, but only some large blur of a dirty walnut color moved about.

"Cool move!" answered the blur in Artur's voice, although Karl-Joseph was not sure how to understand it. That is, he understood these words, yet they did not come together in a reasonable whole—which happened a lot in this country.

Nevertheless, he still made it to the enclosed porch, where he looked for the light switch for an *unbearably long time*, and not having found it, in the ever-thickening darkness, still *more unbearably* and for still *longer time*, he looked for his jacket and Salamander boots. For some reason all of them also followed him to the porch—and Roma was there among them, and while Karl-Joseph *unbearably slowly* laced up his boots, they discussed something *unbearably fast*, this was a terrible argument, terrible because he truly could not understand anything from it ("in such condition? alone? and who of the two of us lost? then I come with him!")—nothing except for the endlessly repeated phrase "13th kilometer," but he already knew without them that there was such a place in this world—the 13th kilometer—now it was inscribed on Zumbrunnen's secret maps, because only there, at the 13th kilometer, there is always walnut *horilka* for sale, as well as any other kind of liquor.

Thus he miraculously managed to deal with the zipper on his jacket, and with all three locks on the door, let himself out to the path he had already walked once. One hour remained until total darkness, enough time to descend through the alpine meadow and cross the forest.

"As you like!" exclaimed Roma Voronych, grabbing the first jacket she found on the coat hanger and jumping out after him. Let it be like this, she thought, like this, and she ran down the same slope after him, and *it* echoed inside her like an incantation: *likethis, likethis, likethis* . . .

"I don't get it," the finally drunk Artur Pepa was offended. "Out of vodka, wife gone, what are we going to do?"

And he decided to take a nap, until *those two* bring back the bottle he won.

8

Immediately after he closed his eyes, Artur Pepa woke up again. What was it—an internal flare, a scream from otherworldly depths, a signal of the start of a tachycardia attack? Did it come from outside—behind the doors, from the hallway, the tactile nocturnal space? For it was night, and Artur Pepa sat fully dressed on the bed in complete darkness. The other half of the bed remained empty and even made up. So, it wasn't that late in the night—otherwise *those two* should be back somehow, concluded Pepa in a surprisingly sober fashion. Although—*you can't hide from the truth*—it was much more important now to find out something about those rustles and moans behind the door, if they existed at all. Research their nature, as Pepa proposed, in a more precise formulation. Yes, research their nature. And although the huge key that became drenched in sweat in his palm screeched with all its force in the lock, trying to wake up if not the whole world, then at least the entire resort, Pepa finally opened a massive door made of yew timber (how did he know that it was yew, is not clear), pressed with his shoulder and silently, like a ghost, fell out into the hallway.

There too it was dark—someone thriftily made sure to turn off all the lamps. However, the moonlight was quite plentiful. "That's right, full moon," remembered Artur Pepa and at the far end of the hallway, and noticed a pointy Gothic-style window from which the pale flour-like substance poured in. Towards that flow Yarchyk Volshebnik the director moved with a Betacam camera on his shoulder. He walked measured, deliberate steps, as if through snow, raising his feet high and putting them down heavily. During this, the camera worked nonstop—Artur Pepa could see from the signal of its red eye, which jumped around the hallway like the laser sight of a rifle, pulling various objects for an instant out of the moonlit fog—various vases, side tables, and for some reason fire extinguishers which weren't here earlier. It even seemed to Artur he heard the monotonous rustle of tape in the cassette, although between him and Volshebnik there remained a good hundred paces. Sometimes it seemed the red light was coming not from the camera but from the long hair at the back of Volshebnik's neck. "Aha, symmetry," concluded Pepa, moving along the hallway in soft jumps from one wall to the other, periodically waiting it out behind various wax figures who chased after him. He was a bit surprised by his perfect agility, but noticing white ballet slippers on his feet, he understood everything perfectly well.

At the end of the hallway on the left-hand side was the staircase—and that's where the director turned. Covering the entire distance in three weightless jumps, Pepa managed to notice down below the same red flash, hence Volshebnik went down the stairs. Moreover, the arrow on the wall above the staircase pointed in the same direction, and the letters above—this time an electronic ticker—informed him of a POPULAR FESTIVAL. Artur Pepa dashed after the director. At the fifth or sixth flight of stairs he saw his large tense back, just a couple of steps ahead of him, and wanted to slow down, just in case, but a powerful gust of wind pushed him onward, so, almost stepping on Volshebnik's feet, he crashed into a loud and diverse crowd of people from whom he had no possibility of hiding. The room turned out to be something like a large party tent, the kind used at weddings, capable of holding about two hundred people (and that was indeed the approximate size of the crowd). There were long rows of tables and benches, and also an elevated dance floor. The gathering apparently had been going on for quite a few hours, noise and hullabaloo overwhelming, clouds of tobacco smoke and alcoholic-gastronomic effluvia transforming the air into a dense and sticky mass, thus even Pepa, not terribly inclined to moral imperatives, thought it wasn't nice to party so heavily during Holy Week. The worst thing was that he completely lost the director, he and his camera vanished somewhere, usually this sort of guy is fond of partaking of free stuff at various folkloric-themed parties, shooting something *for future generations*. But now it was no longer a matter of looking for Volshebnik.

For Pepa found himself in the center of a rapid and dizzying round dance: these were bony old women with incredibly long smoking pipes between their teeth (rather, in their mouths, because over the past hundred years their teeth had totally disappeared), stomping heavily, arms around each other, they danced their special *women's arkan*. And each of them—there were probably twelve of them—in her own fashion boldly winked and grimaced at the lost man they had suddenly captured. Since all of them continued their nonstop swirling and singing, Artur Pepa couldn't turn to any one of them to ask for an explanation. First of all, he was curious why these womenfolk were dancing what is traditionally a male-only dance. Second, why the hell were they circling around him—don't they have plenty of toothless lovers of their own? Third, when was it all going to end? For Artur Pepa once heard at a *retreat for young writers* that there existed a magical arkan, which they danced for seven, eight, even twelve hours nonstop—only the strongest survive, those who in their veins have fire instead of blood or simply have *the hardest veins*. Here, however, it wasn't a question of veins—he was also having to stomp his feet, shake his shoulders, grin foolishly and pretend he really enjoyed the whole thing, a *dancer skillful like no one else*. Besides, the wooden floor had already been polished by countless efforts of previous dancers that Artur's feet, now in shiny leather *kapchurs*,[15] slid out treacherously in all directions. It was hard to fathom how he managed not to fall on his ass in the middle of all this crazy ruin.

He managed only because every now and then one of the grannies jumped out of the circle and grabbed him by the shoulders—then with one hand clasping his own to jump in tandem for a while, each time Artur Pepa surprised by lightness and agility, how good it was to dance with them, even though wrinkles devoured their faces, up close it was especially clear. Their skin resembled fragments of old darkened maps sown together, and these maps were three-dimensional. "Oh my sweet Artur," whispered one of them in his ear, "such a pity, my dear lad, you took a widow for a wife. Many a girl would gladly marry such a fine dancer, and you closed yourself off from the big wide world, you poor thing." Before Artur had the time to think how to respond to this, another of them continued, "Did you drown your head in a well, or did you sell it at the market? How did this widow manage to seduce you? Your reason must be asleep somewhere, and you studied for twenty years to get so wise!" And then the third one, "Grab a good whip, my dear Artur, and chase this viper out of your home, and if she doesn't leave, abandon her with all her possessions, her domestics, her land, and run away to the end of

---

15 Traditional Hutsul sock-like footwear, usually worn with sandal-like overshoes.

the world, to a Czech construction site or to the war in Chechnya!" And then yet another one, "I will tell you nothing, dear Artur, my sweet lad, but you'll stay with us tonight, boy, and make sweet love, kiss until the morning, and then wash and swim around with us, your buxom lovers, at the bathhouse!" And she unceremoniously grabbed his crotch, in which there was nothing except coldness. "How old are you?" asked Artur for some reason, as if it made a difference, although most likely simply to buy some time. He must have heard her answer wrong, for she couldn't possibly truly be *thirty-seven.*

Yes, *you can't hide from the truth*—the magic dance had long become brazenly indecent, *arkan* motifs fused with *kolomyika* tunes, and those in turn, with some measured yet passionate Carpathian ska. Anticipating something *really crappy*, Artur imagined a small-town public bath with crumbling tiles covered with yellowish stains, woodlice and spiders on the walls, rusted faucets with uneven valves, bathtub drains clogged with hair and cotton wool (consider the very mixture of smells—insecticide, industrial soap, and tar soap!)—then the boisterous pack of witches with sagging breasts and buttocks and army-issue loofah between their legs, elbowing each other to get at him first. That's why at the last moment he thought of spinning counterclockwise, breaking the embrace of yet another partner, aiming to disappear quietly somewhere to the side, but at that moment he got his punishment: the slippery, as if sperm-covered soles of his shoes slid out to a critical extent—and Pepa did finally fall on his ass, seeing above himself his raised legs. Oh well, he thought, now they'll rape me.

But instead of a circle of victoriously grinning baked-apple-like mugs that ought to appear above him, bending menacingly, puffing smoke from their pipes and gleefully smacking their blue lips, he saw the tent roof open and reveal clear sky, and most importantly he saw he was lying beneath a tree, and even if he didn't hear a goggle-eyed cymbals player, hoarse from many weddings ("a girl climbed a cherry tree to pick some fruit"), he would still recognize this was a cherry tree—so much red in the midst of green can only be on a cherry tree and only in June. The cherry tree reached the sky, expanded to fill all space above Pepa, its sensuous branches spreading into the surrounding infinity, thus even in this form it manifested one of the few images of perfection in Pepa's absurd life. However, this turned out to be insufficient for the authors of the latest music video. Putting into reality the image sung by the goggle-eyed cymbals player, they placed on the cherry tree a lithe and long-legged girl ("and I help her from below and begin to spy at her," continued the cymbals guy with what remained of his vocal chords). The girl froze at a fork in the branches, her legs wide apart, or moved from one branch to another, smeared all over with cherry juice, and the miracle that Pepa could see from below ("I looked here, and I looked there—and the world started spinning") brought him to the verge of dying from ecstasy ("good people, this cherry tree became God's very Heaven," his brother-musician found the right words just in time). No, Pepa couldn't see her face, but it was enough for him to see those long legs and a cheerful smile where they came together. "Who are you?" asked Pepa of the sky, for he couldn't ask anything smarter. "I'm picking cherries here," answered the girl in the voice of his stepdaughter Kolomea, throwing down a handful of juicy cherries. Unable to move, Pepa tried to catch them with his mouth, but nothing came of it. The cherries fell on his face, there were more and more of them, a soft cherry rain, under which Pepa would gladly stay forever, if . . .

"You snore really loud," said Ms. Roma, touching him by the shoulder. "You always snore when you fall asleep on your back."

She was already in her bulletproof flannel pajamas, ready to lie next to him, at the half of the bed untouched by Pepa.

"Aha, so you're back!" her husband surmised the present circumstance of place and time. "Do you have the bottle?"

"No bottle, sleep," said Roma curtly, for the last thing she wanted to tell *this* fool was how *that* fool began yelling at her in the middle of the forest and how she went back, offended, let him wander around poor villages until the morning if he wants, tough chance anyone would sell him any liquor.

But the First Fool took this news surprisingly peacefully: rejoicing at the opportunity, he rushed to the tree about which only he and we knew, hurriedly turning all the pages between wakefulness and sleep (hallway, stairwell, what next?), although he failed to find the needed page among all of them.

Instead, he found himself at the back of some ethnographic tour group consisting of several dozen people, mostly unfamiliar to Pepa. They filled the entire antechamber, breaking into groups in front of display cases with various old photos, flintlock pistols, hats, studying old looms, spinning wheels, and models of blast furnaces. Pepa now long wanted to ask any one of them, "And where's the cherry here, the tree, you know?" but somehow he couldn't muster the courage: something unclear kept stopping him. Was it the bad acoustics of this room, where sounds froze in a void and lost their expressiveness; was it again the dispersed lunar light, plentiful here as well ("for we're on the Moon!" guessed Pepa). Not abandoning hope for any possible opportunity, Pepa was forced to move with the others, learning in the meantime some previously little-known details about rafting in the Carpathians, the peculiarities of local sheep herding, pottery making, janissary production, the Daco-Thracian roots of most local toponyms ("Dzyn-n-n-dzul," he pronounced one of them, savoring how it sounded), about the methods of persecuting witches and sorcerers by Polish Jesuit clerics and Soviet Bolshevik security forces, the demographic, interconfessional, and hygienic problems tied to this. Finally, Pepa learned that beechnuts exercise a peculiar influence on human and animal organisms close to narcotic intoxication. It was overall fairly interesting.

However, one noticed a certain chaotic manner and confusion in the presentation of the material. For example, the display case captioned "The Dynamics of Oil Extraction in the Chortopil Area, 1939–1985" presented a Paleolithic settlement of primordial humans. The caption "Forced Collectivization of Local Agriculture in the Late 1940s—Early 1950s" brought out a few machine guns, an anti-personnel mine, a red uniform ridden with bullet holes. As for the one announcing "The Best People of Our Area," it presented for some reason photos of various breeds of sheep, especially Merinos. In response to this, Pepa shrugged his shoulders and moved on amidst the dispersed flickering and noise—in equal measure undecipherable and irrepressible.

This lasted for several hours, and Pepa even began to get used to the surrounding strange atmosphere, especially since he managed to recognize a few familiar faces among those present. These were persons whose funerals he had attended recently: first of all that journalist, nosy and persistent, whom they threw off the train in the middle of the night. There was also his upstairs neighbor whom they found with two bullets in the back of his neck inside his private taxicab. There was also one editorial office secretary whom they suffocated with chains in an elevator. *You can't hide from the truth* (for some reason tonight Artur was really fond of this phrase)—*you can't hide from the truth*, there were also other persons from among his family and acquaintances who had died, as they say, a *natural* death—lately Pepa had to help carry funeral wreaths, crosses, and coffin lids. Separately from them stood a freckled and buzz-cut dead guy from twenty years ago—a buddy of his from army service who without any warning or explanation one afternoon aimed a round from a Kalashnikov into his own face, after having started only his third round of guard duty.

Artur Pepa on the whole was glad to see these people. It turned out things weren't that bad for them, and they didn't really disappear anywhere. Although somewhere at the bottom of Artur's soul there remained a small spot of anxiety: he was disturbed by the thought that, sooner or later, he'd have to bury them one more time, that is, experience once again all the blues and depression.

Curiously, a significant portion of those present (and this word seemed to be the most apt to refer to them—*present*) engaged in various useful activities: the antechamber was filled with the hum of spindles and spinning wheels, here too spun pottery wheels, millstones, centrifuges of lumber-cutting machines unknown to Artur. Some of the people focused their effort on carving various heavenly ornaments, others made little horses out of wood or sheep's milk cheese. "A workmen's cooperative, an *artel*," recalled Artur from the days of grammar-school textbooks, where this word sat gathering sawdust in anticipation of its time, somewhere close to *arteriosclerosis* and *artillery*.

In the meantime, Pepa's attention was drawn to a guy with an unremarkable appearance except for his thinness and bushy blond mustache, dressed in a suit that appeared to be made at the Kolomyia factory some time back in the 1970s. Yes, it was drawn—but not because of the medal of outstanding educator and the rhomboid university graduate's pin on his seventies-style jacket, rather by his constantly popping up somewhere close, within Artur's sight. And in the end not even by this, but by his constant coughing and spitting into a large handkerchief, wrinkled and far from fresh, which he pulled out his pant pocket and then, nervously crumpling it, pushed it back in. Finally, the most important thing was the mustachioed guy who several times cast angry glances at Pepa (he saw everything from the corner of his eye) and in a kind of nasal cold-stricken voice called, "You!" For Pepa this call was an opportunity to confirm the validity of his earlier supposition that this guy was some sort of manager here.

"You, you!" repeated the manager impolitely, beckoning Artur with his finger. The latter thought about getting offended but understood just in time this was the wrong place for that. He raised his eyebrows in surprise and, pointing a finger at his chest, asked back like an F student who received a fatal summons to the blackboard: "Who, me?" "Come with me," the blond-mustached guy did not leave him either time or opportunity to hesitate. Without turning back, he swam through the antechamber (why *antechamber*, what sort of word was this if this was a *hall*, a large hall, indeed equal in size to the biggest waiting rooms of this world!), there remained nothing for Pepa but to follow. "But why me?" he wanted to shout at the manager's thin and stooped back, which floated ten steps ahead of him. Precisely here a new attraction appeared: they were passing by some very long tables, where a group of the *present* selflessly worked at painting *pysanky*,[16] from time to time dipping the eggs in vessels of dye, or into hot wax, then arduously working various implements and cleaning the ideal eggshell surface of everything extraneous. The scents of hot wax and homemade mineral dyes reminded Pepa Easter was close. The finished *pysanky* rolled along the table through a specially inclined chute, managing to dry along the way and then fall into a large container lined with cotton wool—each into its own personal cavity. Only one of them, with orange

16 Traditional Ukrainian Easter eggs.

crosses and stars on a black nocturnal background, did not make it into its cavity, as at the last moment it was quietly stolen by Pepa and put into the pocket of his trench coat. "Here's a holiday present for Roma," he noted with a feeling of satisfaction, certain no one had noticed anything.

Finally, they came to enormously tall doors at the end of the hall, and pointing at them with his hand while coughing dryly, the manager issued an order; "Out! Get out of here immediately!" "But why me?" Pepa remembered his question. "Because you don't dare," explained the manager. "How come everyone else does, and I don't?" Pepa refused to agree. "You live with my wife?" the manager was beginning to get really nervous. "Get out of here! Immediately!" He made special emphasis on the word "live," making it come out as a hiss.

Ah that's what it is, understood Pepa. That's who he looks like, Roma's former *life partner*! While he peered with triple attentiveness at this earth-colored irritated face with a droopy mustache, the manager hissed new accusations: "You sleep with my wife, you ruin girls, you get drunk on *horilka*!" Artur was silent, because he couldn't object. "Then go back to them and don't hang around here like a piece of shit in an ice-hole!" Mr. Voronych tried to raise his cold-afflicted voice, but broke into a coughing fit. "And put the *pysanka* back immediately!" he demanded after a minute, spitting into his handkerchief, embroidered by Roma back in the day. "Now I'm going to wake up," said Pepa, for he had had enough of this, "and nothing will happen to me, and you will simply disappear!"

Surprisingly, the threat proved to be effective: Voronych lost his composure, his piercing eyes darting back and forth and he began—literally—to retreat, moving into the giant space of the hall, where he hurried to blend in with others that were *present*. Quietly celebrating his small victory, Artur Pepa again immersed himself in the surrounding foggy lunar rustle and hum. As a consequence of this episode, his self-assuredness grew so much he was already planning to clarify from the people here where one could see . . . but what was it that he wanted to see? Artur Pepa no longer remembered, as the waves of nocturnal wanderings took him far from that *sweetest* cherry tree. Thus he strained, trying to remember and—*you can't hide from the truth*—getting more and more confused in his thoughts.

But then he saw (again, with his peripheral vision, which sometimes makes us fail to recognize ourselves, surprised, in mirrors) another door, unnoticed earlier, open at the opposite end of the hall—this door was truly narrow and small, some sort of *service* or *emergency* exit, as Pepa would joke under different circumstances. And through this *peripheral* door, with his *peripheral, side* vision, Pepa saw Karl-Joseph Zumbrunnen make his way in *sideways*—with the confused expression of a non-local unmistakably his.

He wasn't wearing his glasses and was squinting eyes, looking hesitantly at the hall and those *present*. Although such a *peripheral* arrival should have passed unnoticed, at that very moment Mr. Voronych the manager reminded everyone about himself, uttering a nasal shout that filled the entire room: "Ready! Let's begin!" Well, this nasal shout perhaps did not concern itself with the arrival of the Austrian. Pepa tried to comfort himself with this meek proposition.

Music rang out from all directions—of the kind one can never reproduce when awake. Artur Pepa couldn't read sheet music and did not know musical terminology, but liked music a lot, especially the kind that came in one's dreams. He likewise regretted never having learned, back in the day, to play any musical instruments, so he sometimes considered the opportunity to realize this in the future. And so, enthralled by the incredibly rich, truly luxurious sound of the enormous invisible orchestra (Wagner pales in comparison!), he saw a theater curtain move in both directions (it apparently served as one of the walls of this hall), revealing behind it a boundless stage: an overgrown garden, a *biological poem in two variations*, on a gently sloping hill covered with vines and all shades of green, a neglected and smothered garden, an entire nightingale city with twelve rivers and a starry sky, and in this languidly serpentine environment, between the seventh and eighth water, rose a pedestal covered in moss and stunning sticky flowers, around which writhed two female figures (Artur Pepa immediately recognized both the blonde and the raven-haired).

He also recognized the director: carrying on his shoulder the same camera with the sleepless red eye, Yarchyk Volshebnik circled around them, stepped back and then again came face-to-face, crawled on his stomach and on his knees through thick grass, the brush, the sloping meadow—this allowed Artur to see their dance in minutest detail. The director wittily cut from one angle to another, pulling out of the immense whole the most unbearable fragments of grimaces and poses, then again putting it all together.

Although—*you can't hide from the truth*—on the other hand, it resembled a very expensive and richly decorated striptease session: the dancers indeed gradually shed their colorful clothing, feathery pieces of dress flew in all directions—belts, ribbons, sequins. Only now did Pepa figure out both were dressed as brides, in well put-together traditional bridal folk costumes, thus they had plenty of things to unravel, unlace, untie, loosen, and slowly toss around themselves (Artur tried concentrating on the names of individual pieces of clothing, but in his head only the words *plakhta*[17] and *skirt* kept popping up, while the word *bra* seemed totally out-of-place; the *green* immediately swallowing those details, as if behind each bush or

17 Item of traditional Ukrainian women's clothing: an overskirt consisting of two embroidered apron-like pieces.

tree waited an impatient fetishist animal; when even the final chemises were cast off, it turned out our kind had been duped—where an authentic live bride would have nothing but her *untouched treasure*, both actresses covered themselves with gilded triangles held together by silvery strings!

What was happening to the music? Yes, its intensity grew, moans joined with instruments. Dancers climbed snake-like atop the pedestal. Pepa simultaneously remembered two words: *serpentarium* and *serpentine*. Yarchyk Volshebnik the director in a wooly sweater kept popping up somewhere nearby, spraying ecstasy and sweat in all directions, they almost simultaneously reached the top where the lover, awakened from his sleep, waited on his bed. "The professor?" Artur Pepa didn't believe his eyes, but calmed himself, remembering this was a dream and everything was to be interpreted on a symbolic level.

The girls had summoned the old man from the darkness of suspended animation, jumped on him with increasingly daring caresses, one of them like Gina Wild, the *nocturnal dream of all males*, while the other Doris Fant, *the insatiable tigress of passion* (it was not for nothing Yarchyk Volshebnik trolled the porn interwebs for two months!), they tore the blanket off the old man and, choking their own moans, brought themselves and the music to a state of exaltation. They dipped their sensitive serpentine tongues into the old man's bluish crotch, finding the right zones and spots. Within minutes, the professor began transforming into the *enchanted prince of springtime*, who finally moved spasmodically and with an uncontrolled satyr-like smile on his face, unexpectedly energetically and greedily making love to them both—with lips, nose, hands, head, penis, everything he had—until, brought to the limit, he sprayed into all the forty-four directions of this big wide world, onto the bed, the flowers, the moss, the branches, on their faces contorted with pleasure, and—you can't hide from the truth—onto the camera a powerful black stream of relief, after which he growled, like a possessed antediluvian reptile for all the surrounding mountains to hear.

Then silence fell on the surroundings, and the curtain pulled together again. Artur managed to hear the director's triumphant shout, "Cut! *Vartsabych's Balsam* completed, thank you so much everyone." It came at the right time, for a split second later he wouldn't be able to hear anything over the storm of applause. It was so powerful that a strong piercing wind rose up in the hall. It punched Artur in the stomach and chest, threw clouds of sand, thorns, and repulsive locusts at his face, so he closed his eyes tight and flew down into thick darkness, trying hard not to lose any hairs off of his bandaged head.

And when he opened his eyes again, it was daylight, and he was lying fully dressed under a blanket.

As usual, Roma was no longer on her side of the bed. He was even ready to rush about looking for her to tell her all he had seen—but a minute later he realized he didn't remember anything, so he'd have to make things up.

III.

Caruso of the Night

9

Yes, Roma was no longer there—neither next to him on the bed nor in the room: having finally lost herself before dawn in an unstable two-hour vigil between sleep and wakefulness, she finally moved to the side of wakefulness. Stepping into the hallway, she confirmed what she had already been sure of—Karl-Joseph Zumbrunnen still hadn't come back. As if this listening by his door then careful (but increasingly insistent) knocking could change anything! A quarter hour later she mustered the courage to turn the handle, and the door opened—of course, no key had locked it since yesterday and there was no Zumbrunnen.

The rest were all asleep; the resort was silent.

Then Roma Voronych went to the larger dining room where she could look out the window at the alpine meadows rising up to the building. While doing so she broke a cup and splattered the remnants of her coffee all over the windowsill. "It probably won't be warm today," she decided. Yesterday evening she had to make her way for an unbearably long time across juniper thickets, through a strange cold twilight that quickly transformed into nocturnal darkness (where, where was he going, this moron?); Zumbrunnen must have bolted downhill like crazy. She cast a worried glance at the ski jump but tossed aside the thought of a final flight. Only at the edge of the forest did she finally catch up with him and they went down the path together. "I'm coming with you," she said, catching her breath. "*Sounds cool*," he said in English. Each time when something was wrong he'd resort to these silly English phrases. For a while he was walking a few steps ahead of her. "Look, what a bright moon, you don't need a flashlight," she said. But it didn't work. "Why are you silent?" she said after walking some two hundred steps behind him. "You must finally choose someone," answered Zumbrunnen, resolutely extricating himself from some bog. He turned to face her, stopping next to one of the roadblocks. "What does it have to do with *this*?"—feigning incomprehension, looking carefully at her feet. She wanted to avoid getting splattered with mud up to her knees or higher. "You must choose between the two of us," he exhaled everything he had. "This cannot go on forever," he said in a minute, as she examined the surroundings carefully, getting ready to make her next step. "It seemed to me you felt good with me. Did you simply pretend you felt good with me?" Not having received an answer, he went on, "I thought this was something bigger. I still think so. You should tell him everything—and all of us will feel better as a result." "Did you decide everything for me?" she replied, feeling with horror her leg sink into a smelly springtime bog, "Thank you." "No, I didn't. You decided everything yourself. It seemed to me you had decided everything already, back the first time, at the hotel. And each time after that. I remember each of those times. I thought you also remembered. If it isn't the case, you are simply a . . ." "What, say it!" she demanded, sensing a menacing sound in the bog beneath her left foot. "You really want me to?" he asked, leaning with both hands on that rotten roadblock. "I want you to finish your phrase," she did not leave a means of escape. "You ask so much of me, and in the meantime you . . ." He stood in the moonlight, completely pale. "If this was only a trifle for you," his lips wouldn't make themselves into a cynical grin, "if this was only a temporary adventure with a *foreign client*, then you are but a whore, a prostitute, nothing more. Here, I'm finished!" Then she thanked him again, and said, "Give me your hand, for crying out loud! Can't you see that here it is . . ." So, he offered her his terribly cold hand and, painfully squeezing her wrist (she felt the chill despite the jacket and the sweater), pulled her out of the bog, but didn't let her go, pulling her instead aggressively towards himself. His other hand slid down her back to the beginning of the curve of her buttocks, greedily making its way in the narrow space between panties and tights. He began clumsily feeling with his lips for hers, she resisted with all her strength ("Ah, so I'm a prostitute, really?"). He pressed against her with all his body, enclosing her arms in his, searching with his hands under her sweater and everywhere else. He apparently wanted to take her, right on that damn roadblock. He breathed at her with breath of stale vapors of walnut and alcohol, but when his fingers grabbed the zipper on her jeans, she managed ("No, you won't have the pleasure!") to free her hand and slap him on the cheek with all her strength, sending those glasses of his flying all the way to hell. Of course, she wouldn't be Roma Voronych if everything didn't end with them falling together over that *scheissener Schlagbaum.* He found himself below her, suddenly calmed, so she got up first. "You're a beast," she said, adjusting her messed-up clothes. "Take your glasses and don't you dare touch me again," she added as firmly as she could. He put his glasses on (the right lens now had a crack) and responded just as firmly: "Go away. I don't want you to accompany me." "Well, go then," she said in Ukrainian, "Go get lost! Drunken beast!" She barely held herself from bursting loudly into tears right there and set out directly across the wet dirt. Now foolish tears were going to flow, and the last thing she wanted was for him to see them. Karl-Joseph cast a glance at her, waved his arm, which looked like a scarecrow waving an empty sleeve, and continued in his direction, limping a little.

And now he wasn't there. Between ten and eleven o'clock others came to the dining room, but only three of them: Artur Pepa, Volshebnik, and Kolomea. The conversation stumbled, the clanking of cups and forks made the situation unbearable ("He must be having a good time, there at that thirteenth kilometer"—this, of course, was Artur, he always said something just to break the silence), the director silently built for himself ever-larger sandwiches, the black-turtleneck-clad types (it seemed today's were different from yesterday's) circulated between the dining room and the kitchen, Pepa already puffed on the fourth Prylutska of the day ("Do we have a new guest?" he asked, again to break the silence).

The professor apparently left before dawn ("So we're without Antonych now?" Pepa stared sadly at the deer antlers on the wall. "I . . . eh . . . saw him off a little while ago," said Yarchyk Volshebnik. "He asked to convey his greetings to everyone." "But why did he leave so abruptly," sighed Pepa, shaking off ash into a tray shaped like a Hutsul overshoe). A minute later he caught Roma's gaze, then looked again at the director ("And these cool girls of yours, are they skipping breakfast today?"), understood he couldn't distract Roma's attention this way, and sent two smoke rings. Volshebnik completed the construction of an edible pyramid with a lettuce leaf ("They too . . . you know . . . left. The filming over—good-bye. That's how the contract had it . . ."), then took his latest creation by the edge and sank his teeth eagerly into its multistory structure. Pepa didn't give a flying fuck about all this, but continuing this tense silence accompanied by bird cries from outside was unbearable ("So, you mean to say, they left together with the old guy?"—"Yeah, something like that," answered Yarchyk while continuing to chew on his sandwich). Artur imagined how in the company of the clumsy professor holding his hat with both hands, Lilya and Marlena, dressed in tight Turkish leather jackets jumped into the helicopter, then pulled in the feeble geezer by his hands—and at the last moment his hat, seized by the wind, flew off in the direction of Transylvanian darkness. It could have happened, thought Artur.

Kolya walked out on the terrace, stood next to an unknown curly-haired boy (he was saying something funny, for both of them laughed a bit), then came back into the dining room ("the seventh circle is when you feel easy and free with a stranger, as if the two of you knew each other for a hundred years"), and started picking apples from the fruit bowl ("so we have a new guest?" Pepa repeated his earlier question). Kolya selected the two largest and reddest ones ("Yeah, also from Lviv, came here for the weekend." "With friends?" "By himself, it seems."), wiped the droplets of water off them with a napkin and again went out on the terrace ("Is the shampoo in your room, ma? I'd like to wash my hair.") Ms. Roma followed her with her gaze ("Take anything you want, you'll see it on the side table in the bathroom.")—and then again her eyes directed themselves out the window, where there was nothing, except the same old boring *incomparably beautiful* landscape, nothing: partly cloudy, then a clearing, wind, a large shadow on the next mountain range, a more than half mile long inscription made of river stones: Carpathian initiative: do not shun what is ours ("And where did this come from? It wasn't there yesterday; how did they bring so many stones this high up?"). But yesterday is different than today, she thought. Yesterday things were one way, today entirely different.

Between one and two o'clock they began making hypotheses. First, he could have gotten lost in the forest. Even in daytime you can get lost in the midst of all those pine trees. The forest is a terrifying labyrinth, a large green monster, especially this primordial forest which had not been planted by human hand, it lets frivolous Viennese strangers in, used only to waltzing on palace parquet, but does not want to let them out. Here is no Vienna, not even the Vienna Woods, where all the paths are paved. This forest is a big green thing that swallows you up. But the moon was bright, I could even see a crack in his eyeglasses ("Oh really?" said Artur and scratched the bandage on his head), and first of all he is a very experienced traveler—he has hundreds of miles of hiking experience, even here in the Carpathians he has covered dozens of the most difficult routes, and he can start a fire with one match. After all, couldn't he just get out of this primordial forest, thick though it may be? There are so many signs: billboards, clearings, the old railroad tracks, piles of scrap metal, roadblocks. Et cetera, said Artur Pepa, burying forever his version of a Viennese daydreamer in a black top hat and perfumed gloves lost in a pine grove.

Wild animals, said Kolya, entering the dining room with a towel wrapped around her head. Yes, saber-toothed tigers and cave bears, agreed her *dad.* Not necessarily, contradicted Volshebnik, here one can meet wolves, and lynxes, and these . . . you know . . . wild boars. You're a boar yourself, Ms. Roma wanted to say, but only noted aloud that they were adults and it was necessary to make a decision rather than engage in idle chit-chat. Volshebnik continued his line: you did note in the forest every now and again deer antlers, jawbones, chewed off pieces of ribs and vertebrae! Someone—how should I say—must have slaughtered those deer! Or, for example, an avalanche. Have you ever seen an avalanche descend in the mountains? One should engage search and rescue dogs, giant ones, concluded Yarchyk decisively.

I think he is simply drinking *horilka* at the thirteenth kilometer, Pepa continued trying to calm everyone down. Or perhaps simply he was overcome by sleep and is now napping somewhere along the road, he's not the fussy kind. Would you like me to go and bring him back? I could use this opportunity to buy more booze: the day is being wasted, and a big holiday is upon us. But Ms. Roma did not care for his idea, especially when she imagined this fool going away and disappearing. The worst thing was that he could be right about Zumbrunnen. For a while she was overtaken by this version of a terrible case of alcoholic intoxication, gallons of industrial alcohol, paralysis, coma, or at the very least moonshine-induced syndrome. A local paper, *The Excess,* has been writing about this for several years now.

At 3:15 he still wasn't there, and at 4:27 a human figure appeared on the slope, walking up to the resort along the old military road. The figure moved exceedingly slow, stopping time and again, looking around in all directions, making strange loops in the midst of boulders and dwarf birches and thus leaving some hope for Roma. At four thirty-eight the figure came sufficiently close for Roma to see this was the new guest at the resort returning from a walk, carrying a bouquet of white and blue crocuses (guess for whom?).

At half past five Yarchyk Volshebnik brought the news that he had visited Zumbrunnen's room where all his personal belongings, including the Nikon F5 camera and several rolls of already used film, remained in place. This means he intended to come back here, noted Artur Pepa the private detective. Kolya filled a vase with water and took it to her room, thinking that the eighth circle was the one that gripped your heart.

Then Volshebnik offered to look for a clairvoyant. A year ago we filmed one not far from here, for *Tachycardia*, said the director. *Tachycardia* is the title of a show about various . . . what's the word . . . paranormal phenomena. I know, nodded Pepa, although I don't watch it. I don't watch Channel One at all, he added while he was at it. So, Volshebnik went on without taking offence, this clairvoyant, she is . . . like . . . telepathic or something, she sees, for five bucks . . . let's say . . . she can find you a sheep that got lost, separated from the herd. This clairvoyant only says some incantation and immediately tells you where that sheep is, all of them rush there, and indeed there's the sheep. Well, Zumbrunnen is no sheep, Artur Pepa stopped the police commissar. That's true, Volshebnik went on without taking offence a second time, it won't work for five bucks, it will take at least fifty. Stop it, said Ms. Roma, her hands on her temples.

At 6:12 Artur Pepa observed he had only two cigarettes left and thus in any case one had to go to the 13th Kilometer.

There is also another version here, responded Yarchyk Volshebnik at 6:13. When you exit the forest, slightly above it, by the road, before the bridge, some half a mile away, you have a Gypsy . . . you know . . . Two or three huts, a portable stove and a trash dump. Maybe also some sort of outhouse. There are various rumors going around about them, that this is a really a Gypsy king with his family, you know, servants, a harem, lots of children. Their specialty is assassination on order, especially of priests, no not on the order of priests, but assassination of priests on order. As well as pillaging. So, a king. The sense is that this is a king in this . . . what's the word . . . diaspora. In emigration, corrected Artur Pepa. Yes, in exile, Volshebnik found the right word. His entire court, the palace, the gold, the precious stones, all of it is abroad, in Pennsylvania. In Transylvania, corrected Artur Pepa. And even if it's in Transvaal, it doesn't matter, continued Yarchyk Volshebnik. Apparently according to their religion they cannot return to their treasures until they make a human sacrifice. Blood, you know, the heart, other organs. Obviously, the victim must be a stranger, that is, one of us. I mean . . . white . . . not a Gypsy. And so they are stuck here, between forest and River. The locals, shall we say, have long known about this and avoid this place at all costs. But if some outsider doesn't know they may lure him into their hut and . . .

I don't want to listen to this, said Ms. Roma stepping away from the window. The *wings* of her imagination carried her to the banks of the River, and she saw Karl-Joseph, who in a non-local manner, stepping over piles of empty tins, enters half-bent in a soot-covered black hut, little Gypsy kids all over him. Why are we sitting here and not going anywhere, she asked. And I said the same thing a while ago, reminded Pepa. Let's walk along the river for a while, take a good look, and then set out for the 13th Kilometer. We can split into two, you know, groups, suggested Yarchyk Volshebnik. One group taking the road through the forest and then to the bridge, the other through the forest, but further to the left, closer to those, you know,

Gypsies. If anything—we meet by the bridge.

I would give him another half hour, said Artur Pepa. He felt a forgotten pack of the Prylutska cigarettes inside the lining of his jacket, near an inner pocket with a hole in it.

Can I go with *dad*, asked Kolya, tying her hair, so pleasant to the touch, into a fighting ponytail. No, you are staying here, Roma cut her off, and wait in your room, and I will go with *dad*. In response to such a decision Kolya pouted a little, but not much. For in the ninth circle you remain alone with yourself and there's nothing you can do about it.

And you, Mr. Volshebnik, Roma continued organizational efforts. We must make it before dark. It is better to leave right away, not half an hour later. Are you going or are you staying, Mr. Volshebnik.

Just a second, answered the director, let me run to my room, grab some pepper spray etc. And you, you know, don't wait for me; we will take, you know, different paths all the same.

Thus they decided Roma and Artur would go down the forest road, Yarchyk Volshebnik—the *second group*, so to speak—would descend to the River further to the left, orient themselves by the old railroad track, the noise of water and hazelnut thickets.

Yes, Yarchyk Volshebnik kept telling himself; yes, yes. Nothing forgotten? No one forgotten, echoed, or rather barked back from his long-gone young pioneer childhood with circle jerks in outhouses stinking of chlorine. Nothing forgotten, Yarchyk Volshebnik agreed with his childhood.

What a great invention are these Malta cargo pants! How much you can carry in your pockets! Now one more time, complete check. Four pockets on the left pant leg: the first of them, the deep sided one, contained the original contract signed by both parties, folded into eighths and sealed in plastic. A thinner envelope, held all the necessary resolutions and the seal of the Carpathian Initiative Foundation, a thicker envelope, with the honorarium, and also, sandwich no. 1, a four-level one with mayo.

The second rear pocket contained that very videotape for which all effort had been expended. The filmed material promised to be the bomb. No less a bomb, but of a caloric kind, promised sandwich number two: smoked ham, olives, mustard, and butter.

On both sides of the knee were two symmetrical pockets. The first contained only sandwich no. 3, a symphony of cheese. The fourth, sandwich no. 4 (catch the taste of the Ocean!), as well as the unfinished *Make Yourself Worthy of Salvation*. On his way here, Yarchyk had reached page twenty-eight, but the brochure was fifty-two pages long, and he wanted to know what happened next and how it was all going to end.

On the right pant leg there were three more pockets. The first of them, the side one, just as big and just as deep as the left, contained not only the pepper spray that Volshebnik had mentioned (easy to reach with your right hand—grab and spray!), but also another can, insect repellent, and a half-liter of the local *Vartsabych Premium* light beer.

As for the right rear pocket, it contained one more videotape, with a copy of the filmed material. There was also sandwich no. 5, salami on crackers, just a light introduction to a sustainable diet.

There remained a hip pocket, the last one on the right pant leg, which was quite important for it contained sandwich no. 6, a large omnibus containing all ingredients listed in the previous sandwiches—the apotheosis of Volshebnik's art. A 0.7 liter can of local *Vartsabych Velvet* dark beer, a nine-inch realistic vibrator, rented for the shooting at *Amusement-2* company and two gilded pussy-coverings with silver strings, rented at the same company.

Yarchyk Volshebnik cast a thorough glance over the room in which he had spent a few days and nights. Opened all the possible furniture doors, pulled and shook out all the drawers, looked under the pillow and under rugs. Nothing forgotten? It seems, nothing. Tapes, sandwiches, there must have been something else, but the only word that kept popping into his head was *chains*. And there was no time left for reminiscing. *Outta here*, Yarchyk Volshebnik told himself, *time to get the fuck outta here.*

Yarchyk liked that he was so practical-minded.

He even packed the food he was owed for two more days. That's how it was in the contract: ". . . And also three *balanced meals* a day for the duration of the assignment." Running down the staircase, he thought with satisfaction that he had arranged everything so *smartly.* A clean job, he said, as soon as the front door at the porch clicked shut behind him. Far below, at the border between juniper thickets and the beginning of the forest, he saw that comical pair. Even from far away one could sense their feckless nervousness. Yarchyk Volshebnik laughed silently to himself and turned left.

Karl-Joseph Zumbrunnen lay in the waters of the River, a bit below the place where the stream flowed into it. The current dragged him for several hours. Two or three times it slammed him against the rocky outcrops. It spun him mercilessly in several whirlpools. It had rubbed him thoroughly with sand at several shallow spots. At one point at the rapids it scraped him pretty bad in the tightest of its narrows—but then pushed him onward again. Even though tree branches along its current tried a thousand times to grab him by the sweater or a flap of his jacket, the current did carry him out to the river. Only there did he run aground on a limestone ridge in the center of the riverbed, where his feet-forward swim was stopped: Zumbrunnen's legs stuck knee deep in underwater crevices, but the upper half of his body was thrown with *deadly* force across the ridge. And only his half-submerged head kept bobbing in the current, as if the river decided to wash out of it its glassiness and tentative attempt at a smile. For Karl-Joseph was lucky: his face was almost completely undamaged, and anyone could recognize him. But now he was indifferent to that.

The dead are weird. Our encounters with them happen far less often than with other people. We are used to the notion that a human body has its own special plasticity. It moves through space, gestures, defends itself from collisions, keeps to its own coordinates through consciousness. We are used to seeing it as an indivisible whole that speaks and laughs, appeals to others that are just like it, answers the gazes of others back, examines itself in mirrors. This mobile physical shell carries such weight for us it replaces all other meanings and means of understanding—yes, we are first and foremost corporeal, and any deviation from the norms of our corporeality knocks from under us all the foundations of our relationship to the rest of the world. A dead human body is the most extreme of such deviation. It cannot move or speak, is passive and indifferent to everything, it cannot be agitated. It is unnatural (so it seems to us), for it doesn't behave the way a human body is supposed to behave. It would be simplest to call it sleep, but then what about waking from it? All right, let's call it sleep, but an eternal one. Although now the metaphor called to normalize things turns to an even more horrifying side: there is nothing more inhuman or more terrifying than eternity. So it isn't right to compare death to sleep. Perhaps one can do it the other way round. Still, this horror grows a thousand times when we look at a dead body we recently knew as living, when just a trifling tiny moment ago it behaved like all normal bodies. How is it possible and why? Our surprise is boundless—can you imagine: a dead person! And the most surprising is that all of us, or better to say each one of us at some point, will do the same and *become* dead.

Karl-Joseph loved swimming and splashing in greenish mountain waters. And generally speaking, like all my heroes, he loved water. So, should I reserve a bit of hope for him and me? And write that he *felt* good? That his body did not sense pain, but sensed the current? That his hair flowed in the stream like river grass in Tarkovsky's films? That he felt like a fish in water?

At last he felt good.

Yarchyk Volshebnik looked at him from the riverbank and thought: "Quite beautiful." Such an amazing angle, just shoot away: the head thrown back and ceaselessly bobbing in the waters. The trunk picturesquely spread over rocks. An elbow bent in an interesting way; the other arm stretched sideways but with the wrist submerged in water (Yarchyk did not know that the bones were broken in three places, but this is not essential—we've agreed that *here* there's no pain), so Karl-Joseph was stroking with his hand a languid river-dog.

Unfortunately there was no camera. Yarchyk would have filmed a remarkable episode: a body in the water, interplay of two flowing subjectivities, death the embodiment of being, or rather a return home. Death as the finding of one's niche, sauna, one's nirvanna (Yarchyk Volshebnik was sure this word was spelled with two n's). With close-ups he would show the fragments of luxurious flow, for example, little islands of foam near the fingers. But the head was the best: propelled by invisible mechanisms of influence, it bobbed by force of the current, it kept nodding, agreeing with everything. Thus physics moved into metaphysics, metaphysics into dialectics.

But Yarchyk Volshebnik never stayed an aesthete for more than five minutes. On the sixth minute, still looking at the river, he again told himself, "Get the fuck outta here, right now!" It was first and foremost quite scary: standing on this riverbank, next to a corpse about to start decomposing and emitting poisonous gas bubbles. Moreover, twilight was already beginning and soon it would be dark. It wouldn't be wise to stay here alone. Should he call the alcoholic and his neurasthenic wife? This thought only made him squirm. Run somewhere, report to someone? Then these nasty conversations with the police—such a headache! No, the best thing—*get the fuck out-*

ta here! There was one additional factor: *vibes*. Vibes never let him down.

Thus this time, when a dozen Gypsy runts (whom he had summoned himself earlier this evening) in front of him jumped out of their black huts jumped, he did not turn and run: no matter how long you run, they will catch you and knock you dead, just like they did to the Austrian. The riverbank is long, and the river can't be crossed here. No, Yarchyk Volshebnik went at them, at their puppy yelps (*gimme, gimme some money, sir, gimme some candy, some cigarettes, gimme your palm, your soul, your body!*[18]) and pierced through their ranks (suffering a few losses on the way: sandwich no. 3 and sandwich no. 6, damn it!), they scattered in all directions, and then he ran, although Gypsies weren't really chasing him—but this is what we know, while his fear had such big eyes he only huffed and puffed (the bridge finally began to jump around in front of his eyes) and didn't look back. The little Gypsies whistled at him, but that was all, especially since the oldest and tallest among them suddenly saw what Yarchyk had the opportunity to see earlier: Zumbrunnen in the river.

Only after he ran across the bridge and stepped on the paved highway of the *mainland*, did Yarchyk Volshebnik allow himself to catch his breath.. But this did not mean that he stopped. The same internal re-

18 In English in the original.

frain that did not let go of him all this time continued pushing him forward, in the direction of Chortopil: *outta here, outta here—a kingdom for getting outta here* . . . Entirely captivated by his internal meditation, he walked fast on the side of the road, not willing to notice either the signs that promised the station to be six or even seven and a half kilometers away (and those, without a doubt, were special *Hutsul* kilometers!), nor the transformation of the unstable weather of the day he just lived through, now turning into a snowstorm. Around the twentieth minute of his march along the dead road it began: several flashes of light in the sky, then thunder resounded for the first, then the second, then the third time, and if Yarchyk Volshebnik had a more serious interest in folklore, he could have recalled stories of Elijah emerging for a ride in his chariot on the eve of this holiday. But he did not recall any such thing, only wrapped himself tighter in his jacket and walked faster. Another half hour later, soaked through and covered with snow, he realized he could not see where he needed to go: beyond the stretched out hand began nothingness. And even the still unused can of pepper spray was of no help here.

Right there and then suddenly appeared the first and most likely only car within that *network of local roads*. It jumped out of thunder and snow, or more precisely from behind Yarchyk's back, turning onto the shoulder, squeaking its breaks and almost running Yarchyk over. The car echoed with music, filled with bald-headed men (actually, four of them, but they were so drunk they seemed to be three times more numerous). Finding himself on the back seat, right between two who were the most bloated and hoarsest, Yarchyk Volshebnik for the first time did not feel sorry he resisted the temptation to take with him one of the cameras from the resort (*vibes, vibes* again, he praised himself in his thoughts). All the bald-headed guys, including the driver passed back and forth an open bottle and with their voices tried to break through the veil of cacophony generated by the stereo ("from the sea the wind was blowing, from the sea the wind was blowing, from the sea the wind was blowing") began asking him who he was and where he came from. The car started off and within a minute turned into a shaky amusement-park ride, thrown for an extra effect into the snowy chaos and ready to crash or flip into *devil knows where.* Especially since it takes the driver three times to pronounce the word *Parabellum.* Having heard Yarchyk's invented story about an idiot mushroom picker lost in the center of snowy madness (laughter and hooting ready to blow up to smithereens this drinking joint on four wheels), the *back ones* let him have a swig from the bottle, and from left and right breathing on him the vapors that gathered in their innards during the two or three days of nonstop drinking and smoking, promised to give him a ride anywhere, even straight to hell if he wanted. "Are you from Chortopil yourself?" they asked, to which

Volshebnik answered cleverly, "I know a few people there." So the car dashed on, while Russian-language gangster pop songs flowed from the stereo and this went on an endlessly long time: a limo in danger of exploding, surrounded by four impenetrable walls of snowy whiteness, heart-rending braking at turns, alcohol breath, sitting on one buttock between two slouching assholes and awkwardly formulated questions, snowdrifts, getting stuck, the motor's hysteria, feigned simpleton-style answers, bad jokes, giggles—up till everything calmed, the snowstorm first of all. Then Volshebnik started thinking frantically about the approaching time he'd have to pay for the ride and how he'd be forced to take the entire fat envelope with the honorarium out, so even with their drunken half-closed eyes they would see this fat envelope bursting with bucks. However, there is no better way to avoid trouble than to think of it ahead of time and try to prevent it in a timely manner: with the help of two old ethnic jokes, the larger of the cans of beer and, finally, the phone numbers of Lilya and Marlena (*hey, director, we badly need some good chicks: we're in the money, but there's no one to fuck*), he was fortunately released to be *free, fucking free, fucking free*—and at 10 p.m. he already stood in front of the main entrance to the Chortopil train station.

Two hours later, his still soaking wet back sticking to the mercilessly *hard* train seat, all alone in a sleeping car of the very slow and only train that passed through, he told himself, "Let's go." And getting off later that morning at a gray station platform, continued the thought and immediately completed it: "Lviv."

They managed to get the body out of the River (icy water splashing into their rubber boots) and lay it down on shore, face up, at the edge of the forest. It was easy to see from the opposite—forbidden—riverbank, and if someone were passing, they too would clearly see this large Danubian fish lying on the grass beneath some hawthorns. But that would be tomorrow, for now it was already getting dark.

It had to happen one day. They talked about it since time immemorial: one day the waters of the river will bring a large fish from the Danube. None of them understood how this could be possible, since the waters of the Danube cannot flow backward, nor can the waters of our river. Thus the essence of the prophecy remained unclear, and with the years they started believing less and less, casting more and more doubt on the details of how it had been passed down.

Now it happened: the fish from the Danube turned out to be a man, a foreigner who just a little earlier had strolled here along the riverbank, making heavy steps on the grass in his expensive and massive boots. And all they could do for him was take his fishy dead body, its lungs full of water, limbs broken in three places, head with a deadly injury, onto the riverbank. Let others find him and take care of him—tomorrow.

Perhaps that long-haired weirdo who fled along the riverbank and later disappeared onto the highway across the bridge would do? Perhaps just a few hours later he'll bring a whole pack of cops and there will begin the prophecy of which time has spoken?

For it said as soon as the waters of the river bring a large fish from the Danube, this place should be abandoned. This was a sign that everything had changed and time was entering a new dimension.

Luckily they experienced their last snowfall in these lands, and having gathered some essential belongings, set out across the forest that they had never entered before. Nevertheless they walked confidently: to know the forest you do not necessarily have to visit it. They walked uphill in a line of seven or eight persons, not including the children and the king. The snowstorm covered them with a white cloak, atmospheric discharges lit up fragments of their path, all the border stations of this world were covered in snowdrifts, the guards and their dogs took cover anywhere they could, ahead of them was the mountain ridge, wind, and a two-hour ascent towards the Transylvanian side, where a different future lay in wait.

10

What could two people who had lived together for twelve years be talking about when they entered the forest? Naturally, they were silent.

The forest swallowed them completely at this moment of twilight. Having crossed its boundary they became slower and more attentive. That's at least what each of them thought: go slow, be attentive. Broken off branches, a side path cutting through thickets, an arrow scratched on a tree trunk, a turned-over trailer abandoned in the middle of the road—anything could be a sign when more attentive, indicating a place where Karl-Joseph had possibly taken cover. But nothing gave a hint, nothing pointed to that!

Thus Roma and Artur silently *combed through* the springtime evening forest, every now and then one of them would stop and say to the other in a muffled voice, "Do you hear?"—at which point the other would also stop and say, "What?" But by then the first would already be walking, saying, "Nothing. I just thought I heard something." In general this might resemble a rather nonsensical game for immature teenagers, with its deeply hidden mystical meaning: *do you hear?—what?—nothing, I just thought I heard something* . . . And this repeated over and over again.

However, the forest, this primordial forest full of

hints and symbols, was only a pretext for their much lengthier silence. In reality behind it was exhaustion, disappointment, and the passage of time. Human life in general is a shamefully sad thing. Some would say it is too long, that in reality it is several lives within one chain, but with each successive link it is only one that looks more hopeless and useless. Why on earth did Roma and Artur need to stay together for twelve years? Why couldn't both of them die somewhere in the middle of the journey. Or call each other on the phone seven times a day to hear each other's *voice* (truth be told, to make love to each other seven times a day, for they desired each other so much)?

Now each of them was preoccupied with putting together a list of reproaches for the other. Interestingly their mutual reproaches, although never spoken aloud, formed a certain symmetrical structure. Only you and I are given the opportunity to appreciate the symmetry.

For instance, a significant portion of Roma's reproaches to Artur focused on his ever more obvious physical shortcomings, of which earlier she hadn't the foggiest idea, but they could not help popping up to the surface during so many years inhabiting a *common residence*. So, one year he started snoring, then fillings fell out of his teeth, his nostrils and ears sprouted thick hair, and his poor devil of a penis transformed into an entirely independent and capricious creature often acting against his will (or with equal success did *nothing*). This list could be expanded to other aspects of Artur's turning into a sad old billy goat, such as his habit of spending too much time on the toilet (and that rustling of the newspaper, or my dear Lord!) or, say, fall into bed without brushing his teeth after many hours of drinking, smoking, and dirty talk. Above all else Roma Voronych missed *that* boy (and the twenty-five-year-old Artur she once encountered at an exhibition of colored prints, for her precisely a boy—a page, a cabin boy, a young naturalist)—so, that boy gradually and fully disappeared, leaving in his stead a *dude*, inattentive and at times brutal. This was horrible.

From Artur's side things looked more or less the same, thus he was left to console himself with a cynical definition by way of old Immanuel Kant that *marriage is a legally and socially established agreement between representatives of two sexes for the purpose of reciprocal use of their sexual organs.* And this was equally horrible, since besides this Kantian inert *use,* nothing remained—no trace of earlier experienced joy, thus a quote from another genius of ages past felt especially appropriate: *I can't get no satisfaction . . .*

Roma was feeling more and more irritated by Artur's bohemian ways, by his frenetic attempts to plunge into abysses of oblivion while pretending to be leader of a gang of playboys. Bohemian life was followed closely by lies: Roma was quite sure that wandering from morning to night through all the possible pubs and clubs of their city this man just couldn't help being unfaithful to her through various skirts and buttocks. Buttocks in her imagination were dressed in skinny jeans and belonged to various idiotic Lolitas who only dreamt of seducing aging wasted ladies' men with hairy nostrils.

Men around the age of forty are but an open wound—just touch them. Artur Pepa was just entering this territory.

At the same time he hated more and more her domesticity, this pathological propensity to lie motionless, hypnotized in front of the TV or of any other source of gutlessness. With each year the number of companies they could both enjoy shrank at catastrophic speed. Lately there remained none at all, thus Artur's lies were far from accidental, as she skillfully wove together his imagined wanderings through the city and its suburbs, replacing the faces of *traveling comedians* whom Roma disliked with those to whom she was at best indifferent.

Indifference: this was the name of her greatest reproach. Ten years ago he loved me like a puppy, thought Roma. It was enough for him to spy how I put on (or took off) pantyhose, when I did not close myself off too thoroughly with a wardrobe door or the old screen, and this would be enough for half a night. Not only pantyhose—a smile, a turn of the head, an intonation often sufficed. Now he would *avoid touching* her for months, immersed, indifferent and haughty, in his own play-acting existence.

The same reproach—growing indifference—is what Artur addressed in Roma. We have already mentioned it earlier—he tended to ascribe this fatal extinguishing of passion to their age and inertia. In his passion, he began fatally exaggerating her increasing self-containment and lack of desire. You know, he said in his thoughts to his imagined interlocutors at an imagined civil trial, when a woman is menstruating for half a month and has a cold for another half, it is very hard for her husband to preserve passion in their love relations. Especially after twelve years of married life. And in a religious marriage the same holds true.

At times he would plunge into sweetly masochistic fantasies and imagined true reasons for this growing distance, painting in his imagination passionate scenes of her rendezvous with others. First it was her deceased former husband—he appeared in his *residence* during countless hours of Artur's absence and bossily took her right then and there, on the kitchen table, bringing her to exhausted yelps with forceful thrusts of his mercilessly cold hard piston. But these visions were soon decisively cast away—so incongruous were they with the true image of a kindly Easter egg collector and his chronic bodily diseases and inflamed spiritual ideals. A far more real possibility was surely the rude and powerful *dean of the faculty* who spent two-thirds of his life achieving his inexpressibly powerful social position, and in the years before finally retiring he used it as much as he could, forcing all the female subordinates without exception (undergraduates with incompletes, graduate students, teaching assistants, lecturers) into a state of true *submission*. So, from time to time he would lie on top of her as well, let's say on a leather daybed in his office, and breathe heavily into her ear, while poor Roma was even forced to move around and feign she was dying of pleasure. Later Artur cast off this version as well: for the dean of the faculty turned out to be not a repulsive pig at an apoplectic stage of power abuse but an entirely pleasant and sophisticated woman, specializing in Asian languages and literatures.

The humiliating fantasies kept coming back to him. Think about all those neo-Freudian guys whom she *served as an interpreter* at various small-scale international conferences! Oh yes, they really could show her their *collective unconscious*! Packs of hungry students at dormitories and the surrounding parks, with shaved heads and FUCK ME tattoos on their foreheads and crotches! Say what you will—all the males of this world, including a battalion of soldiers on their way from bathhouse to firing range, could turn out to be Roma's lovers, so she was actually horny as a cat, and yearned for one thing, flirting with any and all *gentlemen* if not with a word, then with a glance, and provoking them into ecstatic madness in elevators, phone booths, in gangways between train cars.

"Pull yourself together," Artur Pepa would say in moments like these to his inflamed imagination messed up by movies. Also in moments like these he sensed how strongly he was attracted to her and how much inside him still hadn't been exhausted. "So, I do love her still," he thought.

And now in this forest, they found themselves together looking for the third one, as he also thought about her bandaging his head yesterday. A gesture of attention he indubitably did not deserve. Artur hated words that were probably invented by dictionary compilers only to increase their size: *velociously, punctiliously, perchance.* Among these favorites of his was the word *indubitably.* However, now for some reason it seemed to fit his thought regarding attention to what he *indubitably* did not deserve, and how well and quickly her hands did everything that needed to be done in that moment. "May the devil take me," said Artur Pepa to himself, "may the devil take me, and her along with me, in this damn forest!"

At the same time Roma was thinking approximately the same thing (interestingly, they *almost always* thought the same thing): this nonstop clowning of his all day yesterday, the chess at which he's so bad, the fencing, and especially the handstands. "Is he really still capable of doing all this foolish stuff for my sake?" asked Roma of her internal gullible interlocutor. And if not, then for whom, and what for? Well, yes, there were also those two small-town tarts, she thought, putting a brake on her too-rapid conclusions. Besides, various mind-altering substances—alcohol, tobacco, pot. Those like him simply go off their rocker from overdosing, lose their heads. But it was precisely this *losing his head* that pushed him into the embrace of her young-widow's loneliness twelve years ago. And this is why she liked this *head losing of his.*

A little later her thoughts guiltily wandered in the direction of the disappeared Karl-Joseph. Over the last few weeks he had become impossible, hinting at each opportunity she should leave her husband and daughter—*those two*—and move with him to Vienna, to Amsterdam, to Lisbon, to hell. ("*Anywhere you want,*" he said, "*anywhere you want. This world is so big, besides we can always come back and visit Lviv, hike in the Carpathians, spend nights under the stars in the local alpine meadows!*") And no matter how many times she begged him to get this foolishness out of his head, forget about these *stars in alpine meadows* and about this brief *history of errors*, stay friends who continue toiling together for the cause of Lviv-Vienna cultural fusion, he only got nervous and sometimes punched the wall with his fists. "*All right, I agree that your daughter can be taken with us,*" he said once, apparently after prolonged painful reflection, and using one of those passive-voice phrases he preferred. But Roma reacted to this not in the matter of an experienced German Studies scholar: "My daughter is not a thing to be *taken*!" Sometimes I speak to him too harshly, this should stop, she told herself to shake off Karl-Joseph. And yes, she now understood her other nagging worry: her little girl stayed behind all alone in that strange large house somewhere up on the mountain, open to all the winds. More precisely, not all alone but with that newcomer boy, what's going to happen there? ("*The tenth circle is a captivity from which you cannot emerge without losing something,*" Kolya told herself at approximately this moment.)

"Look," Artur suddenly called out to Roma in the midst of a forest that had quickly grown dark. She jumped nimbly across a puddle of mud that had been covered by human footsteps but then solidified. "What is it?" she asked. "Look at this roadblock," said Artur, "it's broken for some reason." "So what?" she feigned un-understanding. "Roadblocks are all broken here; they've been broken for a hundred years." "No, this one wasn't," her husband assured her. "Yesterday late morning I went out here and drank a bottle of booze," asserted Artur with increasing conviction. "So, a bottle," Roma tried to confuse him. But he resisted. "I sat down on this roadblock and had several cigarettes one after another, maybe five or six of them. See," he continued, "a cigarette butt, and then another one, and one here." He picked one up and examined it carefully in the fading forest light, then said, "Prylutska." "So what," Roma didn't give up. "I want to say that this roadblock was broken very recently," declared Artur firmly. "It could have happened because of a struggle. Roadblocks don't break so easily." Roma stayed silent. No, it wouldn't be wise to offer him a version that included the wind. A roadblock broken by a gust of wind—what foolishness!

"Oh, see," he spoke up again in a minute. "What now?" she asked a little tensely. "The grass behind the roadblock is really trampled," said Artur the famous detective. "There are lots of places with trampled grass in this forest," she again tried contradicting him. "No, you don't understand," explained Artur patiently. "The trampling here looks like someone was lying in the grass, or even I should say, rolling in it." "But there's no sight of blood," Roma tossed another false clue to the detective. Artur walked around it for a while, looking in all directions. Two or three gusts of wind had already passed over the treetops. The sky between the trees looked almost black.

"No, there's no sight of blood," said Artur. "Then there was no struggle," said Roma as if joking. Artur thought about what he had seen for a little while. "If there was a human body lying here," he pointed to the grass, "they had to drag it away somewhere. But I don't see signs of that." "And what if it got up on its own and kept walking?" Roma almost betrayed herself. "Then we must walk on as well," agreed her husband. After standing in the same place for another minute or two, they set off along the forest road.

And only then, approximately at the same moment, but each in a unique way, they sensed the mystery of this world condensing and bending over them.

A little later, when they were already exiting the forest, carefully approaching the River, a flash of lightning above their heads, then again, and yet again. "That's just what we need," said Roma, buttoning her clothes tightly and popping up the hood of her jacket. "It will hit really hard now," answered Artur and looked worriedly over the surrounding landscape that had suddenly gone all black. The poet, as always, turned out to be a prophet: as soon as he finished saying this, it did hit hard—thunder rolled all across the big sky above them. "That's Prophet Elijah carrying Easter loaves," noted Artur Pepa and took his wife by the hand, which led the thunder to roll again and again, ever more loudly and menacingly.

As they ran across the bridge, a wet snow started falling. More precisely, there was a short minute during which it was at first only cold rain. But somewhere in the middle of the bridge they noticed the rain grow white. Thus when they reached the other shore, they ran as fast as they could uphill along the highway in the direction of a fork in the road where the stream flowed into the River. At that point everything was already completely white.

In a few minutes Artur thought this escape wouldn't give them anything except exhaustion: in his chest the same snowstorm as outside, above their heads lightning continued to strike menacingly, thunder rolled out in all directions with such force it blocked their ears. The potential place to rest at the thirteenth kilometer was still an hour to an hour and a half away by foot; the railway station just as far, but in the opposite direction. Hear and only here, repeated Artur in unison with his run; here and only here, only here, and only here. And only here is a refuge for us.

Pulling Roma by her hand, he—pothole by pothole—crossed the highway and, after running for some hundred yards, jumped (and Roma after him) over the fence above a precipice, then—be God's will—in whatever way they could, a bit on their feet, a bit on their backs, stomachs, and butts, *breakneck-style*, rapidly downwards, to old gray burdocks dusted with fresh snow—to the bottom, to the very bottom of this world where car death rules.

Covered in snow and dirt, like clowns in sawdust, they did finally land next to all those destroyed, squashed Mercedes and Opels; wandering through corridors of this half-labyrinth, half-cemetery, in midst of the other Fords, Citroëns, and Volgas, they did at last come across something larger and not as badly damaged. One could even squeeze inside after playing with the rusted doors—and a roof over one's head, a hideout of one's own from the outside storm. The storm, by the way, at that moment increased ferocity to such extent that all spatial coordinates were lost—white chaos and white emptiness beyond one's outstretched hand.

So now they must catch their breath—Artur in the

torn-to-shreds driver's seat (no steering wheel in front of him, only remnants of its *skin*), Roma next to him, sitting on something similar. It is the right time to let them catch their breath.

Among the strangest collections of this world there could perhaps be found this one—put together who knows for what ultimate reason by the owner of the surrounding lands, Mr. Vartsabych. Bought, or sometimes simply *taken away* from various junk-yards, dead cars were regularly brought to this precipice, where in a few years their number had reached about a hundred. Among them the car into which our exhausted couple had just squeezed could well be considered one of the most treasured exhibits.

This was an interwar-era Chrysler Imperial, one of the miracles of car engineering of years past, yes, the very one that later became more a symbol rather than reality.[19] Clearly each of you has a right to an ironic grin here. Wait, again those phantoms of youth gone by, repugnant repetitions and self-repetitions?

But am I really talking about those? My goal first of all is the truth of *this* story. And it demands *this* wounded iron body, which some ten years ago had been a veritable fortress on wheels (as it was seen then in the midst of fireworks on the streets of Chortopil),

---

19 An allusion to the collaborative poetic project *Chrysler Imperial* in which Andrukhovych participated in the early 1990s (realized on stage as a "poetry opera" in 1992; in printed form in 1996); Chrysler Imperial the car also appears in Andrukhovych's first novel, *Recreations*.

so this body, or rather shell, right now after unknown road adventures and plain adventures over the last ten years, found itself in *this* ravine, hiding two persons simultaneously close to *and* distant from one another.

Even if this wasn't that very Chrysler Imperial, it was in any case something very much like it. For Artur Pepa simply couldn't choose a different hiding place. This had to be the biggest, most powerful, and indeed most noticeable thing out there.

Thus they were sitting in the dark interior of an enormous car, now silently staring at nervous flashes in the midst of thick impenetrable whiteness through the few windows that had survived. Water dripped from their clothes; it seemed they themselves were ready to melt.

"And what if it hits the car?" Roma finally asked, nodding at yet another flash in the midst the outside world.

"Then it seems we'll burn down," answered Artur, not very reassuringly, and lit a cigarette. "I am not too good at physics."

"End of April," she noted sadly.

"Mountains," he explained. "Extremely unstable weather. A paradise for meteorologists."

They stayed silent for exactly as long as his wet cigarette smoked. Then, extinguishing the butt, he said,

"Antonych again. No matter where you go, this Antonych guy."

Roma gave him a look of incomprehension.

"I mean his 'Dead Cars,'" said Artur. "In 1935, when this jalopy was still a luxury super-chariot, the poet Antonych described yet one more of his visions. A cemetery of piled up dead cars. *Like shards of shattered stars, frozen autos sleep in car cemeteries*, etc."

"It's no surprise that here all these crazy things are going on," Roma's shoulders began to shiver.

"You mean, concerning this Austrian guy?" He turned his face to her.

Roma thought that now she had to tell him everything, exactly as it had happened. Otherwise they'll die in this iron sack—from hypothermia, most likely.

"You know, there by the roadblock . . ." she began.

But the sky rattled with so much thunder she had to start from the beginning. Artur turned to her not only his face but also his whole self.

"By that roadblock," she began for the third time and then burst out with everything in one salvo, "where you noted it was broken, I caught up with him at night because I didn't want him to go anywhere, so drunk as he was with that walnut stuff, not sure if you remember how the two of you downed so much of it, well, in any case I thought I'd accompany him so that nothing would happen, generally speaking he is still quite helpless concerning our local circumstances, so, by that roadblock I caught up with him . . . give me a Prylutska!"

She took a long time to light it from his lighter,

then puffed once, twice, and broke into a coughing fit. Artur gently took the cigarette from her and started smoking it himself.

"So," she hurried, "he started pestering me, sticking his hands everywhere, I resisted as much as I could, but he pressed with his whole body, and pushed me against that roadblock, but I resisted with all my strength, then we broke it . . ."

"What?" asked Artur, flashing a little ash-ember glow from his cigarette.

Notwithstanding the surrounding darkness, he sensed his eyes were darkening and that he was overcome with a desire to hold her tight or at least press his lips hard against hers.

"No, it's not what you think; that's why this roadblock's broken, he pushed against me, and I didn't let him, then he went with his hand between my thighs . . ."

Artur moaned, pulverizing the half-finished Prylutska. The darkness in his eyes was darker than all the darknesses of this world.

". . . he wanted . . . you know . . . simply there, on top of the roadblock, but I resisted, and then we broke that roadblock and fell on the grass, I was now on top of him, and I pressed him down with my knees—you noted the grass there had been trampled . . ."

"And then," said Artur with almost his last strength.

"Then nothing," Roma shrugged. "I left him in the

forest alone and returned to the mountain. You were already asleep when I got back."

From all this she couldn't avoid showing her chattering teeth. But she now felt better—she told everything she had to tell. Was it really out of love?

Artur senses the darkness inside him would not let go if this didn't happen.

"I saw it," he said. "I ran after you. And stood a little to the side. In the bright moonlight one could see very well. Then I went back."

In reality he did run that night, but not after her. He told a lie, for he had to tell a lie. Was it really out of love?

"So you were there?"

She moved her whole body towards him. This was the only salvation for both of them—otherwise they could freeze in that metal coffin. They started kissing wildly, painfully—this had not happened for several years. Moving onto his lap, she was now so close to him everything started swimming and spinning: this was a greedy desperate struggle, with occasional biting, a pushing through heavy soaked clothes in hope of making one's way to warmth, to skin. Some rags flew onto the back seat. Beneath her sweater he found her stomach, and the hollow between her breasts, grabbing with his free hand the pocket of his trench coat (*easy, easy*, he repeated the only word he knew), he accidentally pressed some lever, and—glory to the imperialist carmakers!—the seat reclined with a rusty screech . . .

Only then did they calm a little bit and continue in an entirely different fashion, sweetly and deliberately, having found the energy and the rhythm. Her face, now elongated by the pangs of tenderness, rocked above him in the midst of flashes. She closed her eyes. Charges of lightning hit the roof, the fins, the bumper of the enormous jalopy; unable to do them any harm it bounced off with a hissing sound. Everything looked almost like the first night of their acquaintance. His hair had been wet (although now the heroic mark of a head bandage got in the way a little, but it only inflamed their love). Outside the wet springtime snow fell just as it had done the first time. The folding cot in the kitchen had also huffed and puffed and screeched like this old peeling car seat. Roma covered her mouth with her hands both times, muffling cries and moans (back then it was understandable—Kolya was asleep in the next room, but why now?). And both times he excitedly radiated immeasurable joy.

(So when from beyond the mountain range near them flew a pale, snow-covered creature with drooping snowy mustache, bitterly pressing from outside onto the car window, they did not notice, preoccupied as they were only with themselves. And the sorcerer who used to bear Roma's surname, Voronych, only stayed next to them a brief minute, then moved away powerless, disintegrating into white snowy tufts.)

Only then did they arrive at a somewhat hoarse,

animal paroxysm, after which, as always, they stayed still and happy a long time. Surprising as it may sound, the lightning and thunder also ceased. More exactly, they moved away, disappearing into some distant realm. The remaining wet snow continued falling from heavenly reservoirs, but ever more softly and slowly.

"So nice," said Roma when one could again be capable of saying something.

"But you could have crushed the egg," murmured Artur and rustled with his trench coat.

Shaking on top of his chest, she burst into laughter.

"This would have been a terrible loss," she said and again was overcome with laughter.

"It isn't what you think," he replied.

And after making a rustling noise again, produced from his trench coat pocket a painted Easter egg, with orange stars and crosses on a black otherworldly background, and with two golden ribbons, one at the top and the other at the bottom. Now one could look at it closely in the moonlight that suddenly filled the entire ravine with all its car skeletons and car innards and penetrated without difficulty their wheeled hideout.

"Oh, and where's this from?" asked Roma.

"I'm not sure myself," he rubbed his bandaged forehead against her shoulder, "but it's for you. A present for the holiday."

She carefully took the Easter egg and held it in the boat made of her palms. Then she thanked him, touching her lips to her favorite little dip under his Adam's apple.

"You'll give it to me tomorrow," she said and put it back into the same pocket. "It's not yet the holiday. I'll be jumping up and down in surprise. And really, how did I manage not to crush it?"

She again started laughing, remembering the way he said it—just like a purring cat.

"And I do know how it happened," she said entirely seriously a minute later. "I simply stopped being clumsy."

"Since when?" Artur feigned worry.

"Since now," she said proudly.

"But I like it when you're clumsy," he said, resting on his elbow.

"Really? I'd never believe it!" She licked his nose. "All right, just for you, I'll stay clumsy just a little longer."

Crawling back to her seat, she bumped her knee against his side. He gave an affected scream. But thought it would be inappropriate to repeat the joke about the egg.

"You see, everything is OK," she giggled. "I'm clumsy again. Let's have a smoke, just one?"

He clicked his lighter for a long time, taking the first puff, then passed the cigarette to her, and recited,

Sometimes it happens: humans, jackal-like, disturb
these metal corpses
and spread the shabby goods of their greed, and
thirst, and needs, like at market,
and in midst of bluish nights the long-dead trunks
now serve as sinful beds
for homeless lusty grimacers and whores, as evil stars
pour poison right inside them . . .

"That's this Antonych guy?" she asked. "I wonder, where is he now?"

(She uttered the last phrase involuntarily—perhaps because at that very moment her daughter let her first lover inside herself, *the eleventh circle is when two become one*).

"I think he's in his tavern on the Moon," answered Artur. "Where else should he be?"

"So what was he saying about homeless lust?" They started putting on their sweaters, one by one.

"Homeless lusty grimacers and whores," reminded her Artur.

"So, it fits, although not entirely," she agreed. "You are such a grimacer!"

He did not respond to her challenge, only made an offended and cheerful grimace. Artur Pepa could not be a monkey according to the year of his birth, but he was one sometimes due to *life's circumstances*.

"You know," she said, "I'm going to move over to the back seat and take a nap. All the same we can't get out of here anytime soon. Will you share with me *the marriage bed?*"

"If it's *sinful*, yes, of course," promised Artur. "Everything is in our power. You have permission to wake me when you feel like it."

He also made himself comfortable—*ave, Chrysler!*—on that wide and ambiguous-looking leather-clad back seat, much like that couch from the dean's office in his daydreams, and then put his arms around her thighs.

"You give me permission to wake you up?" he murmured in his special way somewhere near her ear. "All right! That is, if I don't sleep through my morning erection."

They laughed a little, then talked, competing in telling silly jokes, then again smoked a cigarette, since—nothing can be done, truth can't be avoided—when after sex there is conversation, more often than not there's also love.

Only later, after a period of time unmarked by chronometry, Roma Voronych slipped out of his embrace, started the old car and went on a joyride through various rooms of the resort, crashing into walls and knocking down vases and fire extinguishers. It is unknown what Artur was dreaming—there is a bit of mystery in everything.

But when he started dreaming of a pack of dogs running along the bank of the River, morning came. For the umpteenth time, the weather changed: everything that had been snow at night now was melting fast, flowing and dripping; an unbearably warm wind tried tearing the heads off everyone's shoulders, even here, in the ravine.

The pack seen in the dream turned out to be only one dog, a rather large one, some sort of German shepherd mix, and he ecstatically barked nonstop, rising on his hind legs and sticking his muzzle against the Chrysler's still-glassed windows. Undoubtedly he could not be a fan of these two-legged creatures, catching this pair in their sleep and now waking stunned. What the hell are they doing here? What is this?

The angry dog was not alone in its irritation. It came running accompanied by no less than three cops, one of them holding a shooting-ready Kalashnikov. Another one—judging by the number of gold teeth in his mouth and his face overall, the oldest among them—ordered with a gesture for them to get out. At the same moment the third expertly grabbed the dog by the collar, which made it bark even more fiercely.

Squinting at the windy sunshine that hit them warmly and painfully, looking somewhat helpless and very sleepy, Artur Pepa and Roma Voronych, after a few unsuccessful and foolish-looking attempts to open the car doors finally managed to crawl out through the front seat. As soon as he stepped on the ground that was melting under his feet, Artur felt a horrible cramp in his leg. Now he had to stand on one foot. And in addition, a terrible wind induced a splitting headache, and the noise of melting water, pain in his eyes, state coat of arms on the uniform caps, and barking pushed to an extreme, a disgusting taste in his mouth, a Kalashnikov half-pointed at them, and all these questions: *who are you? where did you come from? what are you doing here? your papers?*

Artur managed to answer only the first three questions. He did not have any documents, nor did Roma, experienced though she was. "We're tourists," said Artur Pepa (the third cop finally shushed the dog and it fell silent, that old mutt). "We're tourists from Lviv, vacationing here in the Carpathians."

"We're tourists from Lviv, vacationing here in the Carpathians, in Lviv we live at such-and-such an address," said Roma. "And here we were hiding from the storm, we got completely drenched."

"Madam, we are not asking *you* questions yet," grinned the *boss* with all of his teeth. "When your *turn* comes, we'll *question* you as well."

"So as I was saying," continued Artur Pepa. "We went out from the resort for an evening walk, and then as you know, the storm, thunder, no place to hide, so we ran down here and hid inside."

"You hear this?" said the *boss* to his guys. "Do you hear who they take us for—stupid imbeciles! Do you hear, they hid from thunder in a hunk of iron!"

Hearing such nonsense the cops broke into a chorus of laughter, even the dog giggled a little, the sycophant.

"Why are you laughing, guys?" asked Roma good-naturedly. "Why laugh? When we hid from the storm in this car, we didn't think about any physics—we only thought of hiding. And you guys are laughing, not understanding this."

"Madam," the *boss* turned to her again, but in a harsher tone. "Madam, put away that physics of yours! And we are not one of your guys so far—we've not yet *slept* together."

"Mr. Chief Warrant Officer," said Artur Pepa to this. "Mr. Chief Warrant Officer, please don't speak in such tone to a woman. This is my wife, sir."

To which the man responded in an even harsher tone, "If she's your wife, why do you fuck in cars? Maybe she's really a whore to you and not a wife? Maybe this whore fucks everyone in cars like this?"

Then Artur Pepa, Knight of the Order of Noble Sword-Bearers, plunging into his deepest internal darkness, tried pushing his cramped leg forward, to hit the gold-toothed mug of the lousy guy in uniform so that he would never again dare offend the Ladies. But the cop facing him so selflessly pressed against him the butt of his Kalashnikov that sparks flew in all directions, and it's a miracle the bandage didn't fly off of Artur's head.

So Artur only fainted, collapsing onto remnants of snow, sending gray fountains in all directions. They forcefully pulled Roma away so she wouldn't wail as at a funeral. And the dog too got way too excited because of this "*shithead from Lviv*".

But she kept resisting them and calling them bandits and murderers, so the *boss* started thinking about giving her a good kick in the head so she would shut the fuck up and not interfere with their *reporting via the radio.* This is how they led her out—with sobs, shouts, and wails, then suddenly quiet and defeated, accompanied by a guy holding the dog on a leash.

They led her up out of the ravine, a steep climb over slippery rocks, her feet kept slipping from one rock to another, but she somehow made it up. Then they put her into a police van and went in an unknown direction.

Naturally, while she could, she looked back and saw how the other two, the *boss* and the cop with the Kalashnikov, handcuffed themselves to Artur Pepa on both sides and (Artur's head in dirty bandages dangling limply above his shoulders) dragged him between rusty bumpers and car bodies toward the exit.

Only after they drove for some three to five miles and she saw through the grated window not one but two police cars headed in the opposite direction, did she realize they were coming for Artur and nothing more horrifying could ever happen in one's life.

11

Karl-Joseph Zumbrunnen never before felt this distressed, humiliated, or bitter. He wanted to crawl out of his own skin and stomp on it for a long time with heavy merciless boots. Why did it happen this way? Why did he behave like this? Why was he now alone in this forest full of white moonlight?

Weil ich die unglückliche Liebe habe, he wanted to explain to his old high school mentor, who at that moment looked at him with silent heavy reproach, either from the moon or from the nearest owl's nest. The mentor was obsessed with courteousness; for a thousand years he inculcated in his students the idea that *courteousness* is synonymous with *Europeanness.* One must remember this always and everywhere, in all circumstances. The mentor had died many years ago, but now he looked at Karl-Joseph, one of the thousands of his pupils, and wanted to hear at least some sort of tentative justification from him.

Weil ich die unglückliche Liebe habe, repeated Karl-Joseph slightly more firmly, so that the other guy would let him be. The last two words almost rhymed with each other. They came to dominate his limping. Some time later, when he was already exiting the forest, not ceasing to burn with shame and love, Karl-Joseph circled around this mocking pair (*Liebe habe, lie-*

be-habe, Liebehabe). Did this not explain everything, Mr. High School Mentor?

The mentor still ran after him for a while, appearing first on the bridge then simultaneously on both sides of the highway—he clearly did not find the answer satisfactory, thus when he came to a fork in the road near the place where the Stream flowed into the River, he cut the air with his hand and said: "All right, all right, I'm guilty, I am now no European, but a drunken pig!" This was enough for the mentor to finally leave. Self-criticism—that's what it turns out he wanted! Karl-Joseph turned right and, moving uphill along the Stream, started talking to Roma, because this was about her.

Why did you follow me, why did you run down the slope, why were we together, asked Karl-Joseph, although he did not hope for any answers. Why did you speak about that moon, Karl-Joseph demanded the truth. For when someone speaks to someone else about the moon, doesn't this mean the two are very close to one another? When two people look at the moon above, something greater is born between them, isn't that right? I would never speak about the moon to someone with whom I was indifferent. Roma was silent; words failed her.

And if that is the case, Karl-Joseph continued his train of logic, I had to begin saying what I began. For this could not go on forever—these meetings in hotels and other people's homes, secret codes and signs. A few more years of this languishing, and we'll plunge into old age, it will be too late. The only thing I ask for is clarity. Do we not deserve being frank in our relationship? If you at least once, just one time said *enough, I don't want this any more*, I would have retreated and never again gotten even one step closer to you. But you didn't do that!

Karl-Joseph was correct in that he indeed never heard the word *enough* from her. At the same time, he was rather deceiving her and first and foremost, deceiving himself when he claimed he would have retreated. It is doubtful he would still be capable of that. More likely he would follow her like a beaten dog, and still beg for more Ukrainian visas for more secret rendezvous. But at this moment, overcome with a wave of alcohol, he was ready to believe his noble retreat. The main thing was Roma did not dare object to what he was saying; he should make the most of her guilty silence to the very end.

Yes, it seems I told you the worst word you could have heard from me, he started speaking with even more pathos a little later, pebbles flew out from under his decisive boots. Forgive me; I did offend you, that's true. But you did not even show that you felt offended. On the contrary, you asked for my hand. You asked me to give *you* my hand! Karl Joseph stopped dead in front of the trunk of a pine tree. You! Asked! Me! To give! You! My hand! How was I to understand this, can you tell me? Both the pine and Roma stayed silent, so he walked on.

When, in the middle of the night, someone gives another person one's hand, he continued in a calmer fashion, this means closeness, doesn't it? I agree, I may not understand some things about your customs. For example, in your country people kiss on the lips already at the first meeting. You dance with other people's partners, pressing your bodies too closely. Personal private space almost does not exist in your country. You breathe straight into faces of other people and walk around in skirts too short. Now I am talking about you taking my hand! This is something completely different, this is no longer a gesture—it's an invitation.

Here too Karl-Joseph was only partially correct—it is doubtful he had grounds to see in Roma's request, to help her out of a puddle of mud, some higher metaphysical meaning. Deep in his soul he too understood it perfectly well. But in the heat of attack all the arguments were appropriate—the main thing was that Roma was silent. The main thing was she wasn't next to him.

Thus he could allow himself one more frank, indeed insolent statement. I do know your life a little, he said, his feet slipping on pinecones and needles, I do. I'm convinced there are dozens of women you know, both younger and older, who above all else want to be in your place. In your country they mostly dream of marrying a Westerner, at these marriage agencies, professional go-betweens, modeling agencies, prostitution, and so forth. Yes, you are not like this—I still hope you are not like this—but I do not know what kind of person you are. What you want, this I do not know. For you gave me your hand, he clung to the last thing that he had remaining. The hand, the hand she gave him—beyond that his argument dried up. He held to that hand with all his strength, then grew tired.

Then began but white noise inside his head—a muffled struggle, uncontrolled arbitrariness of Eros exhausted by infinitely long waiting, an attempt at closeness that lapsed into brutality, fist punch in the face of his life, the cracking of a roadblock, two terrifyingly hostile bodies plunging somewhere into hell.

Let's agree: this wasn't me, this wasn't you, said Karl-Joseph to Roma in the end, finally letting go of her and her hand.

Saying goodbye took place shortly before he arrived at the 24-hour café at the thirteenth kilometer—a place he had visited once before, a few days ago, when he searched for future objects to photograph. That time he remembered all the details: an elevated pavilion made of aluminum and plastic (Karl-Joseph didn't know that in this country the traditional name for such structures was a *bobber* or, more sophisticatedly, an *aquarium*), front steps made of cement, cracks and pieces missing, and a terrace by the front door, likewise with a cement floor, where in the summer they must bring out tables with various objects around it: abandoned barbecue grills, mushroom-like picnic tables with umbrellas, remnants of bonfires, dumpsters overflowing with trash. Nothing exceptional, then decided Karl-Joseph. In his wanderings across the Eastern Carpathians he had encountered dozens of structures like this. "These people," he wrote in one of his letters, "really do like drinking sessions in the open air, but this is nothing at all like what in our world we call picnics. The mountains and forests I have hiked are incredibly polluted by traces of such excessive joyous partying: broken glass, empty bottles, paper trash and various rags leave you no chance for appreciation of the surrounding beauty. In a tragicomic fashion such sites always include billboards with rhymed (!) appeals to the visitors to protect this treasure belonging to *the people*. On the other hand, it is hard to accuse the actual people—since childhood the system inculcated them with a sense of irresponsibility. By the way, here lies a telling paradox: permissiveness for slaves! Thus it is a question of honor for new generations to overcome this inertia."

This is what he wrote, without even a hint of suspicion that the *new generations* already set themselves the task of surmounting this inertia without waiting for recommendations from wise guys visiting from far away. This greasy spoon, erected back in the days when Malafey, the fierce promoter of mountain skiing, ruled the neighboring alpine meadow, so this establishment, conceived at first as a *trout restaurant for lumberjacks and visitors to the area* (its location above the stream must have helped this concept, as signaled by the original name, Silver Waterfalls—yet it led to a series of financial disasters and many years of standing padlocked and empty)—so, this roadside diner finally waited to see its *true owners.* Some many-branched family rented it from the proprietor, the businessman Y.Y. Vartsabych, and established a 24-7 business. Of course, nobody bothered with things like trout any more: both *lumberjacks* and *visitors to the area,* enamored of the area's natural beauty without trout on the menu, picked this trap to drink away all their cash, sweetly and imperceptibly.

And it was this door another visitor to the area walked through, between eleven in the evening and midnight.

Moving not quite confidently between aluminum tables and chairs in the semidarkness illuminated only by *disco lights*, Karl-Joseph Zumbrunnen remembered he owed a bottle of booze to Artur, which he therefore had to buy here. Inside, some sort of fairly young company was amusing themselves (yes, track suits and tights, and a song in Russian, *you called me your ray of sunshine*). He was elbowed several times while he made his way through the dance floor to the bar (damn it, what a party during Holy Week, on the eve of Good Friday, someone else might have noted with surprise), but Karl-Joseph was no longer surprised by anything. It did not surprise him, pushed by warm suffocating waves to the bar, he had no luck getting the attention from the hostess, who instead flirted with someone much closer and more familiar, or rather with two guys, refusing now for the tenth time to pour one *for the beard.* Karl-Joseph could not make any sense of it, neither of them had a beard, but thanks to a pause he was able to formulate his order (he was not sure whether the correct word for bottle was *pliashka* or *fliashka*—he had encountered both versions). So, some five minutes later, trying to break through the surrounding noise and music (*my little one, I miss you*), he said in a falsetto voice "please . . . *horilka* for me"—when he said it a third time he was heard, and the hostess, a heavily made-up woman of the his same age finally turned to him and said something like "have a seat, someone will come to take your order." Karl-Joseph reflected for a while whether he heard everything correctly ("fuck you over?"), but the only possible interpretation told him to step back and collapse at the nearest free table. From there, he stared for a long time at the dancers, forgotten by everyone, a loner at someone else's party, a stranger, finally his most desperate prayer was heard and a young man in a baseball cap came to him, probably the son of the hostess, although why necessarily the son—he just had the same kind of pear-shaped behind as she had. "Good evening, how can I help you?" said the young man in an irritated voice and after hearing from Karl-Joseph "*horilka* . . . one bottle please," silently walked away.

Karl-Joseph thought none of them have a reason to treat him with such hostility. But he immediately remembered the cracked lens in his glasses—maybe it was because of this? Just in case, he took his glasses off, and his vision dissolved into spots and flashes—terrifying, no less than earlier this evening, to sit in this flashy pit of a place, this overcooked stew of smells among people unknown to him, listening to how they sing along with the stereo in disorderly voices, *and I found a different one*—and not to be able to see anything! Quite a few minutes passed and then a head popped up in front of him, in the midst of green and red flashes. This time it was a young woman with a friendly voice, "Did you order?" After he put on glasses it turned out her eyes were friendly too—and she placed a glass of *horilka* in front of him. "No," he said, "not a glass! Please, I beg you, a bottle . . . one . . ." The young woman asked something like "To go?" but Karl-Joseph did not understand her question so gestured not to take the glass away and thanked her. "Would you like kebab?" she asked with an air of sympathy, but again he just thanked her. The kind young woman seemed to shrug her shoulders and walked away.

He drank several gulps of the vile stuff and thought he had plenty of time to get that cursed bottle for the bet he lost. It was only to get used to what was happening around him and to properly articulate his order. Especially since the first gulps worked with lightning speed, in combination with the *old yeast*, Karl-Joseph soon felt relaxed and in some centers of his body an order was issued to relieve from their posts far-too-zealous guards, he stopped shaking and together with the warmth took in this noise, this stomping, this music. He relaxed so much he no longer sensed the two stares coming from one of the faraway tables (were those perhaps those very guys with whom the hostess annoyingly chatted for so long when he came in?). But he relaxed, and knew nothing about those stares.

Ten minutes later he was ready to head back to the counter and order one more drink. This time the host, apparently the father of that young woman with kind eyes and kind voice, after serving him the drink asked Karl-Joseph whether he'd like kebab. He shook his head (large chunks of charred raw meat with grilled onions wouldn't make it through his gullet now), but so not to offend the owner, he squeezed out something like "one orange please." The owner did not understand him and after some hesitation offered a Snickers bar.

Returning to his seat with a glass and a foolish-looking Snickers bar in his hands, Karl-Joseph surprised himself by the fluidity and agility of his movements, he had caught the rhythm, and this became a true *tango of the white moth*, even the dancers admired his moves. This success ought to be built upon, so after half-emptying the glass in three greedy gulps, Karl-Joseph rose from his table and shouted, "*Achtung! Achtung!*" They didn't stop dancing to their *white moth by an open flame*, but everyone simultaneously glanced at him—guys, gals, the kind-eyed host at the bar, his kind-hearted daughter in the kitchen, and of course those two beardless guys—everyone watched as he plunged headfirst downward and did a handstand . . .

The abyss shook and pulled him towards it, chairs fell in all directions, then there was nothing, someone's hands led him through red and green flashes and when he again was able to see, there were many head-shaped spots in front of him, but for some reason there was no music. He stood by his table and others there talked to one another ("drunk as a skunk"—what does this mean, "drunk as a skunk"?), and the owner's daughter put his eyeglasses back on his face. Karl-Joseph burst out laughing. He very much liked all these people, how they helped him out, so he wanted to cheer them somehow, and, clapping his hands, shouted in English "Go dance!" chasing them away from himself.

They did indeed walk away, and in a little while the music restarted, thus he again found himself alone and felt overcome by a strangely pleasant sleepiness, from the depth of which he still watched more and more dancing, watched them drink and kiss, drink and kiss—and this continued for a very long time, he even threw his Snickers bar at some of them but they pretended not to notice. Only then did a bald-headed guy in a leather jacket announce *last dance for the birthday girl* (*was, eigentlich, soll das bedeuten?*), and a terribly heart-rending song, "Oh birthday, holiday of childhood," began to play. As it did, they spun around for an inexpressibly long time—Karl-Joseph managed to fall asleep and wake again dozens of times, and they kept spinning, and played it again, and then they sang something like "you cannot escape from it anywhere"—but the girl in the center of the circle became hysterical, smashing a wineglass against the floor, the leather-clad emcee mercilessly slapping her on the cheeks ("drunk like a skunk, drunk like a skunk," they mumbled again, and Karl-Joseph understood this must be some sort of incantation to ward off misfortune—"drunk like a skunk, drunk like a skunk").

Next he unglued his eyes as the whole gang was already in the process of loudly exiting the bar. Some were finishing their drinks, others—their kisses. Someone led the *birthday girl* by both hands to the door and Karl-Joseph noticed dirty streaks of vomit on her white blouse. Outdoors, they kept on shouting. Someone returned with more money to pay the owner, then various Jeeps and Nivas took a long time to start, and then Karl-Joseph rested his tired head on the table.

Before he did that he stumbled towards the counter, catching the mostly hostile gazes directed at him by four *members of the proprietor's family* (although there was among them, truth be told, one compassionate, pitying glance)—so he trundled towards a faraway (*infernal*?) corner of this building where there ought to be a restroom. As best as he could, he jerkily grabbed the walls that pulled away and then pushed back, the ceiling with one lonely light bulb plunged down, the floor rose and moved up at him, with his foot he kicked the door with a torn out lock hanging from it—and entered. Inside there were no toilets, only a cement hole with two elevations on its sides, about as big as size 11 shoes. But that wasn't the most important thing: Karl-Joseph also saw a naked behind, tracksuit pants pulled down below the knees, a rhythmic movement of the hips, then a female body leaning forward, responding to pushes in the same rhythm, and its hands spasmodically grabbing the ribs of the radiator. "Who's here?" she screamed, turning her head in all directions. "Wait, wait," answered the male body, breathing heavily and impatiently. While Karl-Joseph poured something dark-colored out of himself into the cement hole (he liked holding his dick in his hand—so massive, so long, now suddenly so heavy), they kept riding, squeezing out of themselves their animal stuff. And as soon as Karl-Joseph finished, the male butt tensed for the last time and finally froze. "So," said the owner of the butt, pulling up his pants. "Now your turn," he said, nodding his head towards Karl-Joseph, then slapped his shoulder, and left.

The young woman got up from her knees, her breasts spilling out of her blouse, turned towards Karl-Joseph, then sat on the radiator. "Will you?" she asked without a trace of any emotion. He pushed himself close to her, although how could he know then that this was the very last such gift to be bestowed upon him, and set his lips and his fingers to explore, full of helpless lust. His tongue plunged into her alcoholic mouth cavity as if it truly was the last time for him. The young woman wiggled in his arms, spread her legs, and pushed him inside herself. He began sliding towards the floor. He suddenly realized how exhausted he was, just like his large and useless dick. She must have understood things in this way, for she opened the lock of her legs behind his back and again pushed them together, stroking his poor head—just like Roma sometimes had to do, at other times and in other circumstances. Then he rested his head in her lap and fell fast asleep. The young woman freed herself and disappeared.

At that moment someone's hand started ever more insistently grabbing and shaking the back of his neck. Without raising his head, Karl-Joseph kept brushing it off (thereby proving to Roma he no longer cared for her much-too-late caresses), but Roma did not let go, her hand was large and hard, covered by horrible thick skin, its fingers short and fat—so, covering in a flash more than half the distance between sleep and wakefulness, Karl-Joseph realized this certainly was no Roma, for her hand could not be so manly strong and so neglected—what about all those lotions he bought as gifts, where were they and their beneficial effects? Only then did he pull his head from the sticky cold aluminum tabletop.

At his table two bald guys—the same ones, of course. They were approximately the same age, between thirty and forty, although in this country, as Karl-Joseph had an opportunity to note, it was easy to make a mistake judging a person's age by their looks. The looks of both of them left much to be desired. And most importantly, why were they wearing those leather caps?

Karl-Joseph clearly saw it all (leather caps, swollen mugs, and the overall *looks*) as soon as he put his glasses on, now cracked in two places. This was enough for one of those two, a rotten tooth in the middle of his mouth, to say, "Hey, bro, get us a couple of shots!" Karl-Joseph silently looked at the two of them through his cracked eyeglasses. He did not like them.

They too apparently did not care for his silence because the other one, with various stupid things tattooed on his fingers, said, "Are you stupid or something? Get me and Dushman a couple of shots each, understood?" Truth be told, Karl-Joseph *understood* nothing. The only thing he could do was order some *horilka*. He looked around the room—at this hour it was entirely empty and quiet. Somebody, though, was napping at the counter—probably the owner.

"You want . . . *horilka* drink?" asked Karl-Joseph. The two bald guys exchanged glances. While they were digesting new information, Karl-Joseph shouted in direction of the bar, "*Horilka* please . . . three times!" The two bald guys exchanged glances once again, and the one with tattoos on his fingers decided to clarify, "Are you in business or something?" Karl-Joseph understood he was speaking about something related to business, hence he *surely* was confusing him with someone else. Karl-Joseph had not worked a single day at anything that could be classified as business, and was rather proud of this fact. Then he shook his head to indicate "no." "Then why the fuck do you speak like this?" asked the guy with tattoos on his fingers. "With an accent," clarified the rotten tooth. It seemed to Karl-Joseph he was beginning to make sense. "I am a foreigner," he said, recalling by some miracle how to say "foreigner" in their language. "Austrian."

The gloomy-looking guy in a baseball cap came to them and put on the table three glasses of *horilka*. "And kebabs!" demanded the one with tattooed fingers. "One for me, and one for Dushman." "Who's paying?" the baseball cap replied skeptically. "Shukhir, I don't want a kebab, I don't care for meat, you know this!" said the rotten tooth. "He's paying," Shukhir pointed with his tattooed finger at Karl-Joseph. "Am I right, bro?"

Karl-Joseph nodded. He did not want to start an argument with these people. It looked like they were down on their luck, perhaps even homeless, and of course hungry. Why not buy them food? He began trying to recall the names of various local dishes so that he could order for them, but he could remember nothing but "*Banusch ist eine typisch huzulische Speise.*" But that guy in a baseball cap had already walked away, thus each of them simply reached for their respective glass. Karl-Joseph stretched his out towards the other two, glass clanked, Dushman grimaced to squeeze out a smile, Shukhir didn't even make an effort to do the same.

Karl-Joseph, as always, only took two or three sips. His new acquaintances downed theirs in one gulp and simultaneously reached for a crushed pack of cigarettes. "Vatra!" recognized Karl-Joseph. "I too have . . . my home . . . pack of Vatra." "Do you want a smoke?" Dushman didn't understand and offered him the pack, spilling dirty tobacco flakes. "Nah," said Karl-Joseph, but then thought, "Why not?" and corrected himself: "Give me one . . . piece." He was feeling more relaxed, the world around him getting palpably warmer, and even Shukhir managed a shadow of a smile, demanding in direction of the bar: "And why're we sitting so quiet. Is the music over, did the player croak?" The angry woman with the sagging behind sighed loudly from the other side of the counter and with the words "May God give you health" shuffled her way towards the boombox, from which all sorts of crap immediately began to flow.

Karl-Joseph sucked the dense foul-tasting smoke from the wet cigarette that smelled of Dushman's pocket. He visualized how gray bands of smoke penetrate his body, fill the chest cavity, envelop his lungs and heart, dumping on them countless pathogenic motes of dust and tiny deadly bubbles. This visualization made him want to laugh but he didn't show it, remembering that those two had their eyes on him from the other side of the smoke curtain. "By the way, what's your name?" asked Shukhir. Or perhaps Dushman—Karl-Joseph could not tell for sure which one of the two it was. "Charlie," he answered into the thick smoke. "Charlie Chaplin, eh?" asked Shukhir, and Dushman burst out laughing, which Karl-Joseph joined , all the while visualizing those tiny cancerous bubbles on his lungs. "You didn't want me alive—here I am dead," he thought with malicious glee, addressing Roma.

Meanwhile, the girl with the kind eyes brought Shukhir his kebab. The ketchup-smothered chunks of fatty meat were still moving on the plate. "Three *horilka . . . nochmals bitte*," Karl-Joseph chimed in with an order. "Listen, Charlie," Shukhir interrupted him. "Order a bottle right away like one normally does . . . Just for three guys. How long are we going to play little boys' games: one round of shots, two rounds of shots . . ." Of all this Karl-Joseph was able to identify the word for "bottle"—but that was sufficient. Looking up at the girl in a slightly guilty fashion, he corrected himself, "*Eine Flasche bitte* . . ."

"And who's paying?" the angry woman shrewishly popped-up from behind the counter—it turned out she had been eavesdropping on them a long time. "Listen," said Dushman in a conciliatory fashion, "give her something so she will fuck off." Here too Karl-Joseph brilliantly seized the context. His wallet with the strange word "GSCHNA-A-ASS!!!" pressed into the leather (was it Eva-Maria's Christmas present from 1990?) appeared on the table. From out of a thick stack he unearthed a pale green twenty dollar bill. "Mama, twenty bucks!" the kind girl shouted in direction of the counter, to which the angry woman mumbled to her "Pour them then." Karl-Joseph, amused at himself for acting in so prudent a fashion, put the wallet back in his pocket. Dushman and Shukhir were already greatly pleased by what they had seen.

About half an hour later (who was counting?) everything began swimming, circling, and flickering—heads in leather caps, unshaven chins, Adam's apples, jaws, the table splattered with dark walnut *horilka*, the incessant clanking of glasses hitting one another, remnants of semi-chewed pieces of kebab on a plate mixed with heaps of cigarette ashes and four squished butts, the last three *pelmeni* in congealed cold fat on one more plate, bread crusts and crumbs, Austrian coins scattered in all directions, bottles—some empty, others half-empty. Bands of bitter smoke now had no time to dissipate, enveloping their table with an ever-thicker, almost immobile mass, a great wall that even the stupid music had a hard time getting through—Karl-Joseph heard in it only three chords, perhaps because from both sides pressing in, mixing and quarrelling with each other, also came bizarre stories from his two table-mates: each of the two tried to look more interesting than the other, somehow pushing through both ears of this *Australian* guy. One ear was just not enough. The result of it all was strange dirty verbal molasses, veritable *kasha spread over the table*—"I, fuck, in Afghan', fuck, platoon leader, dammit, in slammer on the Dnieper, in mouth and in ass, platoon leader says where are you going mines kids, I freak out, fuck, some stool pigeon gang-fucked in the Lenin Room, fuck, they'll fuck you over any which way, APC caught fire, game over, man!" Karl-Joseph wanted to raise his hands and shout yet another *achtung* so they would shut up and let him tell one of *his* stories—he was not sure what about, so slowly in his head he went through the principal adventures of his life, but nothing was coming together, and so he just sat, his hands lowered, his head too, unable to stop this increasingly indecipherable torrent—"they lined everyone up grub to the john the slammer swarmed fuck those goddam Afghans everything was on fire Kandahar the top boss commanded behind him the orderly here fuck for two packs of tea not enough to go round target practice and he has a shiv two hundred six cool you fuckin' lying give it to me for two packs of tea understood fire fuck just stayed there in the field hospital the Georgian struck third-degree burns at the john dickhead fucking fag for three cig his own vein and that's it." Those were ordinary male stories, each wanted to shout his way through to this foreigner, tell him the whole truth, but all this resulted in broken fragments, nothing but exclamations and *auxiliary words*, "chik-chak-there-opa-fuck-tip-top-dammit-watch-it-Kalashnikov-APC-washing-day-checkpoint-SKS-fuck." Both of them fell silent almost simultaneously. Dushman for some reason made a sign of the cross, and Shukhir grabbed his head in his hands.

Then the boombox again began broadcasting shout-like singing, feminine voices repeating *whaddoyawant, whaddoyawant* in Russian. Karl-Joseph decided this was someone's name, she twisted in all directions in the center of the pub in her Russian sarafan, spinning around her long braid and shaking enormous thighs, this Whaddayawant, an enormous *baba* from faraway steppes, Karl-Joseph made signs for her to come closer, but she pretended not to notice, closing her eyes in ecstasy, up till he grew bored with it and everything ended. Whaddayawant made a deep bow and left the hall accompanied by a storm of applause from the audience.

"I buy . . . bottle . . . for myself," announced Karl-Joseph. "Walnut *horilka*. One." He managed not to mix anything in this treacherous combination of words. But he did not succeed in getting up from his chair and he took out his wallet. "Buy . . . for me . . ." he said to one of them. Dushman went to the counter, slowly and monotonously bargained about something with the sleepy owner, emptied the wallet onto the counter, went through the bank notes—dollars, marks, hryvnias, everything mixed up—presidents, Ukrainian hetmans, cultural figures, commercial rates, profit margins. Together they counted, several times stopping to correct themselves and arguing in soft voices. Finally Dushman returned with a sealed bottle, but Shukhir grabbed it from his hands and hid it in the inside pocket of his jacket. "Mine," Karl-Joseph smiled cunningly. "And for us?" asked Shukhir. "I've bought for you. Already," reminded Karl-Joseph. He now truly strongly wanted to walk back, to reach the resort, share this bottle with her husband and tell him how much he used to love her, then finally fall to sleep in his room, but so deeply he would wake decades later.

"And for us?" repeated Shukhir. From the outset Karl-Joseph liked this Shukhir less than the other guy. Thus he didn't give his wallet with the inscription *GSCHNA-A-ASS!!!* to him but to Dushman: "For you." "All the dough?" "I give you," explained Karl-Joseph firmly. Dushman froze with his mouth open, but Shukhir was quicker: "If the guy gives it to you, take it. Why are you staring at it as if it were a louse?" Dushman took the wallet. Karl-Joseph reached his hand in the direction of Shukhir. "I'll carry it for you," Shukhir assured him. "You might break it." Karl-Joseph thought he was right. Why not bring the two of them to the resort? In any case there'll be someone to hang out with, even if all the others are fast asleep.

"Do you have far to go?" asked Shukhir. "Dzyndzul," Karl-Joseph jerked his head up so abruptly his glasses almost fell off his face. The other two gave a whistle. "A fucked-up place," said Dushman. Shukhir answered with a Russian proverb, "For the drunk a sea is only knee-deep." Karl-Joseph was surprised he too knew about the sea that was here many millions of years ago. "Yes, sea," confirmed Karl-Joseph and, pulling himself together, got up at last. He thought about the restroom and started looking with a clouded gaze for *that particular* hallway. Shukhir read his thoughts and as he was getting up, also with difficulty, said, "You'll take a leak outside. Time to go." "Why not?" agreed Karl-Joseph, moving unsteadily towards the exit. Standing in the doorway, he glanced back at the counter. It seemed to him the owner was incredibly tense. Why do they smile so rarely? Karl-Joseph waved good-bye for the last time—the owner didn't even move—and stepped into the night.

They walked in line along the road above the Stream: Dushman first, a few steps behind him Karl-Joseph, and last came Shukhir whistling something like "Whaddayawant." Something pulled him away, to the side. He stopped often, peering into the moonlit emptiness and thought about ways to deal with this *Australian* simpleton so that he wouldn't have to give him the bottle.

While they were on their way, Karl-Joseph decided he wasn't going to stay here until Sunday. Get up the mountain, finish the booze, pack his shit, get out of here for good. But here he thought about the photo. Yes, he saved for himself the right to keep a small photograph of her, this was a banal passport photo, for he himself never ever photographed her—no one knows why. Pushing through the noise of the Stream and the noise inside his own head, Karl-Joseph shouted at Dushman's back. "You! Give back!" Dushman looked back not understanding anything. "My . . ." Karl-Joseph wrinkled his brow feverishly trying to recall the word. "I gave you." He came up to Dushman with outstretched hand. "What's with you?" Dushman stopped him. Karl-Joseph finally remembered the word, "Wallet!" In this horrible noise it was impossible, with these aches in his chest and his head, to formulate a long and unbearably complicated phrase that in his wallet remained her (and who else's?) photo, he will only take the photo and give back everything else, he gave them all this money, he does not need the money, but he cannot give them that photograph.

His hand reached into Dushman's pocket, and here he got a punch in the face. His glasses were completely smashed, a sharp pain in the bridge of his nose paralyzed everything except a feeling of terrible injustice, horrible and dumb misunderstanding, thus he blindly reached forward, caught the folds of Dushman's jacket with his hands but couldn't go on standing. Dushman at first yielded, then slipped out; the abyss again tilted towards him ("drunk like a skunk," whispered Karl-Joseph trying to chase away misfortune, but it was too late)—from behind Shukhir was already running up to him, and his—Shukhir's—hand, heavy with a dark bottle, flew up for a moment then dropped like a rock on the foolish, pain-ridden head of the foreigner—even before his whole body fell into the bushes along the riverbank.

There were no flashes, no stocky walnut-flavored liquid mixed with blood, no shards of glass, no prolonged scream from him. Instead there was limpness, a slide of the suddenly very heavy body—downward, along rocks, past slippery and prickly thickets of branches, past pinecones and needles, past sandstone outcrops—and finally the waters of the Stream accepted a large Danubian fish with its final secret wish never to return.

"No one among us really knows what life is. But

the saddest thing is that we also have not even the crumb of an understanding about death," read his friends in one of his letters.

12

Many years later Artur Pepa would recall this day as one of the longest in his life. Notwithstanding everything else, it truly was exceptionally long. Naturally, this would happen only if Artur Pepa actually succeeds living through this day. But if he succeeds, he would definitely recall it often.

Undoubtedly, among his memories there should be place for that warm—in fact almost red-hot—wind that made it feel like his head was about to fall off. Also a place for the omnipresent, precipitous thaw, the echo of streams, hums, of thousands of pulsating drips, of the dirty thick slush spreading under his feet. And there would definitely be that room to which they had brought him—really dilapidated, with dirty traces of snowmelt streams on the walls, chunks of fallen-off gray plaster, all sorts of buckets and jars everywhere. Every now and then they were taken into the hallway and then brought back again arranged under the drips from a soggy cracking ceiling. In his memories, Artur Pepa would sit on a stool in the middle of this room and be on the verge of dying from tachycardia and a numb pain in his brachial plexus, confirming the kick with the butt of a machine-gun was not something he had just imagined. There would also be two circles on his wrists left by the handcuffs—at first pale, then blood would rush to them and turn crimson and quietly begin pulsating in unison with the rhythm of the thaw.

But even without these details, Artur Pepa all the same could not doubt that he landed in a holy mess. The circling alone, first of one, then of two, then sometimes even three *siloviki* in civilian clothes—walked around his stool, came closer, moved away, disappeared, and then again started in on another circle—but in such a way that there always remained at least one of them in the room. Later it became clear that this guy was First here, but in the meantime Artur Pepa was not able to distinguish anything of the kind, warily listening in on his increasing and all-too-recognizable cardiovascular fluttering. More than anything else he wanted to get off the stool and sit down on the floor—if the next falling into nothingness came it would be much safer. Beyond that he simply wanted to lie flat on this wet wooden floor—he'd look up at the ceiling, catch the dirty water droplets in his mouth, and perhaps in an hour or two he'd feel better. But he could only dream that—has anyone ever heard of an interrogated suspect lying down while investigators tenderly lowered their heads over him, as if they were nurses looking down at a fallen hero?

Artur Pepa clearly understood he was being interrogated. This followed first and foremost from a multitude, answers that were demanded of him ("your surname, first name, patronymic?" "place of residence?" "place of employment?"—this latter was the most hateful question at all times. There is nothing more foolish than calling yourself a poet out loud in front of strangers—and what sort of *employment* is this, and where is its *place*?). He resorted to the familiar device—innocent games, inessential fudging of facts (*all of us are scribblers after all*). So he called himself a *journalist*, which inevitably led to the unbearably irritating follow-up—"which publication do you represent?" Crumbling, inside, from the accelerating destructive pulsation, he mumbled something about work on the Internet and cooperation with several radio stations, thought of the status of an independent contributor ("independent—is that a freelancer?"); all right, they found the term themselves—*freelancer*, so he nodded in agreement to this *freelancer* of theirs, but he didn't manage to gain even a minute of relaxation. This was as impossible as finding something to lean against—the back of a chair, wall, terra firma—no, stools don't have backs! The same with the investigators—they don't give you a minute to catch your breath, especially when there is less and less air inside you. This is the head, understood Pepa, this is oxygen that doesn't reach where it's supposed to, and they at this very moment want to know themes, payment rates at these radio stations, and who funds the programs,[20] and so on—it turns out they could

20 A typical question during the final years of the Kuchma

immediately check it all. Hence one of them slips out somewhere between two streams of water falling from the ceiling—but this is somewhere on the ultimate periphery of the space visible to Artur; in the foreground is the one who, as it would become clear later, ranks First—specifically, it is his head leaning in unbearably close, covered with nicks and cuts from shaving, and—"what is the purpose of your visit, what are you doing here?"

"The Tavern on the Moon," answers someone else from inside Artur's body. "It is a resort of sorts. On Dzyndzul. I was invited, and am staying there at the moment. It is something like a conference." Here Artur realizes that that other one inside his body has tripped him, the fool, for to the question "what conference, what is its theme, its nature?" he has nothing at all to add—what was in fact written in that letter of invitation? The head of Mr. First takes this under advisement along with Pepa's apparent inability ("some conference! you don't even know yourselves what you're doing there!"). Naturally, he doesn't stop with what he has accomplished: "Who else is staying with you on Dzyndzul?" Artur slowly lists them, although each time he misses someone. He starts for the fourth time, leaving Roma to be mentioned last, but they—both Mr. First and Mr. Second (the latter jumps out

---

presidency, when independent media and the NGOs came to be increasingly oppressed and accused of being financed by the West, especially by the US (author's note).

from behind Artur's back) in unison latch onto the Austrian: "Who is this photographer? How long have you known each other?"—and then, all of a sudden, "Why is your head bandaged?" Artur (or that other one inside him) says something about a duel with swords—and it sounds like yet another helpless bit of nonsense. "Swords?" Artur hears from somewhere by the door. "You had the intention of killing him with a sword?" Ah, yes, Mr. Third has come back—and not empty-handed but with a piece of paper—"no, it was a joke, or rather tomfoolery, fencing with swords," Artur manages to squeeze out of himself a completely unsatisfactory explanation, to which Mr. First, reading the just-brought piece of paper, retorts, "Such highly respected, well-known people—and tomfoolery? You came here for a conference, and instead grab swords and start a fencing match?" "This was an idea that arose out of drunkenness?" "Do you drink a lot?" Mr. First catches him. "Did you at some point sign this letter?"

Why a letter, what sort of letter, Artur fails to understand while he's trying to chase away the thought about the inevitability of symptoms: a tensing on the left side of the chest, mad contraction of heart muscles, increasing anxiety ("do You hear? not now, not now, please!"), ah yes, the letter, an open letter regarding that murdered newspaperman, it is doubtful one could explain everything to them here and now, let's say this is *a type of nonviolent reaction to dangerous so-*

cial tendencies, phew, what an awful formulation—no, this isn't right, it was simply scary to see how Nonentity lets itself play with us and take away into the night the best people, causing them to fall to their death onto the train tracks, "yes, I signed it"—clearly now the stakes are life-or-death. I just don't want to pee myself when I pass out! For that's what they're waiting for—maybe it will be enough for them if he peed himself right here? For this goal they won't stop at anything, and they bark over each other, Mr. Second and Mr. Third, attacking from opposite corners: "And he, by the way, this photographer, he, you should know, industrial sites, clear? And military ones too, clear? Espionage, clear? Agent on assignment—nothing but this!"

Mr. First looked straight into his eyes (again so unbearably close, what does he use to shave?): "You're unwell? Why are you getting pale? Is this a hangover? Where were you the night before last? Why did you resist arrest?"—what can I tell you about all this, you have so many questions and there's only one of me. If only there were a couple hundred of us, those who sign open letters! "I need to lie down somewhere," Artur (or the other one instead of him) says, barely moving his tongue, "give me fifteen minutes; it usually passes, it will let go soon, I will answer all your questions, but not like this, not this moment. I need to get a breath of fresh air." He didn't really know whether he said at least half this, or tried to say it—the internal noise made it difficult to hear his own words. Just not to mention this peeing business—then they would definitely take advantage and not let go of him.

"Will you be able to walk?" asked one of them from the side, somewhere very far away. "Yes," Artur licked his lips and got up from the stool. "Should I perhaps hold you by the arm?"—another voice, also from the side, but close by. "I can do it myself," and he waved his hand and immediately saw himself as he lay face up in that muddy snow, somewhere right in the middle of the courtyard, the back of his neck hitting the dirty melting mass, all the springtime streams of this world, next to the *camouflage*-colored fence and an empty watchtower that squeaks horribly, balancing in gusts of suffocatingly warm wind—this dead territory of the former local military detention site where they dragged him a few hours earlier. (In reality not even an hour had passed, but we remember for him that it was a very long day.) Yes, to lie in this snow and fall asleep, up until the snow melts for good.

Now he shuffled along the corridor, just as dilapidated and wet, with the same water stains on the walls, the same moldy stench, walking inside a moving triangle made by three cops. Thus, any hope for *a step to the left, a step to the right* were right away buried—just as well for they wouldn't let him get out, either to the left or to the right. Although one could see some doors, metallic, with little barred windows, three or maybe even four doors on each side—all this testified to eternal heredity, in these cells they broke the balls of many of our men. This is not just a detention center for soldiers, it wouldn't have arisen like this in the later rocket era—no, this smelled of the 1940s, here they killed with a bullet to the back of the neck, and this was considered a mercy of sorts after all prior cycles with barbed wire, red-hot iron nails and blood-filled boots. This is the brief history of *adapted* buildings of the Carpathian region. One more novel not yet lived through to the end.

Artur Pepa, as much as he could, aimed for another door, the building's entryway. Behind it one could already sense the courtyard and the wind, but there stood one of the cops, the one with a Kalashnikov—or perhaps another one, also with a Kalashnikov, he stood smoking at the threshold, and as soon as he saw the civilian bosses together with the *suspect*, he threw the cigarette butt against the wind, slammed the door and busily clanked the keys ("to the left, to the left," someone from behind managed to break through to Artur's ear and pushed him away from the entry doors, directing him instead into another corridor). Yet another cop walked in front of them, clumsily and for a long time clanked with the keys in some other door, finally the lock yielded, and they almost pushed Artur into another, somewhat drier room, where on top of two absurd-looking writing desks lay the body of Karl-Joseph Zumbrunnen, covered to the waist with old sackcloth.

"Do you know who this is?" Mr. First thundered through all his nicks and cuts. "Neva or Sputnik, Sputnik or Neva?"[21] is what Artur wanted to ask of all those cuts, in iambic pentameter, but under different circumstances. Here he only made two or three steps toward the wall where a huge pile of old yellowish newspapers rose from the floor. He had to lean forward in order not to fall. He stood like this, leaning with one hand against the wall. "Do you know who this is?" two more voices attacked him. "Do you hear what you are being asked? Why are you saying nothing? Why are you getting pale? Do you know who this is?"

Pepa only knew that dead people usually say one of two things—either *a completely different person* or *he looks like he's still alive.* But now he could not say either the first or the second, and it was not the absence of eyeglasses on this longish—yes, rather too elongated—face was the reason.

"It's him," said Pepa. His arm started sliding down the wall but the two of them, Mr. Second and Mr. Third, caught him by the elbows and turned him to face Zumbrunnen's corpse.

"What do you mean, him?" Mr. First did not let go. "Can you *articulately* name him? Do you know this person?"

"Zumbrunnen," Artur heard his faraway voice. "Why is he dead?"

21 Brand names of Soviet-era razors.

"Why is he dead?" repeated all three almost in unison, but each one stressing a different word: *why*, *he*, *dead*. And then, as if from the deepest ambush, both Mr. Second and Mr. Third, into both of his ears: "And you don't know why?"

The stores of air in the lungs and in the brain depleted ever faster, the blows of disaster piled on his head ever more deafeningly, clouding the syncopated tongue-twister of Mr. First, from which Artur caught only a few signals: *anonymous phone call—body on the riverbank—according to preliminary—foreign citizen—numerous physical—the death came approximately at—silver plate with the name—resident of the city of Wien—Vienna capital of Austria—as a consequence of a blow with a heavy object—we do not exclude that—seven to twelve hours in the water—clearly a murder*—and something else that existed between these words and apparently endowed them with more sense and order.

And only then, when Mr. First, abruptly changing his intonation, poked him in the chest with a finger (*we suspect you, we you suspect, you suspect we!*), Artur at last realized this guy was First, so there was no need to turn his haggard head in all directions, resisting their *confess!* He needed to shout his way through to this Mr. First, telling him about his—what's it called?—*alibi, alibi, I have an alibi, I too understand a little about detective novels, I was asleep that night, my wife was next to me, in the same bed, where is she now, I don't feel good, please open the window, she will confirm everything, where did you take her?*

"Alibi?" Mr. First was exceedingly pleased by this word. "Of course, an alibi! That's what it is called. Only why did you walk after them that night? Is this your alibi?"

If only there weren't these blows from the inside, thought Pepa. If only not this climate catastrophe, not these three hundred thirty heartbeats per minute. He made two steps backwards—over yellow newspapers—and his shoulders hit the wall. This helped for a moment. "All right, if it were me, what would be the motive?" Yes, *motive*, *motive*—that's the right word! Let them say what the motive is, these good-for-nothings!

But Mr. First waited exactly for this, and immediately started bending his fingers: *domestic drunkenness, a quarrel due to drunken rivalry, a natural desire to dominate a foreigner, jealousy, is this enough for you?* For it is more than enough for them!

"Jealousy!" Pepa tried to laugh but couldn't. "What jealousy? On what grounds (yes, grounds, that's the right word, *grounds*)!?"

Without tearing away his melancholy gaze from the graying corpse on top of the two desks pushed together, Mr. First answered, "For those grounds that your wife for several years slept with this poor guy. She slept with him, do you understand? They were lovers. And everyone knew about it. Didn't you know about it? No one would believe you didn't know!"

"No one would believe you!" Mr. Second and Mr. Third jumped around in Pepa's eyes, or rather, their mouths and cheekbones—*dozens, hundreds of people knew, everybody knew, everyone talked about this—yes!*

Newspapers started sliding from under his feet. He wanted, as quietly as possible—in order not to anger the other one inside him—to lie on his back. But there was the wall.

"You can't speak? Should we fetch you some water? Are you afraid of corpses? Of death? Maybe you caused it? Why are you silent? What did you do the night before last? Eyes! Why are you rolling your eyes? Confess—you'll feel better!" they jumped in front of each other with their questions. No, the questions jumped out of them, but first and foremost what jumped out of them was this *confess*, and no longer even *confess*, their professional phrase *spill the beans*, and now they tripped over each other barking this *spill the beans*, as if inside each and every one of them was put an Oleh Skrypka[22] of his own, and all of them repeated *spill the beans, spill the beans*, and also *invoke an accident*, and then they brought Roma Voronych—her arrival was timed to the precise minute, they kept her in the corridor long enough to kick the business to the end, so now she was here, but she froze somewhere as if in mid-air, one hand reaching toward his bandaged forehead, the other to Zumbrunnen's eyelids. A *confronta-*

22 A noted Ukrainian folk-rock musician, leader of the band *Vopli Vidopliasova*, a.k.a. *VV.*

tion—that's what it was supposedly called, although in reality it was a silent scream squeezed inside a sob.

Thus, already falling through, he managed to address Someone for the last time: "Hey You, do You hear—I asked You, not now, not now!"—and then, slipping out into complete loneliness and isolation past their incessant unison of spill the beans, past Roma's hand reaching out to him, although suddenly heavy and tense, he managed to give them the finger, right in front of their noses, as if he wanted to underscore something. Mr. Second and Mr. Third stepped aside, he—for the second time in one day!—fell down hard, this time onto the piles of newspapers, onto their dusty crunchy yellowness, onto all these portraits, front page editorials, anniversary telegrams, and letters from workers.

But this time the darkness that swallowed him possessed certain particularities. He was being carried through a tunnel—somewhere far from the melting shell of the world, from the omnipresent moaning of meltwater, from an unbearably languorous springtime in the mountains. He found himself in some wide felt sleeves, and when his body bumped against soft walls it caused no pain. Finally, some unknown pneumatic systems shot him as if out of a cannon, and he flew outside—into other corridors, with other lighting, where countless favor seekers of all kinds crowded by numerous closed office doors. All of them continuously talked to one another but Pepa could not decipher anything other than their desire to get to see *Ylko Ylkovych*. Then he managed to hear his own name uttered by the megaphone voice of a dispatcher. This was, apparently, a summons.

All the others, clearly annoyed, stepped aside and freed a very narrow passage for him—pushed by strong air gusts at his sides and back, stumbling, he finally made the threshold of the *control room*, from the depth of which by the main *workstation*, surrounded on all sides by dozens of *monitors*, a yellowish unstable flickering locked inside the imperceptible, fragile contours of a human being staring him down. Artur Pepa began rubbing his eyes in order to decipher anything in this radiance, but that only made things worse.

"Greetings," said the yellow figure in a male voice that made you think of a golden boy, a komsomol functionary, socially active and eternally youthful, with neatly parted hair and a necktie that slid a little to the side. "Unfortunately I wasn't able to carve out time personally to visit you all at Dzyndzul. You know, so many work commitments, the special atmosphere of anticipating the approaching holidays. And somehow one must, you know, find time to make it everywhere."

He nodded at the monitors. In each of them something was happening—dozens and hundreds of films, plots, short videos, a lightning-fast change of camera takes, moving contours and optical diaphragms, changing faces and bodily movements.

"You are Vartsabych?" Pepa ventured a guess.

"Among other things, yes. I have far too many names for me to list them all here. And why would you need them? I hope you are feeling a little better? How's your breathing?"

Artur Pepa felt a surprising lightness, having left his tachycardia somewhere in the bodily shell that stayed behind, thrown on piles of yellowing newspapers.

"I must express my admiration for citizen Voronych, your wife," continued the host. "She asked me to intercede on your behalf, and I cannot refuse."

"What exactly do you mean?" Pepa wanted a clarification.

"Mobile phone connectivity"—the flickering host again nodded in direction of the monitors, from which clownish-demonic voices immediately screamed, as if specially ordered, "Communicating Liberty—Living in Mobility!" And then, from all the monitors simultaneously, caricaturing one another, "Communicating Cleverly—Living Recklessly! Communicate with Dignity—Living in Frigidity! Communicating Stylishly—Living Stupidly! Communicate Politely—Living Crappily!"—after which all this crowd in the monitors broke into nasty laughter and continued until the host waved at them with an intense yellow ray.

"Fortunately, she had this toy with her. It wasn't

even hers, but belonged to poor Karl-Joseph. Perhaps she hoped he would start dialing his own number? Although in these mountains of ours sometimes your call cannot get through—that's true too. But from the other world—why not? Whatever might be the case, it was good she thought of bringing this thing with her, and even better that she managed to retrieve from its memory my—I mean Ylko Ylkovych Vartsabych's—phone number."

"This is totally stupid," guffawed Pepa.

"I wouldn't say so," said the host in a slightly offended tone. "When those so-called *defenders of law and order* summoned her for an *inquest*, so as quickly as possible to make her *spill the beans* on the case of the inconvenient Austrian corpse, she still did not know anything about the murder—just like you. But she knew she had to save you—they had punched you in the chest with the butt of a machine gun as if you were the worst criminal scum, you fell down into the snow. This was all she saw, and then they took her to the so-called *dacha*, the former insane asylum for women, where she was kept in a locked cold cell, and here she had time to think, quite appropriately of me, she spent a good hour trying to remember my phone number, then realized that Karl-Joseph ought to have it saved in his phone, and he did, although the entry was not under the letter V or W, but under B, as if I were some sort of Bartsabytsh . . . What can I say, this Karl-Joseph Zumbrunnen was an incredibly absent-minded man! Good thing he once wrote down the PIN for his phone for her—as you understand, their relations were rather intimate . . ."

The ambitious komsomol functionary imperceptibly transformed into a gossipy lady enthralled with her own witty tongue.

"She called you, and?" Pepa reminded about the thread of the plot, extricating the komsomol functionary from the gossipy lady.

"And she told me the following . . ."

Then there was a ring and *it* spoke with Roma's telephone voice:

"Mr. Vartsabych, I don't know you and you don't know me, but they have seized me and my husband, we are your guests here after all, could you not do something for us, perhaps they'll listen to you, everyone here keeps saying how powerful you are, they're going to kill him, they're going to kill him . . ."

"And this was what she was saying in a passionate woman's voice," *it* continued, having turned off the telephone version of Roma, "especially on and on about my omnipotence, up until I said, 'All right, I'll somehow *intervene*.'"

This word definitely could not belong to a gossipy lady—this was again the activist with neatly parted hair.

"And then she started crying into the phone, and just in time because a female police major came from the district center to search her, and they took away the cell phone, but they were unable to unlock it—their professional training levels are far too low, any specialists with good heads on their shoulders leave for private business ventures, and some even skip abroad—who am I to bust my gut for them for twenty bucks a month?" (Pepa noticed how for a moment Vartsabych turned into a small-town computer genius with airs of a super-tough hacker.) "So they now stare at this cell phone like Arctic savages. Just think of it—they are trying to frame you for the killing, some Pinkertons they are! Parody of a parody! You, a killer?"

"And me too," sighed Pepa, as other depths of their history were beginning to open up for him. "All of us are killers to a small extent. But truly, who did this?"

In the far left monitor, in the sixth row from the top, a large cloudy eye crisscrossed with blood vessels blinked at him. Eventually the camera *panned back*, and the eye turned out to be placed on a worn-out stubbly mug. Actually, there were two mugs—both of them frightened and drooling, they rushed back and forth in the space of the monitor like two flat fish, as if trying to break out of it.

"They are already being made to spill the beans," commented Vartsabych, now a Bull Terrier and a giant brute. "Two morons from the neighborhood, no one special, dirt under the fingernails, riffraff. Got to his dough—to them it looked like a huge sum—and felt like scoring some chicks, having a party. Some asshole—you know him—squawked to them about little Lilya and Marlena in Chortopil, their addresses and phone numbers. So they went, this and that, the usual business, then one of the girls saw Dushman had our Charlie's wallet and remembered that it was Charlie's, purely by accident, it made an impression on her, a fancy foreign wallet with various bells and whistles. And she thought they'd stolen it or found it lying on the ground, imagine. Then they have a drunken quarrel, the morons blew into a rage, abusing the girls, grabbing Marlena and choking her, the two of them together, Lilya roared, calling my racketeer guys—so and so, two morons give themselves airs, throw foreign money left and right, my guys get there in a flash, gave them a good thrashing, you know, and made them talk—aha, so they did bump off that furriner, crazy shit! You know, my guys don't get involved in business like this, they passed the two assholes off to the cops, let them deal with them in their own way. And so now they're spilling the beans, the morons, who do they think they are, bumping off a guest of mine . . ."

"And they *bumped him off* in a literal sense," interfered for a moment a sickly high school nerd, jumping out of the yellow flickers in front of the Bull Terrier. "The body was knocked off and fell into the stream. Here the etymology works with the semantics: they hit him on the head and bumped him off . . . But in reality, they are only an instrument."

At the far-left monitor, the sixth row from the top, flashed pictures of fingerprinting, distorted mugs of the interrogators and interrogated, shaking hands, moans, madness, gnashing teeth.

"But in reality, they are only an instrument," repeated the first voice, Vartsabych-1.

And everyone else (the gossipy lady, the pampered komsomol activist-turned-banker, the Bull Terrier, the virtuoso hacker) confirmed the yellow flickers:

"In reality, only an instrument."

Artur Pepa stayed silent for a little while, watching the flashing monitors. It seemed to him he was already inside the secret, the flash of realization will come any moment now.

"Why did you need his death, what for?" he asked all of a sudden, surprising himself at the question.

"And what is any death for?" answered a maniac inventor from a wheelchair.

"For eternal rejuvenation," answered a circus dwarf with beard down to his knees laughing meanly.

"To honor Antonych," reminded the nerdy schoolboy. "For the sake of his eternal return."

"And so your daughter, pardon me, stepdaughter, would finally free herself from the pressure of virginity," the gossipy lady again made her way to the front.

"And citizen Voronych, your wife," the pampered komsomol activist elbowed everyone aside once again, "in choosing between you and her lover, would choose you after all, and not, let's say, Orpheus . . ."

"Who? What did you say?" Pepa asked, sensing how his lips suddenly turned dry.

"Orpheus, of course!" shouted everyone in one voice—the komsomol activist, the Bull Terrier, the nerd, the maniac inventor, and the circus dwarf, and the old-fashioned lady, and the virtuoso hacker, and a whore, and a tramp, and a hawk-nosed young witch, a she-wolf, a crow, a snake, and even a dream, for all of them were Vartsabych, or more exactly, that intense yellow substance by the controls.

"And you hadn't guessed?" it asked from the inside.

"So it was a ritual murder?"

"All murders are ritual murders," it answered. "But you are correct in that this was, for me, an act of my free creativity."

"So you're the devil?" Pepa decided to push straight ahead, although he wasn't sure whether he was heard, so dry had everything become inside him.

"I am an author," it answered cheerfully, mockingly. "Or at the very least, the copyright holder. And this is precisely why now the time comes for me to join the action. In other words, now I'll become a *deus ex machina*. Do you remember by any chance Zumbrunnen's phone number?"

But Pepa did not remember anything of the kind, staring intently at the far-right monitor in the thirteenth row from below—with that very room, the fussing about of the *siloviki*, a body covered with sackcloth on two writing desks pushed together, with Roma, and with one more body, his own and another unconscious.

"All right, I'll remember without your help," it shook with laughter by the monitors and started dialing an incredibly long series of numbers.

From the monitor there was a ring, and Mr. First grabbed from the table the phone taken from Roma during the search—his *hello* sounded slightly wary and surprised.

"Major Voshyvliuk?" it spoke from the controls. "This is Ylko Ylkovych Vartsabych troubling you. You've heard of me, right?"

Mr. First lost his breath for a second, but he managed to produce his disciplined "Yessir, Parshyvliuk here" and then bent in half, overwhelmed by the otherworldly tirade of the Master.

"Parshyvliuk, how are things? Everything cool? How's the mood before the holidays? OK? Are there problems? But who is without problems these days? Listen, Voshyvliuk, here's why I'm calling. Your guys over there got too excited, grabbed two of my guests for no good reason, a husband and a wife—alleging they bumped off some Australian or something. So, Pereshyvaniuk, my guys purely by accident found the real ones. No, the ones who did in fact rub out the guy. No, they've already passed them on to your guys to work with. They're already spilling the beans. So, how about letting my guests go? Do you understand me, major?"

He managed to bend down even further, and then repeated thrice his "No problem, Mr. Vartsabych, Sir."

"So," said the god from a machine contently, "let my guests go, I'll come get them them there, all right? And time to go home, pal, it's already Saturday, time to bless the Easter loaf, the eggs and all that stuff. And to you too, Zashybliuk, go, take it easy, we'll talk next week."

The monitors went dark one after another, going downward from left to right, all the movies, plots, short videos, froze all the holiday eve stories with distorted camera perspectives, human grimaces and gestures.

"Artur Pepa?" it said thunderously from the controls.

"Yes," he said, stepping back towards the exit.

"You have been released. You can go. Good-bye."

"Coronary spasm," Artur Pepa heard somewhere above him. "Note the sweating," added someone else. "Yes, it's letting go," added another voice knowingly. Roma was the closest to him. She carefully undid the now-gray bandage on his head, and wiped his brow and temples with a wet sponge, so he'd returned to this driest of rooms, and although at the moment it was very hard to judge by the color of the skin who of these two men was more dead, Artur Pepa did in fact feel he had been released (the darkness grew thinner and gradually transformed into a flashing, there appeared the first contours and colors, the ringing in the ears quieted down, the sound of water draining outside the wide-open window, lungs rediscovered the happy capacity for air and—what was most pleasing now—this abundant sweat of relief, the sign of salvation—here is another deferral, another greeting for you, motherfucker).

Then everyone went out somewhere and went back in, for some moments there remained two of them in the room, Zumbrunnen and him, then Roma said the car was already waiting, *would you be able to get up and walk*, asked Mr. First compassionately. Artur Pepa got up from the floor, the newspapers that had stuck to his back fell down with a rustling sound, then they gave him his raincoat and the Easter egg taken away during the search, he put it in his pocket with a mechanical gesture. In the corridor that very cop on duty with a Kalashnikov carefully helped him by the elbow, but beyond the threshold Pepa impatiently freed himself from his care and dashed behind the corner of the building. He urinated at length, with infatuation, with his clear stream boring something like an opening in the soft clay newly freed from snow. Having done its job, the warm wind now ran away somewhere further. Spring exploded all around them with more and more scents. Pepa buttoned his fly. From behind him came the final, somewhat guilty parting words of Mr. First ("if I were you I'd see a doctor—

you know, two whole minutes without consciousness, this is no joke"). He crossed the courtyard of the former slaughterhouse, yeah, military detention center, in the direction of the fence and the exit to the road. Already by the gate, half fallen off the hinges and half-open, he caught up with Roma and asked,

"You slept with him, right?"

Notably, they were provided the same Jeep-style car with the same engine of a military-issue truck. And the driver too could very well have been the same—big ears, strong neck, black leather jacket. And the same sign above the car, "Charitable Program *Heroes of Business for the Heroes of Culture*." And now there were only two of them there, somewhere far in the back, sitting as far as possible from the guy at the wheel—true *heroes of culture*, Ms. Roma Voronych and her husband Artur Pepa.

The road was getting ever bumpier. The back seat kicked them up into the air more and more often. Roma gave her husband a worried glance a few times. Along the road walked locals with Easter baskets in their hands, the big-eared driver overtook and passed anything that came up in the road, the passersby dashed to side ditches and the rocky shoulders, trying to save themselves from streams of dirt from his wheels. There was not a trace of snow left, only broken poles and trees testified to the nighttime storm. When they again crossed the wildly roaring river and continued along the muddy forest road, Roma grabbed the sleeve of his coat.

"Why did you ask about this?"

Pepa woke from his daze and answered—not so much to her but to the forest beyond the window, to all its branches that nervously hit the car's sides,

"I wanted to know what one feels in situations like this."

She did not understand, but he did not try to explain—about the body that made love to her, about seeing it dead, about immobility and the writing desks pushed together. He had no words to explain this.

Women always cry when they look at the dead. Pepa had experience to prove this.

"I am the one to blame for everything," said Roma a little later. "You should leave me. I bring death. He is already the second, you know?

"I know. And this is why I am going nowhere. I'd like to be at least third."

She did not appreciate the joke, if this was a joke.

A little more time went by, allowing Pepa to hurl into the air,

"Do you still love him?"

"I feel sad that he is now alone. All of us will stay on here, tomorrow is a holiday, and he will no longer be there."

"All of us will stay, but not for too long," reminded Pepa.

He took her by the elbow, and making his way

through to her ear, somewhere between the first sob and the first shaking of the shoulder, he breathed the only thing he could,

"Although we do not know anything about this."

Surprisingly, she calmed down.

Then they remained in the middle of the forest by themselves: the big-eared desperado turned his car around stuntman-style at the same clearing and let them out in the midst of wilting anemones. As a good-bye he rattled off something like "you go about seven kilometers, you'll get there in about two hours, tomorrow after three o'clock they'll bring the copter, pack your things and wait, they'll come and get you in time, before the fire," then slammed the door and went back to where he came from. Far above, covered in sunset light, Dzyndzul stood covered in snowy spots, waiting for their return, with an indistinct dot of the resort on the very ridge.

They walked uphill, from time to time giving each other a hand and holding each other in slippery spaces. When they reached the lower juniper thickets, they stopped to catch their breath a little. Pepa looked at the mute mountain peaks and said the first thing that came into his head,

"In reality, everything could be much better than we think."

IV.

Wrapping Up

Karl-Joseph Zumbrunnen looked at Karl-Joseph Zumbrunnen. The second of the two was a corpse lying on two writing desks pushed together, covered up to the waist with old burlap. The first, however, was now a different, infinitely finer being. This night, the moment of his liberation, had arrived. It was strange for him to see himself from the outside, yet not in a mirror: in fact, this had to do with the meeting of the two greatest mysteries of existence, Death and the Self.

Karl-Joseph, the one who had separated himself, stayed somewhere higher—perhaps, on the ceiling. In any case, he saw from above what so recently had been his body: the first signs of decomposition—a few spots on the skin. Its manifestations to come later were likewise perfectly predictable—subcutaneous emphysema, cadaveric green, detachment of the epidermis, formation of blisters with fetid watery discharge. Karl-Joseph knew all this, although he had never studied forensic anatomy. But now he knew and understood countless things.

Did he sense regret? Did he feel embarrassed in this darkness pierced with moonlight coming from outside?

That is unknown. The only thing known for certain is that he didn't want to and couldn't remain hovering here for long—the Moon was calling him. In the morning the body was to be dispatched to Chortopil for medical and legal examination, although the autopsy itself couldn't take place before Monday: the likelihood that an anatomist would cut up a stiff on Holy Easter Sunday was zero. Monday was highly doubtful as well. Perhaps on Tuesday or—even better—after the holy days, on Wednesday. Thus, in the morning, he was only to be taken to a *refrigeration chamber* to stop the *process of saponification*. But still Karl-Joseph saw how it would end: the pale light of an argon lamp; the chilly metallic clanking of sharp objects (coldness is sterility, and sterility coldness!); the painstaking filling out of the protocol in a special journal, hand-stitched and sealed; the monotonous recording of anomalies and potentially incurable diseases, as well as the extraction from the dissected body of various river pebbles, two or three darkened aspen leaves, and pale slime-covered larvae and chrysalides. And then—Karl-Joseph could clearly see this as well—the cynical and crude sewing up. This was when a torn-off piece of intestine would be quickly stuffed into the groin or somewhere else. Karl-Joseph now could see the thick coarse thread and sewing awl, as long as half a pencil, and the morgue orderly not entirely of a sound mind (*twenty-nine years of experience at the same job!*), with an enormous bust, yellow eyes, and formalin-smelling breath.

As a photographer, Karl-Joseph loved darkness no less than light.

But now he acquired countless new possibilities: to see; to know; to feel. And also to pass through, for his structure was now finer than the finest of material structures. Without any effort he emerged outside through the ceiling and the roof of the former military prison. He rose slightly above its roof and now could see it all, together with the two cops on duty who presently were "letting go" in the guard annex (state-issue rags thrown here and there; a classic rectangular electric heater, white-hot; a table littered with glasses, half-empty bottles, leftover food, cigarette butts; the Vesna tape recorder; two loaded Kalashnikovs leaning against the wall; and two cops, sweaty from sleep, on the same narrow bed, in nothing but long johns—no, not gay: cousins, relatives, Ivan Mykuliak and Stefan Drakuliak). They were to guard this corpse till tomorrow morning. They were, in fact, guarding it.

Karl-Joseph for the first time sensed something like a wondrous painful lightness when he succeeded—again without effort—pushing higher and reaching the proverbial altitude of bird flight. He found himself in a stream of moonlight, dense and somehow even palpable. The moon looked full and therefore slightly menacing, although in reality it had reached its fullness back on Wednesday. Now it was already in decline, and this was well known to all the church astronomers. And to Karl-Joseph too. He swirled fish-like in a stream of light and for an indeterminate moment (time for him had already turned into something else) he froze. No eyeglasses needed, he thought, no binoculars, magnifying lenses, or extra diopters! He now saw all the way through and into the depths—across the entire expanse open to his eye.

For instance, how the grass grows, how oil flows through pipelines, how fish swim in rivers and streams, both with and against the current. Skeletons on the floor of filled-in caves and skulls at the bottom of abandoned wells. Innumerable long-haul trucks frozen in endless lines at border crossings with half-alive, half-suffocated Pakistanis (this time he was certain they were Pakistani and not Bangladeshi) lying still in rows under the floor.

He also saw thousands of churches lit from the inside, across the entire country.

Karl-Joseph made a small circle above the valley of the River and, without hesitation, set in the direction of Transylvania. This cannot be explained—one can only accept this as a given. The dead usually travel westward. The memory suddenly produced the children's game of pilot, and for some reason also the lightness of jumping into water and the greenness of the warm river cove near the mill.

But can this be called memory?

He reached the Mountain Range above the Dzyndzul alpine meadow and—nothing could stop him, not even the call of the Moon—he descended sharply. This turned out to be stronger not only than the Moon but also his very self: not all ties had been broken. He rustled above the snow-dusted tops of juniper bushes, bypassed the ski jumping hill, and arrived directly at the building of the resort. Something *pulled* him here, this was his Place, this chimerical building with porches, terraces, turrets, and its dozens of windows. But only two of them were lit. Zumbrunnen thrust himself, glued himself to one of them, pressing against its impenetrable triple-pane insulated coldness.

Behind the window the room of Kolomea Voronych. She reclined on an unmade sofa bed, scribbling nonstop in a formerly thick notebook, tearing out text-filled pages one after the other. This was already page one hundred thirteen of her letter to the disappeared friend—the one who had left yesterday at sundown.

"I know," wrote Kolomea on page 113, "You are split in two, and because of that, eternal. You, who only a night ago were still here and took me so magnificently [she crossed out the last four words] tenderly liberated me from this brand, from this sticky stain—I mean my vanished virginity—so, You are the one for whom I waited all my life [she crossed out the last three words] I won't say how long. But at the same time You're different: a heavy, balding, old, Hobbit-like ancient bullshitter [last word crossed out] chatterer. For as I know now, You exist in two versions. Young—that's when you are eternally twenty-seven. That was apparently the age of That Poet on the night of his death. And old—when yours is the age That Poet would have been today. If he hadn't died young, of course. Just don't tell me it isn't so and that I am off target again! I saw you step down from the terrace toward the Ambassadors of the Night! They hid in the dark bushes waiting for you. You think I hallucinated? [The entire sentence crossed out.] And when You looked at me for the last time over your shoulder—it was not You! [the last two words and the exclamation mark crossed out], aha, it was that professor, for half a second he burst through Your shell: You and him are one and the same, I know. I think because of this you can be both here and on the Moon. For in reality we are allowed only one thing: to be either here, or on the Moon. We are now forever apart, aren't we? By the way, I know that now You're already there. Ha! I saw You dissolve in that wretched [last word crossed out] moonlight; I'm so sick and tired of it! And then the Ambassadors of the Night flew out as three owls from their hiding place in the bushes. You rose in a ray of moonlight, and they flew above you and slightly behind, like a kind of escort."

She had to write the word "escort" with a hyphen: "esco-rt." Two letters spilled over onto the following page, and page 113 was resolutely torn out and tossed on the floor next to the sofa—joining its 112 predecessors. Karl-Joseph guessed that what was about to come next concerned him.

"You know," she wrote on, "I'm writing to You now, but how would I be able to deliver this letter to you? For You will never come back to me—it's clear. You have so many—countless—untouched girls. An entire Eden full of girls! As for the ordinary postal service, it's hopeless—You know very well how slow the mail is between us and the Moon. In fact, it takes one's entire life. Although I don't give a flying [four words crossed out] am not that concerned about it: I will all the same finish this letter, bring it to the final three dots: I am sure it will be read. Also, we have news. Last night mom and Pepa reported that this Austrian photographer guy got killed here. I think about him more and more often. [She crossed out the last sentence.] He is no longer in this world—and I, it turns out, didn't know anything, anything at all about him! And now it looks like I will never know. What sort of guy was he? Why did he come here, what force dragged him in our direction? No, it's not like that—it's not that I'm thinking about him, I am tripping because I feel like he is somewhere here. For example, behind this very window. I close my eyes tightly, turn toward the window, and then count to ten: *one—two—three—four—five—six—seven—eight—nine—nine-and-a-half—nine-and-three-quarters—al-*

most-ten—almost-almost-ten—ten! I open my eyes—behind the window there's no one and nothing, only the night. But he's somewhere here. Perhaps I don't yet have the permission to see him? But through him I understood what the twelfth circle is. It is the circle of eternity, the beginning and end rolled into one, Alpha and Omega, all of us and each one of us . . ."

Karl-Joseph Zumbrunnen, quite appropriately, at the moment of *almost-almost-ten* dove into the windstream and disappeared from her window. Clearly he did not want to get caught. Because of this he never learned what the twelfth circle was. In general, the letter written by Kolomea amused him by its high pathos, this eternal feature of the young and living. Besides, he remembered, this girl read too much fantasy fiction and listened to Jim Morrison. This was nothing but mysticism, decided Karl-Joseph.

In reality he had long wanted to go to another window—and you can guess why. In just as resolute a fashion he thrust himself against it, gluing his face to the glass.

And his face now saw the room of the Pepa-Voronych couple dimly lit by a night-light. Artur and Roma, it seemed, were asleep. They slept the way people who love one another sleep. That is, so tightly, so together, so closely, and so breathing in unison, as do the people who sleep together out of love. This was an inexpressibly deep sleep. Karl-Joseph did not even try to call *her*. The night-light only showed that at some time prior they could have been making love. The giant face as big as the entire window frame, on the other side of their room turned for a moment into a mask of pain. It appeared he could still sense *that*.

Breakup; breakup . . . Farewell; loss; breakup.

He pushed himself as strongly as he could away from the window. And then, resolutely piercing the night air, rushed up high. And only looked down again at the Mountain Range, milky white from the snow and the streams of moonlight, when the building of the resort diminished to the size of a useless mole on the world's skin.

No radar, of course, could detect his aerial movement across the border. Already on the Transylvanian side, Karl-Joseph for the first time understood *who* always crowed like a rooster here. He barely managed to escape from a whirlpool of air that turned out to be a powerful turbulence of astral energy. Dozens, if not hundreds of souls spun in this space-time warp, unable to escape it. Most likely the majority of them were fated to remain forever in this centrifuge of sorts. Karl-Joseph managed to slip through a cylinder of vacuum between two cyclones heading for each other, both of which could have sucked him in until the end of time.

Only after that did Zumbrunnen finally set on his flight path. On his left he passed Suceava, from which came the sounds of a choir singing matins, mixed with the trombone roars of a Gypsy wedding and the train whistles at the station Suceava Nord. On his right, Bistriţa and Piatra Neamţ. He doggedly followed the Carpathians and with all his strength strove not to divert from the rocky outcrops on the mountain ranges. On the Transylvanian side there was no snow at all, and spring was already so far ahead that, it seemed, orchards would burst into bloom any minute now. Humans stayed further below, this high country generally did not belong to them. Between humans and mountain ranges spread the forests. Karl-Joseph did not only remember this, he heard every stream in the undergrowth, saw each tree separately and all the trees put together. He was capable of even greater stuff: could hear every leaf on every tree, heard buds burst open and moss breathe, and—without any strain—he heard the annual rings grow on tree trunks, and also the hearts of both hedgehogs and wolves beating. He noticed in front of him the first outlines of the Transylvanian Alps but, before reaching them, he made a sharp turn westward. Yes, westward, definitely westward—away from sunrise.

At first, an array of possibilities opened before him. He could, for example, take the shortest route, through Slovakia. There were plenty of mountains if he absolutely needed to see mountains beneath himself. He could go slightly to the south and stay close to the Slovak-Hungarian border—if he preferred not the mountains but the sandstone hills and the vineyards. He could in fact cross this border, in a manner unnoticeable not only to the border guards but also to himself, and emerge over Zemplín, all green on the maps and then, drifting not so much to the south as to the west, finally reach the Danube slightly higher than Budapest. In fact, the Danube was inescapable, both in the Slovak and Hungarian version of the flight path. And thus bridges, barges, and reed-covered shores all the same would be waiting for him.

But if he desired not the shortest but the longest route from the very beginning, he could set on a northbound course and cross Poland. This would mean he had inevitably have to fly above Lviv. Karl-Joseph loved this city with more strength and honesty than the majority of its inhabitants. Now it is possible to say out loud, not hiding the truth any longer what during his life had to remain a secret: Karl-Joseph often saw Lviv in his dreams. In them, fulfilling assignments from vaguely indeterminate superiors, he entered dilapidated secret dwellings, and then went to underground caverns cluttered with thousand-year-old junk: his task was to find water—the hidden riverbed, the river itself. In the final such dream he did find it, but this led to a rupture of the locks underneath the opera house. Zumbrunnen could still remember how the dirty foam rushed in from all directions, how he stood in it waist deep, unable to move, how—despite being a fish—he ended up being fully covered by it and suffocated.

And still, this time from the outset he was moving away from Lviv. No one would ever be able to answer why. Perhaps, since his childhood days, used to drawing on maps, he decided to close the half-oval of the Carpathians with the half-oval of his own flight? Create a virtual oval named after himself around the center of Europe?

Perhaps there was another reason. Maybe this was a tunnel—*his* personal tunnel—and he simply did not have another choice.

Everything is for the better in this best of possible existences.

The same night, in Lviv, director Yarchyk Volshebnik, utterly drunk, crushed and miserable, by some miracle found himself at a train station where in the back pocket of his pants he scrounged for the last small change to buy the right to enter the *extra comfort* waiting room. In reality no comfort, let alone extra, was to be found, but a clear advantage consisted in the absence of the insufferable gypsies, who of late seemed to be following him everywhere. Yarchyk Volshebnik threw his hefty body onto the train station bench and tried looking around in search of human compassion. Focusing his exhausted and wet eyes did not produce a result. But as soon as he took out a half-finished bottle of Vartsabych's Herbal Balsam from the deep side pocket of his cargo pants, a young soldier sat down next to him. The soldier turned out to be a deserter waiting for the first morning commuter train to get home for Easter.

"You know," Yarchyk said to the deserter, while the latter took a swig of the dark foul liquid from the bottle, "you know . . . I get in on Friday, right? Film the clip, cash in the envelope, right? Everything's cool, right?"

He was now telling this story for the fortieth time. The soldier understood almost nothing, but pretended to listen.

"You know," Volshebnik went on, "I have a good night's sleep, then have breakfast, and go to watch the tape—and there's nothing! Imagine, man, nothing! Diddly fucking squat! Everything lost, man! The hottest video of the season, definitely in the top ten. So sexy—the best, man! You know, man, the best!"

He sighed, then took another swig from the bottle, wiped his tears. During the day dozens of random strangers had already listened to this story. At first it seemed easy to understand, but gradually it became murkier. Now too it was getting hard to grasp:

"Then, you know, I reach for the cash—there was a stack this thick, and all of it in bucks, man! And what do you think? I look into the envelope, and there, you know, is a pile of scrap paper, all covered in shit: an entire pile of ass wipes! Man, it was a pile this thick, large enough to wipe two hundred asses, man!"

It had already been verified earlier: as soon as Yarchyk reached this place in the story, he broke down. This time too, he started howling, "The tape's empty, and the honorarium is shit!"

By then the soldier had long been quietly cursing the hairy dumbass. The booze in the bottle was long gone, and listening over and over to "it was all those gypsies, man, it's the gypsies—the tape's empty, and honorarium is shit" was getting to be too much. But still, he only cursed quietly: two hours remained until the first commuter train that morning, and there was *fucking nothing to do.*

Thus here and now we have the final opportunity to see them up close.

For instance: Volshebnik, much battered by life, his exhaustion taking its toll. His speech getting softer and more incoherent; he swallows entire words and phrases ("honorarium fucking stolen, Austrian guy bumped off, tape covered in shit"). Finally, he abruptly dozes off, as if falling into a pit. For now the soldier tolerates this head leaning on his shoulder.

A few minutes pass—and the director Yarchyk Volshebnik, without opening his eyes, notices: taking advantage of the moment when everyone, including the ticket lady and the security guards are fast asleep, bent figures in dirty rags quietly entering the *extra comfort* waiting room. They noiselessly move towards him, open their switchblades. His horror rises to his throat. He cringes. The gypsies raise their knives at him. Yarchyk Volshebnik screams, waking the entire train station.

Karl-Joseph Zumbrunnen could hear this scream

if he really wanted. Although he was now moving away, not only from Lviv but also from the memories of Lviv. Presently, he recognized the city of Braşov underneath himself, and a flock of crows covering the belfry, the spire, the roof of the Black Church. Apparently recognizing him as a fresh astral body, the crows hurled themselves frenetically into the surrounding space. A turn in the sky above Braşov resulted in Karl-Joseph flying along a southerly range of the Transylvanian Alps. And just for him perhaps, the moonlight was getting brighter. He saw each valley and each rocky outcrop with such clarity as if he had invented them himself. That night parties had been held at castles and palaces, but now they were winding down. Ladies' translucent, pale exposed shoulders dusted with lunar specks now wrapped in furs. The similarly pale gentlemen bowed to one another, their medallions and monocles glistening. Refined groups of aristocrats gracefully took their seats in horse-drawn chaises and carriages in order to get through serpentine mountain roads to their residences well before sunrise and, having drunk a glass of nicely aged blood for better sleep, took their places in coffins.

On Karl-Joseph's right remained Sighişoara and its labyrinthine streets. Soon thereafter the silhouette of the citadel, the medieval arcade connecting the Upper and Lower Town, and the Lutheran Cathedral leading him to recognize Sibiu (well, yes, he had never been there during his lifetime, but he was now able to recognize any building, street, or square of any city or suburb in this world—this was one of the advantages of his new abilities—and thus he repeated to himself several times the words "Sibiu, Hermannstadt"). Then the rapid emergence of an enormous cloud of mixed poisonous odors—yes, of course, petrochemicals; and sulfur, definitely sulfur—led him to remark that also on the right, but at a greater distance, about one hundred to one hundred fifty human miles, he was bypassing Timişoara.

Transylvania generally reeked of oil, and everything in this world reeked of it.

Sighişoara, Timişoara—these names sounded like an incantation. This was one more thread still not torn—his childhood and the childlike fondness of incantations.

But naturally there were not only castles, not only market squares of toy-like old German towns. What there was the most of was emptiness. The second place was taken by iron and concrete, by nine-, ten-, and twelve-story slums, working class neighborhoods covered in rag-like linens on clotheslines, studded with satellite dishes. Then came city dumps, littered industrial spaces, vacant lots, miners' settlements. Everything exactly in its place.

Close to the Serbian border the mountains gave way to a plain. Karl-Joseph sighed and looked for the last time at this fatal land, the Carpathians.

At that moment, or perhaps a moment later, Artur Pepa and Roma Voronych woke for a second, their lips met each other's. Then falling back into the same episode where the pause button had been pressed, they unfolded their embrace and turned away from each other. Part II of two persons sleeping together is always a temporary distancing, a return to the individual shell with the saved signal from depths of a slowed-down consciousness: this is only the middle of the night! This is only the middle of our lives.

It is doubtful a statistic exists as to how many human couples sleep together at one and the same moment in time. It is even more difficult to find out how many of them sleep together out of love, how many out of habit, how many out of exhaustion, how many out of calculation, and how many out of despair. It is absolutely impossible to figure out the proportion of opposite-sex and same-sex couples among them. Thanks to Karl-Joseph, we have found this night not only cop cousins Mykuliak and Drakuliak sleeping in the same bed. We also saw Volshebnik leaning his hairy head on the soldierly shoulder of the young deserter.

And in the dorm of the Chortopil Art and Culture school, Lilya and Marlena slept in the same bed. And this was nothing like the *lesbian shows for lonely romantic men* one may find in some classifieds. This was inevitability itself. This was love.

Now they pressed tightly against one another: two *gal pals*, a dyed blonde and dyed raven-haired, only one of them had a bruise under one eye and a loose third tooth, and the other had a hickey under her left breast and several bruises on her neck and forearms.

Nothing could ever separate them. Except perhaps a Schengen visa.

Above Vojvodina Karl-Joseph finally reached the Danube. First he veered to the left towards Novi Sad, but the smell of dirty bandages quickly pushed him northward. A year or so ago this place had been fiercely bombed, thus he was unable to see a good half of the bridges over the Danube. Things did not look any better in terms of riverboat traffic: his expectation of moving ship lights proved to be terribly naïve. However, Karl-Joseph still decided to follow the path of the river further and further to the northwest. Inside him still were remnants of the Danubian idealism of his recent life. Or more precisely, this was already only a memory of the memory, on the level of the finest cell structures of his present *body*. So, for a while he moved upstream above the Danube, but right from the start this path turned out to be packed with angels moving in the opposite direction. It was not like they created any barriers for him— every time he simply had to explain who he was and where he was coming from. This, first of all, was an unfamiliar experience (like reporting to a corporal in the army), and second, it was a bit humiliating. Somewhat soon he figured this would continue all the time as long as he followed the path of the Danube: this the so-called Danubian Angelic Corridor, a site of regular patrolling, a zone of special attention. Therefore Karl-Joseph sharply turned westward. This happened somewhere above the Hungarian border. Next came Pécs, where yet another flock of crows reacted to him with nervous cries, circling worriedly round the minarets. Then he flew over the great emptiness of the Hungarian Puszta where night lingered—all the time aiming northwestward. Yes, he was running away from daylight, for he already belonged, already *almost* belonged to a Different Light.

But in the meantime earthly electric lights were becoming more and more numerous. The further to the west, the more he encountered well-lit highways, train tracks, embankments, Lake Balaton all aglow with a garland of searchlights, reflectors, and lighthouses. Then after Sopron one could see an all-encompassing sparkle, it was getting closer, it expanded like Western Civilization—well, yes, that was exactly it: Austria, an integral part of the Empire of Electric Light. Only Neusiedler See still beckoned at him with its black longish spot, and he was able to sense the saltiness of its lukewarm waters, the rustling of its reeds—in general, this night he could feel anything and everything. But already not like that, *not like that*—and this is the saddest thing.

He approached Vienna from the southeast. For

this he needed no compass or astrolabe: the scattering of multicolored lights below, surrounded by a giant curve of light with two irregular ovals at its ends, confirmed that below him was Schwechat. At this hour there was still nothing happening—dozens of larger and smaller planes simply spent the night in the airfield. True, the UPS6612 from Cologne was already descending, while the OS3016 from Bangkok was twenty-one minutes late. After that a veritable kerfuffle was about to begin: Liège, Copenhagen, Sydney via Kuala-Lumpur, and then—believe it or not—Odessa via Lviv. Then departures for Budapest, Istanbul, Athens, and Frankfurt. And then more flights each minute.

For some time Karl-Joseph kept up with the Cologne flight, and managed to peek through one of the windows at the half-empty cabin with a large group of Indians in orange turbans (what on earth do they need in Vienna at such an early hour?), but bearing in mind the ever-increasing light coming from the eastern side of the sky, *behind his back*, he dove sideways from the wing of the Boeing and continued his own flight path, independent of any airlines.

Besides, it would be completely erroneous to imagine Karl-Joseph a kind of anthropomorphic plane, with horizontal trunk and legs, arms spread like wings, and a head with the pilot inside. In reality, he left all his *anthropomorphic qualities* behind on the writing desks pushed together, in the building of the former torture house, later a military prison, somewhere in the Eastern Carpathians. In reality he was a little cloud, a Drop in the Ocean, simply a drop, a full stop, a particle of lunar light.

In reality, he was everything.

Without abandoning his lunar corridor, Karl-Joseph reached Simmering and then flew above the rail line, which then led to the tangle of train tracks at the Kidering railway depot. Vacant lots spread along the tracks. Behind them now appeared some not terribly expressive buildings. Somewhere, on the left, not far from Kurpark, Eva-Maria apparently lived now, after her wedding—but he did not even make an effort to see her bedroom, her bed, nor her in that bed, to hear her breathe while sleeping. Instead, touching the territory of the Central Cemetery, he quite clearly saw the cremation of his own body that was to take place. It was to happen eight days later: the summons of a consul from the Austrian embassy in Ukraine. Then the processing of the required paperwork. The flight from Kyiv to Vienna with a special escort. Three or four acquaintances brought together by the cremation ritual—then only fire, fire, fire. This was exactly how it was going to happen, ending with a fistful of dust, a fistful of ashes that once knew how to take photos and how to kiss. But Karl-Joseph did not care for this dust.

Now came the Südbahnhof, the Southern Train Station—it was its turn. Yes, the much-loved oasis with its palm trees, winged lions, with the homeless, the insane, the Turkish and Arabic taxi drivers, the Balkan prostitutes: the train station for the poor, the southeastern outpost of *the best of all worlds.* Yes, he had wasted many a night in this area, a weak-sighted seeker of adventures, a photographer with his present name, who back then planned an entire book about Vienna's nighttime train stations, with their overflowing trash bins, dozens of crashed beer cans—for some reason always Ottakringer and never Zipfer—plastic bottles, paper bags, boxes, newspapers, ads. Now too he recognized familiar faces in the waiting room: Predrag, Marica, Dejan, Willi, Natasha, Ismail. Have they ever left this place at all during these four—no—almost five years?

They didn't even sense him. It was useless trying to give them a sign. He picked up speed, faster and faster. He now swept above Wieden, above Karlsplatz, above junkies frozen in horizontal positions in underpasses, above the first streetcars on the Ringstrasse, above the depths of the subway and everything further below. He now saw before him, beyond the historical and cultural cloaca of the Inner City, the northern suburbs and the Vienna Woods, green and sticky at this time of year. He suddenly wanted to fall onto this forest.

However, somewhere in the triangle between St. Stephen, the Maltese Church, and the Emperor's Tomb he hit an invisible yet impenetrable barrier. And was blinded by an intolerable flash of white light.

A Wall of Light rose in front of him, and a somewhat raspy, jazzy voice asked,

"Who are you? Who demands to be let in?"

Karl-Joseph answered without realizing how these words flew out of his mouth,

"I am His Majesty the Emperor of Austria and the King of Hungary."

The viewers (and there were hundreds of thousands of them, all invisible, at this concert) whistled and stomped their feet.

"I do not know any such person. Who demands to be let in?"

To this again out came a response,

"I am Karl-Joseph, Caesar of the Holy Roman Empire, Apostolic King of Hungary, King of Bohemia and Gypsia, King of Jerusalem, in my young days a fan of Judas Priest and Iron Maiden, Grand Duke of Transylvania, Grand Duke of Tuscany and Cracow, Duke of Lorraine . . ."

This was met by an even angrier response from the stadium.

"I do not know any such person. Who demands to be let in?" the Wall asked for the third time, in an even raspier voice.

And then the newly arrived hit upon the right response:

"I am Karl-Joseph, a poor sinner, a photographer and adulterer, now surrendering to Your mercy."

The invisible Spectators grew quiet. Only for half a

second, although it seemed nine thousand years had passed.

"Then you may come in," the Wall finally said.

And then the Wall stopped being a wall, and became a Staircase of Light, and it led—surprising though it may seem—upward.

(Let us imagine that everything happened exactly like this. For what else remains there for us*? A body on the pushed together writing desks?)*

At this very moment Artur Pepa puts the palm of his hand on a warm curve of Roma's body. This happens halfway on the road between sleep and wakefulness. In his dream there was a crowd of noisy people, something like a Hutsul choir or theater. They stole an Easter egg, covered in stars and crosses from his pocket, and refused to return it. Seeing he is now beginning to wake, they disappear en masse, bowing, dancing, singing something bawdy.

Let this be the departure of the characters, but already different ones: from a different novel by a different author.

You and I should also take our leave now. Here's hoping this time Artur Pepa will not yet again sleep through his morning erection.

YURI ANDRUKHOVYCH was born March 13, 1960 in Ivano-Frankivsk, Ukraine. In 1985 he co-founded the Bu-Ba-Bu group, which stands for бурлеск, балаган, буфонада, burlesque, side-show, buffoonery, together with Oleksandr Irvanets and Viktor Neborak. Andrukhovych writes in Ukrainian and is known for his pro-Ukrainian and pro-European views. In his interviews, he said he respected both the Ukrainian and Russian languages and claims his opponents do not understand that the very survival of the Ukrainian language is threatened. During the 2004 presidential elections in Ukraine he signed, together with eleven other writers, an open letter in which he called Sovietic Russian culture: "the language of pop music and criminal slang". Andrukhovych has published five novels, four poetry collections, a cycle of short stories, and two volumes of essays, as well as literary translations from English, German, Polish, and Russian. His essays regularly appear in Zerkalo nedeli (Mirror Weekly), an influential trilingual newspaper published in Russian and Ukrainian with excerpts published in an online English edition. He was awarded, along with *Pussy Riot*, the Hannah Arendt Prize for 2014.

Made in the USA
Charleston, SC
28 January 2016